In memory of our daughter Michelle (1993-2014).
A unique, inspiring person,
who was taken from us too soon.
Thank you for giving me the courage and inspiration
to write.
You are always by my side!

The Oak Tree
Prologue

When it first rose out of the ground, was anybody there to notice? For it was only a simple acorn giving rise to a simple sprout of life, nothing more. The terrain, the land may have been much different. When it sprouted up, was it next to the creek or did the creek come later, changing its course over time so that it slowly moved closer to the tree, giving the tree a much needed source of water throughout the year.

How was that little acorn carried there? Had it been carried there by an animal, rode the slow current of the creek or had it been dropped by a low flying bird? No one would ever know. However, it eventually wound up in that spot. Was it predestined to be there or just a chance occurrence. What forces were at work to cause this tree to grow? Against all odds it took root. Certainly there were humans in the area who might have seen its first tiny beginnings. Maybe only animals and birds witnessed the first few years of the oak. Over time, Native Americans in the area may have passed by, maybe not really taking the time to notice. What they thought of the small sapling and its few oversized leaves is uncertain. It would have brought forth a few green leaves each year for the first few years, and as fall arrived they would have changed color and dropped off. During winter and spring the tree would have been at the mercy of nature and the elements. Its end could have come quickly to a hungry deer or rabbit looking for nourishment in the harsh climate. But against all odds it continued to grow.

As time passed, nomadic Indian tribes would come down to the creek banks from time to time in search of wild game or to grab some water. They would have come across the tree as it continued to grow. As it became taller and broader they would have relied on its shade in the summer or taken advantage of what little protection from the elements it could provide in the winter.

Maybe they even stayed along the banks of the creek for an extended period of time making it the location of their base camp. No one really knew; and those who were there to recall part of the oak's story were long since gone. There was nothing written down. What was the tree's age? Who knew? Was it one thousand years old? Younger, older, ageless? Had it always been there? No one could really say. The tree had grown for many more years than any people who were first there at its birth.

It had become a defining statement of the surrounding landscape. It created its own habitat. Creatures large and small relied on it for food and shelter. Scavengers made use of the many acorns for a food source. Birds used it broad branches as a sanctuary and place to call home. And so it continued to grow strong and wide, courageous against the elements, weathered and statuesque.

If it could speak, what stories would it tell? What secrets would it care to disclose and what knowledge would it impart? Was it wise? Was it weary? What had it seen over these many years? It was part of nature and yet it beckoned to men: behold the power of my beauty and strength. But, use my many attributes wisely. For I am a part, a piece of nature. No, I am more than just a piece of nature, I embody the essence of nature Be mindful, nature is never tame and the beauty it provides at first glimpse always comes with fair warning that there is raw energy underneath. Respect its beauty, but don't corrupt or spoil it. For man does have a way of bringing evil to even idyllic natural places, peaceful settings, and natural beauty. It is not nature that is evil, but man who has a tendency to transfer his evil nature to those things he comes in contact with from time to time. And so it was with the giant oak.

The old oak tree held a wealth of knowledge that it was willing to share with anyone who came along and showed the proper respect. How it shared that knowledge depended on how it was treated. It also held many dark secrets as well. Some secrets maybe left well enough alone; secrets that some men might be unfortunate enough to unlock; secrets that over time had been left hanging in or underneath its many broad branches. And so one might ask what becomes of a mighty oak?

> **You shall become like a tree with falling leaves, like a garden that has no water. The strong man shall turn to tow, and his work shall become a spark; Both shall burn together, and there shall be none to quench the flames. Isaiah 1:30-31**

Chapter 1
The House First Noticed

My name is John, John Stogh. We were new to our neighborhood, that is my wife and me. I had always wanted to be right in the city. Right in the thick of things where the action happens and it's easy to get around experiencing it. It's where you can truly say you live in a neighborhood because there are sidewalks, streetlights and not too overly manicured lawns. Plus you're closer to your neighbors than the suburbs. The houses don't all look the same and you aren't concerned about getting lost or explaining to people who are coming to visit you, how to get to your house because you live on Plum Tree Circle which is near, but not the same as Plum Tree Court, Plum Tree Lane, Plum Tree Street and Plum Tree Blvd. No, I liked the diverse group of people I lived around, people I could call neighbors. I was slowly getting used to settling in to our new home. I hadn't yet gotten to know everyone in the neighborhood. That process, I realized just took time. For me, getting to know them was more about knowing their names and where they lived, rather than actually having to get involved with them. Good neighbors were ones that kept their distance. Seen but not heard if you know what I mean.

One thing I enjoyed most about the neighborhood was the fact I could take a walk at night. After dinner I'd take a stroll through the neighborhood. During my walk I could check into what was going on; new fences going up, gardens being planted and then harvested, or fresh coats of paint going up on the houses. I could keep an eye on the neighborhood and make sure it was all living up to my expectations. Plus, I would run into different neighbors along my walk. Brief conversations with them slowly allowed me to get to know them a few words at a time. There was Jim, the retired Ford plant worker, who was always out walking his little bulldog, Digby. Jim was always there with a friendly, "How's it going? Looks like the weather's going to change. That's one thing you can count on, the weather to change."

Digby on the other hand he was all business acted like he owned the sidewalk, didn't want to stop and chat, just wanted to keep going.

Samantha was something else all together. She'd turn the corner coffee in hand, with her little poodle that she always had to half drag down the street. It always seemed that I'd run into her just as I turned the corner of a block. I would never see her coming. I began to believe that she stood waiting for me to turn the corner. Many times she didn't know or didn't seem to care whether her poodle was keeping up with her or not. She'd want to stop and talk, but she was one of those people who was always concerned that all wasn't right with the universe. In her case the universe was her neighborhood. She continually complained. I don't know if it was just to me or it was to anyone who happened along. She'd complain about the dog barking next door, the loud party last week down the street, or the decaying fence her other neighbor was slow in getting fixed. I quickly grew tired of listening to her for any length of time, but I did have to admit that she was a wealth of neighborhood gossip. I could pick up more information about our neighborhood in a few minutes with her than I could hope to pick up in a week from anyone else. That was the main reason I didn't mind running into her.

Then there were other neighbors that you only caught fleeting glimpses of as you walked through the neighborhood. You might see them going in their house or out in their yard. What they were doing in their yard, I could never be sure. It was up to me to interpret. Gardening? No not dressed for it. Taking out the garbage? No they weren't carrying anything. Must just be checking the grounds of their city lot pretending it was a large country estate and they needed to make sure there weren't any poachers wandering through the distant corners of the estate. I was sure they wouldn't leave any tree or shrub unturned. I always wanted to know a little more about each of them.

For me though, it was certain neighbors down the street that I was particularly interested in. They always seemed charming and interesting; they were people I wanted to get to know a little more about, probably because I really didn't know much about them at all. Maybe it's just human nature. You always want to compare your situation with those around you. It always seems that other people lead more interesting lives than the life you lead. It's so easy for imagination to get the best of you. Their lives become exactly what you would want your life to be. And so it wasn't any different with me. I was always looking for a change. I had more time on my hands than I knew what to do with. I was in between jobs. The economy had tanked and the job search was going slowly. Anybody else's life seemed more interesting than mine. I did take more than a passing interest in these particular neighbors though. The longer it went in between the days that I would run into them in the yard or out on the street it made me wonder even more about who and what they were. Maybe it was because of where they lived.

I remember the first time out on a walk, when we first encountered one another. She had aged gracefully. Looking up at her face, I was captured by her long and expressive silhouette against the backdrop of the autumn sky. In fact it was almost as if the upper reaches hung in the clouds. Even though her charm was muted under the staleness of worn paint, I could feel her elegance, her sophisticated grace. Her majestic size captivated me. She was a forceful presence in my eye, requiring me to stop and admire her each time I passed. She held her position in this spot on the street well, unyielding after all these years. She challenged other houses to match her charm, age and simple complexity. None could. She was from an era before those other buildings on the blocks that surrounded her. She was the first here and one of the few remaining of her kind in the city.

I imagined what fresh colors from a new coat of paint would do. Maybe vibrant colors that would splash forth, "Here I am. Look at me," or more sedate colors that would subtly say "status". In my mind, I could see what some much needed repairs and an overall cleaning might do to bring back her original character. Maybe she was best just the way she was. I wasn't sure if any of those changes would protect her future or hide her past.

Like a blanket, the front porch gently wrapped, curving around two sides of the house. Large glass windows offered an eyeglass lens into the interior of the first floor beyond the porch. What mysteries lay beyond the white lace curtains that hung gently down the inside of the panes like ancient spider webs, I could only imagine. Ornamental woodwork dipped here and there, breaking up the line of the porch roof drawing attention to the rounded pillars that stood like sentinels. The house was made of wood, wood siding, windows, floors, and doors. The only non-wood structures on the house were the ornamental railings that broke up the slats of the wood siding in strategic locations on the upper two floors These black railings contrasted with the long unbroken trim that defined the roof line. A rounded spire framed in wood siding reached above the entire square outline of the symmetrical roof line rising straight above the square wood and frame outline, changing her simple symmetry, adding an additional layer of sophistication. It acted like a beacon, standing above the other houses in the area, beckoning people towards it. But it also stood out, warning them to remain at a safe distance, lest you become trapped in the single round hidden room laying within the spire.

Whenever I passed, I would catch myself pausing from time to time caught up in the small details: colored paint that attempted to hide rotted wood here and there, little imperfections, blemishes that couldn't quite be hidden. Here and there were some decayed floor boards in the porch making me aware that she had stood here a long time, a silent witness to time passing. I wondered what secrets lay inside. I really didn't know anything about who lived there. It is always that curiosity to know more about something or someone that makes them interesting. And so it was with this house and its occupants. It's funny how our minds wander as we conjure up all types of scenarios about what a person or thing is really like. If a person doesn't talk much, it means they are reflective deep thinkers who take their time to assess new situations and new people. It couldn't be that they are just boring people who really don't think or talk much at all. No these neighbors had to have more behind the scenes. Houses don't lie; and this house was a definite sign that there was more, much more behind the street view.

My passing curiosity with the house and its inhabitants began to change from just a passing interest to a nagging desire to know more, yet torn by my need to not turn into a nosy neighbor. I would look forward to those infrequent times when we would see them out in the neighborhood, taking a walk, or working in their yard. But at most, our conversations included,

"Hi."

"What's new?"

"Surviving the winter?"

"We're your neighbors down the street. We should get together sometime."

Until now it had never gone beyond that. Until now, that is.

Well, now the polite "We should get together sometime," had come back to haunt me. The other day I was stepping out of my car focusing on end of the day relaxation. Not that the majority of my day isn't usually relaxing. Well it is, except for the occasional anxiety attack when I realize I don't have a job.

That particular neighbor caught me off guard. Getting out of the car, I looked over and there he was waving me over from down the other side of the street. At first I didn't connect his face with the house. Quickly though as the realization sunk in, I began to look forward with anticipation. I was being drawn into a conversation with the person in the neighborhood I was most curious about. Normally, he wouldn't even acknowledge me with more than a simple, "Hi". This time however, he was waving me over. Bad timing, long day, maybe both. At first I wasn't sure I was up for personal contact, much less conversation. Not at this moment. But finally, I turned and looked up. I quickly turned my annoyed grimace of what-do-you-want-I've-had-a-long-day on my face into a faked smile.

"Hey neighbor," I said as I walked across the street towards him.

"How's it going?" he said.

I was still uncertain. At first I was hoping that the pleasant wave wasn't going to be more than a simple hello. Now that I was being offered the chance, I really didn't want to get to know him any more than I already did. The occasional pleasantries were more than enough for me. That way I could maintain the mystery in my mind. I wouldn't have to face the disappointment that the owner was an accountant who only wanted to talk tax season hardships.

"Oh, Hi didn't see you there. What's been going on? Survive the winter?" I couldn't resist adding that line. It was my best superficial line to use to show I sort of cared about what was going on in someone else's life. In reality it was just a way to avoid the current topic and deflect any discussion about myself.

"Not much," he replied.

"A little water in the basement with the melting snow. The house just doesn't soak up the moisture like it used too, and we're down to our last jars of canned beets, but yes, we did survive the winter."

I couldn't tell if he was serious about moisture and the canned beets and why do they call them "canned beets", they're in jars for gosh sakes. Before I could really get lost in the random thoughts of canned versus jars, he continued on.

"Say, Alona and I have decided that we want to invite you over for dinner when you have a free night. You and your wife, of course. I know we always say we should get together and now we just decided to take you up on it. We'll cook the dinner if you two want to bring the dessert. Would this weekend work? I suppose you'll have to talk to Rachel, and check her schedule."

I thought for a moment. I didn't know how he knew my wife's name. I didn't even know his wife's name. "Alona" it was then. I'd have to remember that. Now I'd have to figure out what his name was. I was simply terrible at names. I wondered how he knew my wife's name. She was always better at mingling with the neighbors and getting the important details like their names. She must have run into her at some time. When it was, I didn't have a clue. I didn't want to bring it up with her and give her the satisfaction that she had done some better detective work than I had done. But, then I resigned myself to the fact that I'd have to have that conversation with her.

"Sure," I said.

"I mean, yes I'll check with Rachel and let you know, although I think we are free this weekend. Let me get back to you tomorrow. You want to give me your phone number and I'll give you a call tonight?"

"Oh," he replied, "our phone hasn't been working. We're in the process of getting it repaired. Tell you what; just drop a note in our mailbox tomorrow with a date that works. I'm sure I'll see you in the next day or so."

"Sure," I said, "works for me. Have a great rest of the day," I continued as I turned and headed back down the street towards my house.

"Oh, always do rest most of the day," he replied in a lazy tone, as he turned and headed up the street towards his house. I wasn't sure if I heard him right but I didn't bother to clarify and simply continued on across the street and up the stairs to my house.

When my wife got home that night I mentioned that we had been invited by the neighbors across the street for dinner this weekend.

"Oh a neighbor function, which neighbor?" she asked.

"Alona and her husband. You know they live in the old "Painted Lady" down the street."

"You were talking to Alona? How would you happen to have a conversation with Alona?" She asked truly wondering what I would have in common with her.

"No I ran into her husband."

"You can't remember his name, can you?"

"He never mentioned it."

"Well, it's Darrah and you've got to be kidding me. Aren't they the ones that all the other neighbors have had problems with? Don't they call the police every time there's a loud group of kids walking through the neighborhood or playing in the yard next to theirs? Don't they really try to stick to themselves and not want to get involved with the neighbors or much less the neighborhood. I don't know that I'm interested in getting to know them any better. Based on what I've heard about them I know them enough already."

"Oh come on," I said, "Darrah seems nice enough. And wasn't that the reason why we moved to this neighborhood. We wanted to get to know our neighbors, wanted to feel like part of a community. I think we should go. Plus I think Darrah really was looking to get to know us."

She hesitated, but then I gave her that little smile that said please and I knew I had her. When she broke the silence with, "I don't like it, but I'll go," I knew it was a done deal. But then she added, "We won't stay all night just for dinner and dessert. And we won't commit to have them over here. Agreed?"

"Yes. Works for me," I added.

Chapter 2
Making Plans for the Get Together

For me, making friends has never been easy. So when I take that step I take it seriously. Whenever I start the process of making friends, I like to get a little background on them before I actually get together. Usually you've already had the occasion to meet them in advance and exchange pleasantries. You already have a preconceived notion: who they are and what you might expect during an evening together with them. All too many times though, I've really been off-base altogether. An older balding gentleman, quiet spoken at my first meeting with him, turned out to be an avid thrill seeker, sky diving, hang gliding, lady chasing. I spent the whole night listening to his exploits involving women, adventure, or both. Then I met a real outgoing individual, talkative, funny and able to hold a decent conversation. Well, I didn't do my background on him. I get to the event and nothing but silence. Turns out the first time I met him, he was a heavy recreational drug user. Next time I met him, he had decided to quit cold turkey. He didn't say ten words the whole night. That brings me to my next point. You need to come with your own discussion material. I usually think forty-five minutes worth is about right. Never come loaded to discuss, politics, religion, or guns. Any of those topics, if brought up, will usually lead to a heated debate, choice words by both sides, and you leaving realizing you don't want to get together with them again anytime soon. No, you need to arrive with fresh material that is not controversial: current events from the entertainment section. Most people are interested in the latest movies or what's going on in Hollywood.

Weather is good too; you can't lose with weather. Everyone notices it and it's always a good five minute filler. Well, you get my drift. Keep it fresh, keep it diverse, and keep a wide variety of topics in mind.

In my mind, it's best to know what you're dealing with. The more you know about your friends-to-be, the more you can decide where you might want to start the conversation, or how you might want to approach difficult topics, or for that matter, to be prepared for difficult topics that they might arise. If you haven't done your homework you aren't going to be at your best in a social get together. My wife calls it cyber stalking. I just call it due diligence. It's all about evening the playing field so I don't get caught off guard by any unpleasant, unknown facts. I do the standard background check, look up their name on the internet, check the property records on their house. You know the usual. I see when their house was last bought or sold. Just to make sure I know who I'm dealing with.

Well, I started the process to pull up the names of my neighbors on the internet. Then I realized I hadn't taken the time to get their last names. I could hear my wife's voice in the back of my head, "You just don't pay attention, he probably told you his last name, but you just didn't pay attention." I couldn't recall. I don't think he had given me his last name. Not to worry, I could pull up their names off the county records. I had their address. They would be listed in the county tax records. Then I could check to see if they'd paid their taxes in full, were delinquent in their payments, or if they had paid in installments. Any information would help me learn a little bit more about them. I pulled up the property tax records on their house. Odd, under when the house had been sold last it listed, "No Data Available". I checked under the name of the owner and there appeared the names: James and Maureen McMasters. Who were those people? I pressed the "More Information" tab, but then all it said was "No further information available." But, Darrah and Alona lived there. Maybe they were related to the McMasters. By my conversation with Darrah, I got the impression that they had lived there forever. Maybe I was mistaken. It was odd, but there was probably a simple explanation. Maybe it was just a glitch in the system data records. You rely on the public records people to be current and have the correct data but no you're let down again. I was going in blind.

Now I realized I'd have to go forward with our little get together with a blank slate. The dinner would no longer be a simple evening of chit chat and small talk. If I was going to get any more info or if I wanted to get to know them any better I'd have to be alert; I would have to pay attention to the details and actually listen to what they were saying. Yes, I would have to pay attention to the details.

The next day I went to drop a note in their mailbox. As I headed across the street to drop the note in the mailbox, my thoughts turned to what I would provide for the dessert. Premade chocolate chip cookies, that was it. That would work. Nice, hot, gooey. Everyone liked homemade cookies.

Lost in thought, my eyes caught the sidewalk in front of me. At the edge of their lot I noticed it. The sidewalk in front of their house wasn't standard slabs. It was smaller slabs, each one-quarter of a standard slab. And they were old. You could tell, they had weathered over time, the individual stones in the aggregate protruded through the surface polished to a smooth shine. I looked over the entire walk in front of their lot. It was all old slabs, never replaced. It was original to the house. I kept walking, admiring the old-fashioned concrete work. Here and there, the alignment of the slabs was uneven, heaving up or settling over time. But all in all it was amazing the condition it was in. It had aged nicely, just like the house. Before I realized it, I had walked to the edge of the lot line. There in the last slab was some writing, fairly worn, but still legible. It read: "McMaster Const." and "1910"; Ah, something to talk about on Saturday I thought.

I turned back from the edge of the lot line and walked up to the front door. I reached the door and started looking for the mailbox. There didn't appear to be one. That was odd. There had to be a mailbox, everyone has a mailbox. I was about to give up looking and just tuck the note in the curved elongated antique handle of the door when I spotted it.

I wasn't sure if it really was a mailbox, it was a heavy brass flap built right into the side of the house. It was in the form of an elongated oak leaf with acorns for hinges. I took a few seconds to marvel at the craftsmanship. Then I tried to lift the leaf upwards. It wouldn't move up more than an inch or so. But, I could see an opening. So I stuffed the folded note up under the oak leaf, hoping it would slide down the narrow chute. It was then that I thought to myself that I should have spent more time on the note when it was going into such an ornate receptacle.

The note simply said:

Dinner at 6:00 on Saturday would work for us. We'll see you then and will bring dessert. Looking forward to it.
Sincerely, the Stoghs, John and Rachel

Sincerely seemed too formal, but it was the only way I knew how to sign a note. Plus I had forged my wife's signature or at least first name. I didn't want to ask her again and give her another chance to back out.

A couple of days went by and I have to admit I forgot all about the note and the Saturday dinner. Well actually, I tried to forget. The note kept nagging at me. I was concerned that they hadn't received it. When you have few things to occupy your mind, it's those little things that can start to drive you nuts. By Thursday I was beginning to wonder whether I would have to drop off another note, or God forbid talk to them in person.

But that night, when I pulled up in my car and began getting out, I heard a familiar voice, "Hey John, got your note. We're looking forward to this Saturday."

I turned and waved as I headed across the street towards him.

"I couldn't find your mailbox at first. But when I finally figured it out it really is some piece of craftsmanship. It's really unique," I said, wondering to myself at the same time how long he would have waited to tell me about Saturday if he hadn't run into me today.

He looked at me and then said, "Oh, I forgot to tell you, we're working on getting that fixed. We don't really have a working mailbox. Right now we pick up the mail at the post office. They don't deliver if you don't have a mailbox to put the mail in. Well, anyway I'm glad we're set for Saturday."

"No shit Sherlock," I thought to myself. That made no sense to me. No working mailbox. For me, mail was the high point of my day. How could you not get your mailbox fixed, and fixed as quickly as possible? I was getting a little annoyed.

"Oh, I understand," I said to Darrah. "And I know you should have your address numbers above your front door too. Let me see my address is 765. Yours must be 775," I said, as I pretended to count down the houses on the other side of the street for his enlightenment. I figured I needed to get him going on some of those repairs. He needed to know there were certain standards of care to maintain a house and that he just couldn't continue to ignore them. Plus, he had annoyed me. It was my way of paying him back. Also, I wanted to make sure I had looked up the right house in the tax records the other day.

"No," he corrected me, "It's 777."

I had checked the right house.

"That's a lot of sevens," I said.

"I don't know if it's too many sevens, but I guess it really does make a statement," he said and then continued, "You are right you know I need to get those up as well. So much to do and always so little time to do it. With this old house it's really a balancing act. You want to maintain its old charm. You don't want to make too many changes that might change its character. At the same time the modern world is always dragging you forward to adopt new technology, new ways or new trends. See you on Saturday," he continued, "and don't forget dessert," he added. "We are so looking forward to it."

"See you then," I said, "and we won't forget dessert," I said as I turned and headed back across the street.

I thought to myself. Putting numbers on your house, how could that be a new technology or trend? He must really be old school or just old. Then I wondered, I always knew 666 was supposed to be an evil number. I wondered what 777 meant. Maybe it meant nothing. Oh well, that was for another time.

Chapter 3
Dinner with the Neighbors

Saturday arrived. As it got closer to evening, my wife became more nervous, wondering what to wear. I told her casual was fine. Her response was that I would have worn casual to our wedding if she hadn't stepped in to let me know in advance that it was a formal affair. After she mentioned that to me, I decided to take the listen and not respond approach. Evidently she wasn't looking for my expert advice; she just wanted to use me as a sounding board. I got it.

I couldn't adapt quickly enough when she changed her concerns to the dessert. I was still in the listening, not responding mode. I could never keep it straight whether or not she wanted me to just listen or just respond. She kept asking me about the dessert, what were my plans, what was I going to do about it. Finally, I used my best response that seemed to work in most situations. I said I had it under control. Having it under control in my mind was: don't bother me at the moment, I'm busy with something else; when the time comes, I'll figure something out. Before I knew it, late afternoon had arrived. Panic set in, my one responsibility: the cookies. I hadn't even begun baking. What to do? It looked like plan B would have to work. So instead of homemade cookies, I bought some cookies at the store. I did put my best effort into it, putting the cookies on our best non-holiday-themed plate, covering them in clear wrap, and hiding them from my wife until we headed across the street. They were presentable.

The moment came at last. I made sure I carried the plate of cookies in a white bakery bag to reduce any suspicion from my wife. Then we headed across and down the street. Once up to the door, I looked for a door bell to no avail. In looking around I spied door knocker in the center of the door. It was a large, tree-shaped knocker with a round acorn at the end of the knocker itself. I lifted and dropped the knocker twice. Inside, I heard footsteps moving towards the front door and in a moment the door opened. There stood Darrah in simple attire which included a tweed overcoat.

"Welcome, come in please," he said. "John, good to see you again. And you must be Rachel. Please, both of you make yourself at home and welcome to our home." He ushered us inside and there we were standing in the entry way. It was a large open square entry area. I looked up. There was a multi-layered chandelier that hung down almost reaching the tops of our heads. The light from the adjoining rooms bounced and redirected off its glistening crystals. I looked at the ceiling. The chandelier base was surrounded by a plaster relief of oak leaves that slowly fell away into the flat plaster ceiling. Dark crown molding framed the room where the ceiling met the walls. The molding was ornately carved, oak leaves strewn along the length of the molding. Ahead, a banister, stained in a rich dark color rose upwards from the first floor, slowly rising and curving like a serpent, framing dark wooden stairs. On the end of the banister, perched on top of the bottom post at the foot of the stairs was an oval orb of dark wood. It was a large acorn. And so it seemed the theme of the house was "the oak".

A fire was burning in the fireplace to our right through a curved entryway into the living room and a three- pronged candle holder sat burning in the center of the dining room table to our left. The shadows danced in the corners of both rooms and I realized that the only light in the rooms was being produced by the fire in the fire place and the candles in the dining room and a couple of candles placed along the wall in the living room. What a quaint relaxing mood it set, I thought to myself.

My wife piped up breaking the silence.

"What a nice house you have and that fire is a nice touch. I hope you didn't do it just for us."

"No," he added, "We usually have a fire going. It really soothes the soul and Alona and I are students of the philosophy that natural self-sufficiency is better. We try to use more basic non-traditional energy sources. Try to use as little electricity as possible. I guess you could say we're throwbacks to a simpler era."

As those words trailed off, I just hoped that the simpler era meant something good and home-cooked for dinner.

"Come you two; sit down next to the fire. Let's chat while Alona finishes up in the kitchen with dinner."

"Oh, here's the dessert we brought before I forget," my wife added, "Chocolate chip cookies."

I had handed her the bag in a quick exchange at the door and now I was confident she would be none the wiser that they weren't homemade, but bakery bought.

"Does she need any help? Can I help her with anything?" my wife continued.

"Oh no, I think she's pretty close to being done. Come here, sit down. Relax. Can I get you anything . . . wine, beer, sparkling water, soda, or wintergreen or spruce tea?" he spoke in a low soothing voice.

"Glass of wine would be great," my wife said. I knew she had just stopped listening after the word wine came out. But did I hear him right. Did he say "wintergreen or spruce tea?" What the heck was that, I thought to myself. Before I could say anything my wife added.

"Anything red, I'm not picky," she added.

"Oh, a woman after my own heart," he not so subtly added. "I have just the right thing. And you, John, what would you like, the same?" He asked turning to me.

"Oh, well I'm not much of a wine man myself. Did I hear you right? Did you say you had wintergreen or spruce tea. What is that? I've never heard of either of those two types of tea."

"I'm glad you were listening. Yes, I did say wintergreen and spruce. They're Native American teas. They're traditional Lakota teas. My wife and I have been trying some new traditional things. We're trying to get back to our roots, do some more healthy kinds of things. Are you interested in the tea then?"

"Well, yes I think I am," I said.

"You pick which one you think is better, OK," he added.

"No, either one is fine," I continued.

"I think you should decide, that way I won't be responsible if you don't like the taste. You need to take control of your own fate, otherwise the powers that be decide for you. Then you never know what will be decided. It could be good or not so good," he said trying to end the debate.

"Well, alright," I said, "I'll take the spruce." I thought to myself, how did deciding or not deciding what kind of tea to drink decide my fate.

"Spruce it is then. I think you'll like it."

He left the room. My wife and I settled into our chairs facing the fireplace. Starting to get comfortable we began checking out our surroundings. The furniture or at least the chairs and loveseat were older and overstuffed, with carved legs and sturdy arm rests with worn fabric that felt slick to the touch, worn down over the years. Above the fireplace mantel hung a large, ornately framed picture of what looked to be a large oak tree. Odd thing to hang above your fireplace. It did look quite majestic sitting on a mound of a hill spread out with its green leaves on what appeared to be a late summer day. It just added to the comfort of the room. It slowly dawned on me; the oak motif ran throughout the house.

"Oh I see you've noticed our masterpiece," he said breaking the silence upon entering the room with a small tray with three drinks on it, noticing that we were both looking intently at the picture above the fireplace mantel.

"Wine for the lady, hope you enjoy it. It's a local vineyard that really does a nice job, not too heavy, not too sweet and the price is right. And here's a spruce tea for the gentleman," he continued without pausing in his low voice.

"That picture really tells the story of this house. It's the tree that built this house. The wood from that tree was used for the timber to frame and provide the planking for the floors you are sitting on. You know an oak tree can live for more than a thousand years. Then the wood is harvested from that tree. Well, that can last for another thousand years if you take care of it correctly. That's if the oak isn't corrupted."

Strange use of words I thought," corrupted". But the more he spoke the stranger he seemed.

"Interesting story," he continued, "The tree used to stand at the edge of an apple orchard set in the corner of the Marcellus Magogson farm which used to make up the land this whole area was built on. The tree itself sat right where this house now stands," he said informatively. Then he paused as if thinking to himself. "Interesting. The tree gave its life to build this very house that we live in. I think the picture has been with the house since it was built. We found it in the attic when we moved in and put it up above the fireplace where it sits now. It fits perfectly, don't you think?" He added.

"Yes," I said. "Well, when was this house actually built then?" I asked.

"Good question. We think it's really ageless," he added.

"Well, the other day when I walked up to drop off the note, I noticed your front sidewalk. There was a stamp in the walk '1910' and 'McMasters Const.' was that when the house was built?" I asked.

"When is a house really built? Is it the day the tree used for the wood to build the house first rises from the ground? Who's to say when it is built? A sidewalk, that's something different. A sidewalk doesn't define the character of a house like this, not in a thousand years. I don't know what that stamp really means in defining the true nature of a house. No, a house is something all together different. You can't even include those two things in the same sentence. I don't know anything about the sidewalk," he said his normally steady voice growing ever so slightly agitated.

"Well, I just thought you just might know something about it. It's really nothing, just something I noticed," I said backing down and hoping to move on to a different topic.

"You've shown some interest, John, let me show you something," he finally said. "It's over here. I'll show you what the area looked like before it turned into this, this urban city."

My wife and I stood up. But before we could move he motioned us back into our seats.

"No stay there, I've got it," he said as he walked over to the left of the fireplace standing beside my wife. In his hands he held a small framed picture the he had grabbed from the far corner of the room. He brought it closer so we both could see it, just near the edge of the light dancing out from the fire that burned with a steady, medium heat.

"Here is a picture of the farmhouse with Marcellus, his wife Eleanor, and their three kids standing on the porch. And there to the right, in the distance, see that? There is the large oak tree sitting off to the side. That's where we sit right now. Same spot."

Sure enough, that looked like the same tree above the mantel. Same low-hung branch to one side and that rounded over-arching canopy that looked like a long, tall sentinel watching over the farm and its inhabitants. But realistically, one oak tree was just like any other oak tree I thought to myself.

"Finally, dinner is ready," Alona said, as she poked her head around the corner. "Sorry for staying in the kitchen, but I wanted to make sure nothing burned. Us Braddocks normally keep to ourselves, but I dare say Darrah has been telling me all about you. So nice to meet both of you," she said.

My wife nudged me. I knew she was letting me know that I now had been given the husband's last name and that I better remember it because I may not get a second chance.

Alona didn't appear as old as I would have expected. Dark brown hair was swept back in a bun to the back of her head and she wore small, oval glasses. Her face was oval, almost elongated like Darrah's. There was warmth that radiated off her face that displaced the warmth of the fire.

"Come," she continued. "Let's sit down at the table. I've put everything out to get started. John you sit here at the head, Rachel you sit here next to me."

We sat down and before I could speak or move to adjust my plate and napkin, Darrah started in.

"Let us say a prayer."

Wow, I hadn't done that for quite some time, at least not since last Thanksgiving. I guess it was the right neighborly thing to do. I clasped my hands and Darrah continued on.

"Dear Spirit:

Be watchful, and strengthen the things which remain, that are not yet ready to die: for I have not found thy works perfect before thy spirit. Remember therefore, how thou hast received and heard, and hold fast, and repent. If therefore thou shalt not watch, I will come on thee as a thief, and thou shalt not know what hour I will come upon thee. Watch over and protect this great house and its inhabitants from harm. Likewise protect the Great Spirit that looks over this house. Amen"

"Amen," my wife and I both mumbled as an afterthought.

"Not your average lighthearted prayer," Darrah added. "Sometimes you just have to remember to be vigilant and know that a spirit is always watching over us. We always need to be ready. Well, are you ready to eat?"

We all nodded, and plates started moving around the table.

"I hope you like this traditional fare that I've prepared," Alona chimed in, lightening the mood a little. She then pointed to the different dishes spread out before us.

"Here we have succotash, it's a mixture of beans and corn from our garden; this main dish is buffalo stew from an old recipe I came across, a mix of buffalo stew meat of course and various vegetables from our garden; here's some fresh cornbread, that I made today; and finally some acorn bread. Oh, and over here, we have some wojapi. It's a cross between a soup and a jam. We made it from berries that we grow out in our back yard. But before anything else, to start off, over here in this soup terrine is "wohanpi". I can't say that everything in it is from our garden but I know you will like it. Oh, I almost forgot and here is a salad direct from our garden as well as some fry bread. The fry bread is a little modern for my taste. I hope you enjoy it."

I couldn't help but think to myself, "traditional food to whom."

"I don't think I've heard of some of these dishes, "wohapi" and "woapi" and bison stew and acorn bread. What traditional types of foods are those? I mean how did you come across those dishes?" I asked.

My wife nudged me under the table, thinking I was being impolite by asking.

"It's wohanpi with an 'h' and 'n' and wojapi with a 'j'. These dishes are actually traditional Native American dishes. They come from the very people that originally settled this area. Alona and I like to celebrate their culture from time to time. We just appreciate their culture. That's all. Maybe it is a little bit different, but we like keeping their legend alive so to speak. I hope you enjoy the food as much as we do," Darrah added. "Here, start with the wohanpi," he said as he passed me a medium-sized bowl filled with brownish liquid.

As I started to sample the different dishes I had to admit that it wasn't half bad.

"So buffalo stew, that's something you don't see every day," I added. I could see a slight glare from my wife out of the corner of my eye and I knew I had started the wrong topic.

"Actually it is quite healthy. It was a traditional dish of certain Native American tribes. Did you know that buffalo is leaner and healthier for you? We enjoy having it from time to time," Darrah went on.

I tried to continue holding the conversation while I was eating, but I kept getting lost in my food and more often than not found myself nodding yes when Darrah spoke, not really paying attention to the conversation and only catching words here or there. Other than that, the night was rather uneventful, except that I began to dread the end of the meal knowing that everyone was awaiting a dessert that couldn't come close to rivaling the rest of the meal.

Alona did her best to arrange the cookies so they filled the plate. A few stuck together. I could sense that my wife was either a little nervous or mad or both. She sat fidgeting in her chair. I knew she was weighing in her mind the lack of effort that I had put into the dessert and what, if anything she could do about it. I knew there would be a discussion later, a one-sided discussion.

"You know," Alona broke the silence, "you really make a house a home by the care you take in preparing the meals within its walls. Rachel, thank you for providing the dessert."

I didn't know if she was really trying to be nice or whether it was a way to let my wife know that she needed to step up her cooking efforts. In any event, it led to a few more moments of awkward silence until Darrah started in.

"We really can't say how much we enjoyed sharing our house with you two this evening. Thank you for allowing us to share the history of our home. And you know what they say. History eventually catches up to the present."

After a little more small talk we wrapped up the evening. Looking at my wife, I couldn't decide whether or not she actually had a good time. Sometimes she could really put on a facade that my male cluelessness couldn't crack.

My wife and I left them that night agreeing that we would have to get together again soon. I offered to host the next event, but Darrah and Alona kept jokingly saying that they would be happy to host the event again so that we would have a chance to make our own dessert next time to rival the sumptuous dinner they had prepared. Plus, they said they were true homebodies, feeling most comfortable in their own home. No, I didn't question their intentions; they simply offered the hospitality of their home for the next event whenever that might be because they felt more comfortable in their own home. Plus, I was focused on something different all together. Knowing I was in trouble, I had come clean to them about my cookies, all in an attempt to save my wife's reputation. I just hoped it wasn't too little too late. We headed out the door with our empty cookie plate in hand.

I looked back over my shoulder and our two hosts were standing in the frame of the doorway, not really waving, but just standing. They really looked ageless with the glow from inside the house warmly outlining their muted features. For a moment, it almost seemed as if they were joined at the hip. I suppose when you're married for that long, you really almost become one. At least, that is what I had heard.

Heading up the short walk to our house, I again looked back, down the street. The house was now almost dark, except for a low flicker of light coming from a dying fire. I don't know if the night, the food, and the drink all hit me at once but the outline of the house looked just like a huge oak tree. It was probably just the stories and small talk rolling around in my head. I grabbed my wife's hand and headed up the last couple of steps to our front door. Interesting neighborhood we lived in, I thought.

Chapter 4
The Morning After

"Well, that was a great meal last night, don't you think?" I said lowering my paper as I sat at our kitchen table the next morning.

Neither of us were morning people. And so it was we spent the first half hour of each morning waking up in our way. For me it was reading the paper and taking in a couple cups of coffee, waiting for the caffeine to hit. For my wife, it was popping open that first can of diet coke and checking out the ads in the paper, looking for deals at the grocery store, the dollar store, or big ticket items we really couldn't afford. No, we were both zoned out in our own little worlds waiting for the proper energy levels when we could begin interacting with each other and the world around us. By speaking, I had acknowledged that I was ready for the day to begin.

"And the company was very interesting as well," my wife added in an uncertain tone, after taking a long draw on her can of diet coke.

"More like unusual is a better word. It wasn't just the company, that meal was unusual as well. What did they call it, classical American fare? Native American? Who would pick that classic food to prepare? I've never heard of anyone doing that. I don't think they were Native American. Do you think they were?" I continued.

"I don't think they were. Hard to tell. Maybe they were just part Native American. That's possible," my wife added.

"You might be right. It was odd that they wanted to preserve that culture. Not that I'm saying it's not worth preserving. It's just that you don't really hear much about Native American culture in magazines or the newspaper. It just doesn't come to mind. But I guess everyone has a hobby of sorts. Maybe their hobby is cooking different cultural dinners. I really don't know," I added. "That whole history of the house and the neighborhood was really a little over the top, too. I'm not sure if that really is the background on the house and the land before the house was built. Something just seemed odd. They were so into "our" home this and "our" home that, it was just a little too much. Plus, did you notice the overwhelming 'oak motif'? When the house was built it was probably all the rage. But you know sometimes things become outdated. I do admit that the craftsmanship was something else. It was pretty amazing. But all in all, maybe it was just a little too much. With the candles and everything, I almost thought I was in the middle of a horror movie. As the night progressed I didn't know what would happen. Unique experience is probably the best way to describe it. People do get hung up on their importance in the world. If they don't have a family crest and a title, they create a history for themselves; a history of positive stories that boosts them up. All of a sudden they are larger than life. No I think they were lucky enough to buy that house and well, whatever history they discussed, well they just went and created it. And one more thing did you notice how he became a little upset when I brought up the sidewalk stamp?" I continued starting to get away from myself.

"Wow," my wife said cutting me off, "I sense a little envy here. Are you upset the timing wasn't right and we didn't find that house before they did? We didn't even know about this neighborhood when they had already been living in the house for years. No, I think they do have bragging rights. They have the most magnificent house in the neighborhood and well, the oldest for that matter. Or are you upset about the fact that he challenged your notion that a neighborhood isn't a neighborhood unless there's a sidewalk in front of every house? You and your sidewalk neighborhood," she cut me off.

"It was just a little too much, that's all I'm saying; and why would anyone get worked up about the fact that they have a date and name stamp on the sidewalk in front of their house? Maybe he knows more about that name on the stamp then he cares to share," I said trying to calm down a little.

"Well, you are getting worked up about it, that's what. Listen to yourself Mr. Conspiracy Buff. Maybe it's just the tip of the iceberg. Maybe it's a fake walk and we're actually living in the suburbs without sidewalks. What do you say to that?" she said smiling. "If you're so concerned why don't you check into the history of their house and while you're doing that you can check into the history of our house. Maybe we have an even more unique history. You've been promising me that you would find out about the history of our house. Plus, right now you have plenty of time on your hands," my wife said.

"I don't know if I really have the time," I added, trying to ignore her attempt at humor. I was weighing in my mind what this project might entail and I didn't want to commit just yet.

"No seriously, what else do you have going on, you know you should really check into it. You know how to look up records at the county. Why don't you spend a few hours one of these days and look it up? I've always been curious who owned our lot. Maybe you could talk to Darrah some more, if you need to get some more detailed info. He seemed like a wealth of information."

Here she went again, I had just finished one project, painting the extra bedroom and she was sending me off on some new project. She was always trying to redirect my focus. Just when I would get settled in a regular schedule, there she would go and change everything. She always made it impossible for me to keep my life on track. I didn't need the added stress this new project would bring on. I already had enough stress. What did I want with another new set of tasks, no a new project, that would take my focus away from what I was currently working on. I took a deep breath, trying to stop my thoughts in mid-stream. I realized I was getting myself worked up. I was heading down a path I didn't want to go, but I couldn't stop myself. Wait, I could. I was in control. Then for a second, I had to admit that the stories from last night had peeked my curiosity. It was all very interesting I had to admit. I calmly began to talk, hiding the flurry of disjointed thoughts raging through my head. I began talking slowly, thinking through the process I would have to go through to do what she was suggesting.

I could hear my thoughts as I spoke, "That was quite some time ago that I spent my days in the county records searching documents. I don't know if I still have it in me, if I still know how to look up records. Things may have changed," I said.

In college I had worked part-time for a title company making copies of records and updating title records for new loans. I knew I could handle the task. I just didn't want to commit.

"Come now. You're the one always saying you have all this experience. You used to say how easy it was, that you could get a full day's work done in half a day. Remember you're talking to the one person who still knows you from those days. I just won't take no for an answer. Plus, a change of pace would do you good. Maybe you'll run into someone you know down there. Networking is always a good thing you know."

She stopped and gave me that look of challenge, knowing I couldn't resist.

"OK, I'll try to figure out some time that would work," I said reluctantly. "You know, I'm not sure which story, the one about the tree or the history of the farm that I found more interesting." I added, looking for an answer in my mind.

"Oh, I liked the history of the farm. It was all about building America, taming the open land," she said.

"I know I can locate the history of the farm, at least through the county records. I don't know if I will be able to find any more information though on the tree. Maybe I could check with the Historical Society to see if they have any information. You know pictures or maps. They would probably have more in depth information on both. Do you really think their house sits exactly where that old oak tree once stood? I think it is highly unlikely. But, maybe I should find out. Maybe I can find out," I said.

"See I told you, you're already getting interested; it's just up your alley. Just make sure you don't get carried away. I'm not looking for a novel, I'm just looking for a little background on the history of this area. Give me the Reader's Digest version and I'll be happy. Remember, you still need to get back on track with the job search." Then my wife added, "Anyway, the only real mystery I'm concerned about is where Alona got those interesting recipes. Wasn't the food just great?"

"You have to be joking," I said realizing just as I finished speaking that she had the beginning of a smile on her face. I hesitated for a moment more and then I realized she was joking for sure when she cut in with,

"Yes and those cookies you decided to bring, those just topped off the evening," she added giving me a dirty look. "Now we'll have to follow up with another dinner with them just to prove we can bring a decent dessert."

I hesitated for a moment and looked at her.

Then she continued talking, "Actually, that wouldn't be so bad. They actually are a cute couple. Darrah can be somewhat long-winded, but he certainly tells some interesting stories and is a gracious host; and Alona, she just has that quaint motherly charm about her."

I cut her off "Are you thinking of moving in with them? I'm sure they wouldn't mind. Remember, you were the one who didn't even want to go over there. Are you forgetting that strange prayer before dinner? I'm going to check into that, too. Now it's as if you want to be their new best friends," I added getting a little worked up.

"Mr., you just worry about what you can bring for dessert the next time we get together and please . . . I'd really like it if you'd look up the background on both houses. That's the only way you'll put your mind at ease. It would be interesting. And now that you finished the painting you really need a new hobby to keep you busy around here. Waiting for the mail on the weekdays just isn't what I classify as a real hobby." She ended the discussion by turning and heading into the other room.

"I'll see what I can do," I yelled after her, "No promises."

I was now a little ticked. There she went again making it seem like I really wasn't doing anything around here. I had my own way of staying busy. I didn't need her to meddle in my daily routine. Now though, it was the lesser of two evils. I could string her along for awhile, but I knew that I would eventually have to check up on the history of their house and our house as well. My wife wouldn't forget about it. I finished and got up too; I needed to be on the move before she'd have a chance to poke her head in the room and add something else to my plate.

Chapter 5

I Check the Records

For the next week, I didn't see Darrah or his wife. Although I had to admit I didn't ever really recall seeing his wife outside the house. She must head out the back way. Finally, after a few more times of my wife mentioning when I might have some time to check, I woke up one morning and decided I'd put the rest of my busy job search schedule on hold and instead head downtown to take a look at those county records. It really shouldn't take long, if I still had the old touch. Plus, there was a great soup place downtown that I hadn't been to in years. Edwintons it was called; bottomless bowls of soup were their specialty. The soup was great, but the main reason to go was actually the endless, fresh, garlic bread sticks they served. Lightly browned, hot, with a sprinkle of garlic salt on top. That was the motivation I needed.

I let my wife know what I was up to. You never want to have your wife call you at work to ask for you and get the response "Oh, he called in sick today, didn't you know that?" For me, work was at home. I was handling my job search just like a job. That's what all the experts said to do. Yes, I had a job. My job was going through the motions of looking for a job. I knew she was getting worried about my job search. So she would check up on me, calling on the home line at eleven sharp every day. Today I wouldn't be there. I would be handling some important business. Keeping the wife in the loop is the key to hassle-free wedded bliss. That, and if you keep the wife in the loop, you usually have a little extra time to do things on your own.

Looking up records at the courthouse is really like detective work. You look up properties by the legal description of each parcel. Usually the description of a parcel is a lot number, in a specific block, in a specific subdivision. I had looked at our tax statement which had the ID number and lot 14, block 3, Apple Orchard Addition. Lots can be any size; it's really up to the city and the original developer when the subdivision is created. Most city lots aren't that big. That was the case with my lot and most of the lots in our neighborhood.

That was my starting point. Maybe, this was all a waste of time, maybe old Darrah was right. Well, I wouldn't know until I actually started looking. With the name of the subdivision being "Apple Orchard", maybe this land was really part of an apple orchard that once sat on the Magogson farm.

But as I recalled I had seen it all too often when I searched titles. More often than not, the name of the subdivision was whipped up by the developer, a marketing ploy to make the land appear more inviting. Overlook Creek usually had a dry creek bed. Oak Tree Farm was five miles from the true location of the oak trees and so on. No, you really couldn't rely on the name of the subdivision to know the land's location to old physical markers. You would have to find real people to talk to, or old photographs, or information at an historical society to check up on it. No, today I was just looking up records of who owned what, when and how it was legally described when they owned it. It was pretty straight forward, just a bit tedious. But I liked the idea of solving a puzzle. Wading through these records would give me some much needed satisfaction. I would get to complete a task that would have a beginning and an end, short and simple. Nothing like the long, drawn out process of searching for a job. No that entailed numerous interviews, stops and starts, almost landing a job, then getting the form e-mail notice that another candidate had gotten the job. It was all a big game. It was a game I no longer wanted to play. No, this would take my mind off that whole useless process. This morning, I would be doing something worthwhile. And after that, my reward was lunch. Hopefully, the facts were there, I just needed to find them. Hopefully, I still had the skills to do it.

I headed up the stairs of the old government center. The steps, even though they were made of stone curved inward in the center, a reminder of the tens of thousands of people who had gone up and down those stairs over the past hundred plus years. I reached the top of the stairs. A wooden and glass partition stood at the top. A heavy wooden door was propped open. Beyond the glass enclosure, the entire floor opened up into broad rows of metal bookcases packed with large, tan, bound books. The bookshelves stretched out in front of me and around the room on three sides. Directly in front of me stood a simple counter with a young clerk behind it and beyond that were a few rows of metal tables with some of the bound books laying open here and there.

I walked up to the counter. I could never understand the lax procedures undertaken to allow someone to go through the records, all you needed to do was sign your name and have your ID checked. It was like getting let into a vault full of precious artifacts without so much as a quick check to see if you were actually alive. You were able to look at history as it was made; the names of the different people who owned the land, the transactions that revealed how the land was divided up over time, and sometimes unique information about the transfers of the land. Yes, I was now in the midst of the land records of the entire county.

I methodically worked my way through the records, starting with our home. It's pretty simple if you know what you are doing. You start with the current deed for a specific lot. The lot name and number you can get from the tax records by looking up the street address. From there you work your way back. By looking at the current deed you can usually see the reference number of the prior deed to the property. Working slowly, you can find out when a named subdivision was created. Before being subdivided into city-sized lots, land is usually bought and sold in larger tracts. Farmland is usually described in terms of acres.

I worked my way back through the various deeds. I was disappointed that my house stood on a tract of land that wasn't part of the tract of land to Darrah's house. It didn't matter though. I was concerned more about that house than the history of my house. However, I did know my wife would ask about our house, so I quickly jotted down some info about the history of our house. It was just enough info I hoped, so that she wouldn't ask any further questions.

Now I could move on to look up the real information I came for. It took awhile, working my way back through the dated records. I found deeds running from the developer for individual lots in the subdivision; and of course the developer had a fitting name "Apple Orchard Development Corp". I could barely make out the signature of the person signing on behalf of the corporation for the deeds to the different people who purchased the various "Apple Orchard" subdivision lots. It looked like "Cornelius Rademacher" I made a note of the company name and the individual in case there was information on him from other sources.

I wasn't done yet, though. I needed to find out who owned the farm that was sold to the development company, if that was what happened. Finally, I found the deed for the original farm. Sure enough, the development company had bought the Magogson farm back in 1899. It was like finding the jackpot.

Maybe it was just me, but I always found those old deeds interesting. There were always restrictions put in them. Land could not be used for a rendering plant (slaughter of animals), no facilities serving alcohol could be run on the land. Most of these restrictions were not valid legal restrictions that would hold up in a court of law and even the valid restrictions normally expired over time. I even remember one restriction in which an elderly couple sold their home with the restriction that they be allowed to occupy the upper rear bedroom for the rest of their natural lives. Odd request, but I guess they needed somewhere to live out the last years of their lives and back then, there really weren't any retirement homes to speak of. Anyway, I began reading the deed. It transferred the farm from

Marcellus and Eleanor Magogson to Apple Orchard Development Corp. I read through the body of the deed to find more specifics and finally got to the legal description of the land being conveyed. It was described by metes and bounds . . . running the SW 1/4 of the SE 1/4 of section . . . Ramsey County . . . . In all it covered 80 acres. At the end of the legal description was an additional paragraph, that read "except the current owners, Marcellus and Eleanor Magogson, retain the right to occupy the residence and buildings which are currently known as the Magogson homestead located on not more than 1 acre of land for their natural lives at which time all right title and interest shall transfer to the Apple Orchard Development Corp." That's interesting. Normally there should be a better and more precise description. That one acre could be anywhere within the 80 acres. I looked at the date on the deed. It was dated October 21, 1892, but wasn't filed until 1899. That was weird; seven years had passed before the deed was filed. I made a note of it in my file. Where was that deed for seven years? When did the Magogsons die? Well, I was sure the Magogsons were long since dead. Still I wondered where the homestead sat in relation to all of the lots and houses currently sitting in our neighborhood. Was Darrah right? Did their house sit right by or on the Magogson homestead? Darrah had made it clear that the current house he resided in wasn't the original farmhouse. His house was old, but not that old. And why, even back then, would the county allow that type of vague document to be filed? I looked at the bottom of the last page and stamped with a square stamp with the word "Approved". At the top was the signature A. Rademacher? I wondered how he fit in. Was he related to Cornelius Rademacher? I was more curious than ever. I had one more piece of info to look for on the document: the notary. The notary, for the Magogsons' signatures was listed as "Mary Percy". I added her name to my short list of names that I would check up on at the Historical Society.

My stomach was starting to grumble. It was getting close to lunch time so I folded up my notes, tucked a copy of the deed I had made in my pocket and headed out. I was off to lunch and then to see an old friend. I had a list of questions that I needed some answers to and I also needed some background information on oaks. I knew my old friend could help.

As I walked down the stairs of county records building, I felt pretty satisfied. I still had the touch. I had tracked back the ownership of the lot that the Painted Lady sat on. Now there were just a few loose ends and I'd be done. First I'd have lunch, then I'd meet my friend, and then off to the Historical Society if I had time. I could already taste the soup and breadsticks.

I was used to getting to Edwintons through the skyway system. The skyway system was a maze of second floor walkways that allowed people moving throughout downtown to travel from block to block without going outside. Your landmarks moving through the skyway were totally different then when you were on the street below. Access to first floor shops and businesses was sometimes via hidden stairways through poorly marked doorways. That was why most of the well-traveled restaurants and shops sat along the second floor corridors of the skyway. Edwintons, though, sat on the street level. I knew how to access it from the skyway, I just wasn't a hundred percent sure where to access it from the street. The day was nice so I decided to head out along at street level. I gathered my bearings by looking up at the different skyways that crossed over the street. I was enjoying the fresh air and marveled at how the people moving through the skyways looked like hamsters in their own maze. I wondered if anyone would let them out at the end of the day.

Finally, there it was a little restaurant tucked in the corner. It wasn't much from street level. All they had was soup and homemade bread sticks. The soup of the day changed every day. But, there was always a special soup that they had on their menu every day: wild rice. It was real wild rice in a creamy thick base. Served along with the large bowl was a handful of bread sticks brushed with the garlic butter concoction. Once you got going you couldn't stop. In fact, it was an endless order you could keep refilling your bowl of soup and get more breadsticks at no additional charge. I couldn't resist, that was why I chose my trips downtown carefully. Going downtown everyday could be dangerous to my health.

After my fill of soup and bread, I began to continue my journey on to my next destination of the day. I was running ahead of schedule for my appointment with my friend. I cut down on my usually quick pace, wondering what I could do to waste some time. Halfway down the street, I could see the County Courthouse up the block. Yes, I had time for a little field trip. What the heck. Why not? I couldn't resist.

You might ask why I would want to go through the County Courthouse if I didn't have a reason. The County Courthouse was an art deco high rise some twenty-one stories high, built in 1932. It had been years since I was last inside. It was sort of on my route. I only had to cut through the first floor, that's where it was located. Something about the marble and multi-wood interior always had a soothing effect on me. Then there was the large statue that sat at the far end of the first floor, rising three stories, that was what I was going to see. I could never remember its name, but it always carried a sense of power and peacefulness at the same time. At the moment I couldn't remember all the details about the statue. I needed to check it out again.

I continued walking, feeling the glare of the sun off the buildings that lined the street. As I drew closer to the Courthouse, about halfway down the block from it sat a man, legs folded in front of him just sitting with a worn coat, pants and boots, with his hat face up in front of him on the pavement. I started to walk by when I heard him say, "We can't all go back to the beginning."

Not sure if I heard him right I stopped and turned. Looking at him I could see the weather-worn reddish brown of his face creased with lines that showed the timeline of his hard life. His nose was broad but bulged out at the end in a round, red, veined bulb.

Again he repeated, "We can't all go back to the beginning."

"What do you mean old man?" I asked not understanding him.

His voice was deep and clear, but I wasn't sure I understood him correctly. Then it hit me, not only had I disobeyed one of my rules of thumb by acknowledging the existence of a panhandler, now I was starting up a conversation with one, as well. Normally a panhandler strikes up a conversation for one reason, to ask for money. I didn't mind giving out money to a worthy cause, but with individual panhandlers I never knew how worthy the cause was. However, I was in control at the moment and I had some time to kill. Quickly he started into another chain of thought, "You are in need of some information, no, I think you are lost about where you might find some information."

Information, what was he talking about, I thought to myself. I had just gathered up all the information I needed this morning. He sounded like a fortune in one of those Chinese fortune cookies.

"You're not sure, just trying to find your way. You know all things begin and end at the tree. You just don't know where to find it yet."

He must have really caught me off guard because I answered back. "What do you mean old man?" I asked again.

"You need to know where the tree grows now not where it once grew. The thousand year old oak is what you must find. This land where I sit was once my people's land as far as the eye could see. It is still my people's land, it has just changed its shape; and yet, the Great Spirit watches over all. And I, I am still Proudfoot; no one can take that away from me. My ancestors were here before this city even existed and before your people arrived to spoil this land and they will be here long after you are gone, like the Great Spirit tree, we shall never cease to be, we just change . . . ."

"I understand," I said cutting him off in mid-sentence, not wanting to hear him ramble on.

"Can you at least spare some change then?" he said realizing I was growing short with him. "I'll give you one more piece of advice. Then you can decide if it was worth parting with your spare change."

I thought for a moment, and then I reached in my pocket and felt around, grabbing a few quarters but not all of my change. If this would make him quiet, I could then continue to move on down the street. I dropped the loose coins in his hat.

"Well old man," I stated in a disbelieving manner, believing that I had already parted with my money all for no good reason, "What words can you add to make my day?"

"Thank you," he said.

Then he paused for a moment.

"Beware of what appears to be a vision of peace. Peace is rarely brought forth by the hands of men. It can't be crafted or made. Peace is natural. It comes directly from the earth from which it is brought forth in its untainted form. It takes root slowly over time, growing wide and tall. A true vision of peace comes from the spirits of our great fathers, long since passed and is created out of the earth by the will of the gods. Like a great living tree, we can only stand back and be awestruck at its greatness. But, too often we try to create a likeness of it. Being simple men, sometimes we unwittingly corrupt that likeness and end up turning it into something evil. You might seek the vision of peace, but beware of what you may really find."

He was about to start into another thought, but I said, "Thanks for the advice, Proudfoot." And I started to turn.

"Wait, I have one more thing to leave with you. Give me your hand."

I started to get a little nervous, but not wanting to make a scene, I obliged and held out my hand. He gently placed something in it and said, "It is for your own protection. From now on always carry it with you. You don't know when you might need it. May the Great Spirit keep you safe."

I tried not to acknowledge the exchange of what he had placed in my hand and started walking down the block, trying to cradle whatever it was in my closed fist. After I was a couple strides down the street I opened my hand. In my palm was a large white feather, an eagle feather. I turned and glanced back. The Indian was gone.

I continued heading down the block and then there in front of me was the large building that housed the Court house. My pace quickened as I reached the front doors. I pulled hard on the handle of the large glass and metal door. In relation to the building, the doors seemed overly small. They were made of shiny stainless steel with full glass making up the center. I felt like I was entering a fifties diner for a minute, but when I grabbed the handle, to open the door, it had substance to it. I looked upwards across the front facade of the building. I was no longer able to see the entire front of the building from my vantage point. It was at that moment that I realized how truly massive the building was. For the first time I noticed the stark vertical lines that made up the front. Stone, alternating with indented panels of glass, streaking up the front as far as I could see. It looked like prison bars to me. I walked inside and immediately the darkness and serenity hit me. It took a few seconds for my eyes to adjust from the bright light of the outside world. I looked down the first floor expecting a large open space. In front of me though, were three uniformed deputies manning a checkpoint station. I moved up to the counter and they asked me to remove my belt, coat and any valuables and place them in the tray. I thought about placing the eagle feather in the tray, but kept it tucked in my front pocket. My peacefulness was replaced by a sense of uneasiness. I stepped forward through the electronic sensor, wondering if I would hear a beep. After I collected my personal items, I moved on down through the first floor atrium. It seemed much smaller than I had remembered. My eyes adjusted and there on the opposite end of the open space was the statue.

I walked across the hard marble floor and the clicking of my heels echoed off the wood and stone walls. I stared at the statue as I walked up to it. The statue reflected off the mirrored ceiling many feet above my head, making the statue look stories taller. The statue itself was polished like glass, golden from a distance. As I drew closer I could make out the veins running through the individual blocks that made up the entire piece of work. As I stared, the stark white color changed to a more cream color. The curves of the statue gave it an unreal dreamlike image, heavy and solid yet fluid and in motion. My eyes lowered to the base of the statue. There in a ring at the base of the main statute were five seated figures smoking pipes, peace pipes I assumed, because they were dressed in Native American dress. From their pipes swirled stone which rose into the great three story monolith that rose between them. I looked down at the plate in front of the statue. The plate read "Indian God of Peace" by Carl Milles. This is exactly what that Indian was talking about. He must say that to all the passing tourists. He knew most people heading that way would stop in the Courthouse. Nothing unusual there. The rest of words were just words that he had quickly put together as he sized me up during our brief conversation. That was all it could be. There wasn't any more to it.

But this in front of me, this was real. I was standing in front of it looking at it. Then it hit me, what did he mean about the true form of a vision of peace? I took another few minutes standing there pondering the statue. I wasn't too sure that the Native Americans from long ago would have approved that this large building now stood where plants, animals and nature once thrived. I could only wonder if it was really their god of peace or the white man's twisted interpretation of peace. The more I looked at it, the more I realized that the onyx statue wasn't alive, it was stark and cold stone. Here it was housed inside this huge angular edifice, never seeing the sun. No, I was pretty sure Native American ancestors wouldn't have thought it peaceful at all. Maybe that is what that Indian was talking about. Heading out the rear door on the other side of the block, I caught my bearings and let my eyes adjust to the sun.

Chapter 6
My Discussion with the Priest

I had lost touch with him until recently. We went back to my college days. He was a character all right, one of the more rowdy people I knew during college. He was one of those freethinkers always off on his own adventure, not concerned about what others thought. He never needed to be having a drink in his hand to be funny or hold a real conversation. No, he was the real deal. Just a down to earth guy who enjoyed living life for the moment. There was deepness about him, though. I could never put my finger on it. I always sensed that he was struggling with issues deeper than most of us dealt with, like the midterm coming up or a party this weekend. It wasn't really a surprise when near the end of our senior year he came up to me with a question. Actually it was more of a statement. He said to me, "What would you think if I told you I was seriously thinking about going on to seminary school?" I knew he had taken a heavy load of philosophy courses. He appreciated any discussion about different ideas and religions and was one of those rare people who could always look at something from many angles. In my mind, he was the perfect philosopher and maybe becoming a priest wasn't that much out of his calling. So, in the end after our lengthy discussion about why he was heading in that direction, I wasn't really surprised. He liked people, especially the part about dialogue with them to better understand where they were coming from and he was the most knowledgeable person I knew in the areas of philosophy and religious dogma. I just didn't think he had the ability to focus on only one religious viewpoint.

I hadn't seen him for a few years. He had officiated our wedding, but since then he had drifted away. Maybe it wasn't that he drifted away, I just hadn't stayed in touch with him. But I thought someone had mentioned that he was assigned nearby to one of the churches. Maybe he was even a Pastor by now. I didn't know. I really didn't know how I would get a hold of him. The internet might help, although I couldn't be too sure that he would have any type of listing there. I punched in "Father Tom Kelly" not believing I would get much of a lead. But there it was, fourth down on the screen, a blog by Tom Kelly "Ask Your Father", was the name. It had to be him. I hit the link and it took me to a rather plain looking website. It seemed to be set up in the form of a question and answer board focused mainly on concerns of faith and how to handle personal crises that someone was encountering. I scrolled down and there was an email link: "Ask the Father". I started in creating my e-mail: Dear Father, Is religion man-made or is it made by God? Please send me your answer in 25 words or less because I really am busy and don't have much time to spend on the issue." Getting together for a cup of coffee when you have the answer would work as well. I will buy, Sincerely, Roger." I knew I would get a response from him. The next day, a short e-mail was in my inbox. It read: "Roger, Man is God made, but man's ability to know God is up to man. Meet me at the rectory of The French Church, 8th and Wabasha next Tuesday at 1:15 for the remaining 11 words. That's if you have the time. The words are few but the advice is worth it. – Father Tom."

That was him. He still had that strange sense of humor I liked. I was looking forward to our meeting.

It was now Tuesday, I had timed my errands well. Lunch was good and feeling full, the walk to The Little French Church turned into a leisurely stroll. I didn't think Father Tom had any type of French background. But that really didn't matter now; the French part of the church name was ancient history. Originally, it was called the Church of Saint Louis King of France (*French*: L'Eglise de Saint-Louis, Roi de France) which is known commonly known today as "The Little French Church". It was the third Catholic Church built in St Paul and was originally built by the local French Canadians to serve the large French-speaking population. Since that time it was just one of a number of downtown churches swallowed up and surrounded by the city. The French Canadians were long gone, but the church still stood as a reminder of the past that was part of St. Paul.

I soon arrived with time to spare. I walked up to the front of the church or should I say the street side of the church. I was always confused which part of a church is considered the front. I always wanted to call the part of the church that faced the street, the front of the church, but then I realized, I was actually at the rear of the church, the end of the building opposite where the altar was situated. It was a miniature version of what I thought a larger, grander church should be; and so I understood why it was called the "little" French Church. It had tall spires on either side of the rear of the church that faced the street. At one time, it must have stood out, rising above one and two story buildings. Now it stood nestled among taller, modern buildings that rose above it, crowding it; as if trying to nudge it back into the dated history that defined it. Its neo-gothic look and size gave it charm and strength at the same time. The smaller size of the building made it appear as if it was simply a down-sized replica of something much more important. Yet here it stood, defying time and continuing to impact the downtown area in which it stood. It was too ornate for a simple church. Small for its size, it still held some surprises. Stone pillars were tucked in between the two spires and framed large sturdy doors accented the main entry into the church. The spires, square at the base raised three stories and were each capped with round white domes. As if it was an afterthought, the side front of the church had a shorter, exterior domed entry way. It was in that direction that I headed, after seeing a small sign with an arrow that said "Rectory" along the side of the building.

I followed the walk around the side of the church and then as I almost reached the front of the church, there was a large wooden door with inlaid design rounded at the top, almost hidden under the small white dome. Next to the door it said, "Rectory". This must be it. I pushed and the heavy door swung in.

A bell rang and I heard a familiar voice say, "Have a seat. I'll be right with you."

I didn't sit down right away. Instead, I paced around the small entry way. There was a small bench against one wall. I noticed the polished stone floor with different sizes and shapes of stone that fit neatly together like a large jigsaw puzzle. Curved stone edging divided the floor from the wall. Nothing hung on the walls. The only thing that broke the cut sandstone blocks of the wall was a small, square stained glass window. The multi-colored glass let in a mix of light. I looked at the picture inlaid in the glass. It was a tree with a male and female figure on either side beneath the tree's canopy. A serpent was coiled around the tree's trunk. The caption in the glass and under the scene read "Scit enim Deus quod in quocumque die comederitis ex eo, aperientur oculi vestri, et eritis sicut dii, scientes bonum et malum." Interesting, I thought, not being able to decipher what I assumed was Latin. Just at that moment Father Tom walked out into the entry area. He started in.

"Are you deciding on whether you have the right kind of knowledge so you can be saved?" he said in a joking tone.

"No, I'm just wondering whether it was really a talking serpent that made them do it or the challenge of the great tree itself. And seeing how I don't know any Latin I'm just going off what's in the picture in the glass," I answered.

"That's an interesting perspective on it," he said. "And yes, it is Latin. It's from the Book of Genesis and translated into English it reads 'Through true knowledge your eyes shall be opened and ye shall know good and evil.'"

He waved me in.

"Well, it's good to see you. Come on in to my office and sit down. It has been quite awhile hasn't it?" he went on. "I think the last time was at your wedding, if I'm not mistaken. How's your wife doing? I hope you aren't here because of problems on the home front," he said as he ushered me in to a small office, just a little bit bigger than the entryway but with no window.

A large desk piled with papers with a high-backed chair behind it took up two thirds of the space and two cushioned chairs in front of the desk took up the remaining space.

"Sit down. Sit down," he said. "So what do I owe this pleasure?" He asked.

"Well, Tom, thank you for meeting me; and no my wife is doing well and it isn't problems on the home front that bring me here," I said. I just didn't feel comfortable calling him Father. Now calling him Tom, as he had gotten older didn't seem comfortable either. Before I finished my thought, he started in again.

"Can I get you a cup of coffee?" he broke in, pointing to a coffee pot sitting on a shelf next to his desk.

"No, nothing, thank you," I added, as I sat down in the chair opposite him I was about to speak when he started in

"I don't have anything else to add to answer your question. There, that's eleven words," he said smiling after he spoke.

I leaned back and laughed.

"Oh, you knew that wasn't the reason I wanted to meet with you didn't you. Anyway, how you been. Saving plenty of souls?" I added trying to be humorous.

"John, it's not really about saving souls, it's about breathing life into them. I don't give people anything they didn't already have within them. I just awaken them to who they are and where they should be going. I just give them some insight. That's all," he continued. "Other than that, things have been well. I'm the Assistant Pastor here at 'The Little French Church'. That keeps me pretty busy. Actually, it's really three parishes now. You know with the downsizing at all levels, it's now just Pastor Robert and me working two churches. The third parish church was sold last year. It's a fitness center now. Can you believe that a Catholic Church is a fitness center, who would have thought? I hope this church here that I've attached myself to at the hip can keep moving forward in the right direction under my leadership. That's a little of my most recent background." He paused for a moment as if to catch his thoughts and then continued. "Enough of my thoughts. What's on your mind? And don't say it's the question you sent me."

"Well, I called you because I have an interesting puzzle I was hoping you could shed some light on. What do you know about oak trees? I asked.

"Oak trees? Let me see. They're great to make furniture out of, roasted acorns are a great poor man snack, and oh, oak leaves can be used for great grade school art projects," he said smiling.

"No, I said. What do you know about oak trees from a religious or maybe historical perspective?"

"Why do you ask?"

"Well, I have this neighbor. He's really hung up on the past and construction of his house. He's just really caught up in the fact that his house is made of oak, was made from an old oak tree that sat on his land. I was just curious, if he was just an eccentric old man or if there was more to that oak infatuation," I said.

"Hmm, that is interesting. He probably is just an eccentric old man. But, all joking aside, the oak tree really does go back a long way, to the roots of mankind, no pun intended. It comes up in many different cultures. Oak trees were found in basically all of the countries around the Mediterranean, and in ancient Palestine certain types of oak trees grew to a large size; and lived to a very old age. For many ages after Christ, there was an oak tree near Hebron that was thought to be one of the oak trees that Abraham lived under at Mamre. Throughout history, it is always under the shade of large oak trees that public affairs were carried out, sacrifices made and kings crowned. There are those types of references right from the Bible. I can think of two bible passages that come to mind that back that up, Joshua 24:26 and Judges 6:11. Anything specifically you're looking for?" he continued.

"No. I'm not sure. Like I said, I'm more curious than anything else. It's interesting because he seems to be a very religious man as well. Well, not religious in the normal meaning of the word; maybe spiritual is a better word to use. He's hung up on tradition and history. A number of his reference topics appear to be tied to Native American ideals. I think I'm just really curious as to what are the mythical or religious references to an oak tree?" I added, as I felt myself beginning to wonder why I really was having this discussion. It was beginning to sound strange as I spoke about it.

"It depends. Different parts of the oak have different types of meanings. The wood from the oak of course was used to make tools, shelter and many other implements going back to ancient times. Because it is such a hard wood, it holds up well for many different uses.

Plus, the acorns were used as a food source. I can't remember the exact Dickens novel, but I remember that they used to roast acorns as well. In Korea, after the war the people made an acorn jelly to stop from starving due to food shortages. To this day it is a traditional side dish at special occasions.

Many oak trees can last for more than a century or longer. Interesting enough, the tree is tied to the birth of fire as well. Because many oak trees were struck by lightning, it was considered a sacred way for the gods to communicate with us mere mortals. In Greek mythology, the tree was tied to the god Zeus, In Viking lore; it was used for Thor's mighty axe handle. Hercules carried a giant club made of oak."

"Wait a second," I stopped him, "Are you just making this up?"

"No, not at all. I did some research on the oak for a practice homily I had to do when I was in the seminary. I tied in the idea of the mighty oak being similar to God: that his canopy, his spirit, spread over us, protecting us from harm. That as the tree of life, god created us, the acorns, watching over us until we started to grow and expand our own families, keeping in mind that we always came from the one mighty oak," he said. He paused for a moment.

"Now it's sort of corny looking back on it. But interestingly, there are plenty of references in the Bible to the oak. The oak tree at Shechem is the site where Jacob buries the foreign gods of his people. In addition, Joshua erects a stone under an oak tree as the first covenant of the Lord. In Isaiah 61, the prophet refers to the Israelites as "Oaks of Righteousness". The oak is woven throughout many cultures," he continued.

"Is there any meaning that the Native American peoples tied to the oak?" Not expecting him to know about their rituals.

"Well, I'm not sure; I pretty much gave you my wealth of knowledge. But, as I mentioned the oak appears throughout history in many cultures. The oak was present here in this country long before the white man came. I would think that the Native Americans may have attached similar importance to it, just like other cultures." he finished.

"Is there any negative connotation associated with oak that you're aware of?" I asked. "I was noticing the stained window in the entryway. Is that an Oak tree?" I continued.

"No, I don't think so, to answer your question about the stained window. But, I couldn't be certain of that. As to your first question, it's hard to say. It depends on what you consider negative. As I just mentioned, oak trees are referenced throughout the Bible. I think it really comes down to what it symbolizes. That tree in the window is the tree of knowledge of what is good and evil. It's not that the tree is good or bad, it's what it represents and how we choose to use it for good or evil. That is my two cents. I don't think anything is inherently good or bad, it's how we interact with it that makes it good or bad," he added.

"Well, so you think we can turn something good into something evil?" I asked trying to egg him on.

"That's a whole other discussion. I believe man is great at changing things in many different ways. He's either improving something or making it worse. Man doesn't usually want to just sit and look at something and appreciate it the way it is. When we're looking at things from the spiritual perspective, many times man corrupts something to change it into his own image, not God's. Many times, man thinks he is doing what God wants him to do but he loses sight of the actual purpose that God has planned for him. He gets the interpretation all wrong and thus goes down the wrong path taking whatever it is along with him. But, don't get me started." He stopped for a moment. "That last part was just my personal perspective on things. Now you mentioned your neighbor was religious, maybe that provides a context as to why the oak tree is so important to him. How is he religious in your mind?"

"Well, it was more in his demeanor. As I said, it was more a spirituality than an adherence to a religious belief or beliefs. It was how he carried himself. Oh, and in fact at dinner he said an unusual prayer before we ate."

"What did he say?"

"I can't quite remember, something about being watchful, protecting the house, something like that. I'll have to think about that."

"Let me know if you come up with it. I hope I was helpful with information regarding your search for knowledge. I don't want to cut you off, but I do have to run a prayer session in a couple of minutes. Can we set up another time to get together? I actually found your line of questioning very interesting"

"Yes, I would like that." I said. You're my only outlet for a connection to God these days," I jokingly said. "But seriously, thanks for meeting with me." I finished.

"Not a problem. Good to see you again. Remember religion and spirituality are sometimes worlds apart," he added.

He ushered me out through the doorway and I couldn't help but look at the stained glass window one more time as I exited the entryway.

Chapter 7
Meeting at the Historical Society

I knew it was getting to be mid afternoon, but my curiosity was still running wild. My day wasn't over yet. I was an experienced detective hard on the trail of solving a mystery; and I didn't have anything else to do at the present moment. Plus, The County Historical Society was on the edge of downtown and on my way home. I might as well swing in and see if they could shed some more light on my quest for additional answers.

I walked back to my car. Thinking about what my friend, Father Tom had said, I agreed with him: things aren't inherently good or bad. But was a tree a thing? Wasn't it somehow alive at least in the sense of a plant being alive? I guess a tree really couldn't be good or bad. But then again what did I know. I was just an unemployed private investigator.

I pulled up to The County Historical Society. It was housed in a true Victorian home built well before 1900. The house was built and originally occupied by the first governor of Minnesota. It was only fitting that this is where The County Historical Society was located. I walked up the sidewalk and looked at the old house admiring the asymmetrical stone front and the tidy black wrought iron fence that surrounded it. The house looked sturdy, rising three stories, capped by its gabled roofs and large square windows uniformly set into the hand cut stone facing. The house itself was made of oversized cut sandstone blocks. A newly laid brick walk led up to the front door. It was the only feature that suggested this wasn't completely out of the past.

I walked up to the front door. Hung on the inside of the door, but in front of a lace curtain that ran the length of the oval glass set in the wooden door was a sign that said:

"Closed

Hours: Monday, Wednesday and Saturday 9 to 4".

I thought about leaving, but as long as I was here, a simple knock on the door wouldn't hurt or how about just a ring of the bell, as I saw a doorbell to the left of the door. I rang the doorbell but couldn't hear any resulting sound. I was getting ready to turn and walk away when I heard the sound of footsteps moving closer towards the front door. A hand pulled back the lace curtain and a face appeared. It was a thin frail lady in a simple dress.

"We're closed," she said, "You'll have to come back during our regular hours."

"I'm not here just to visit I'm here on official business," I said stretching the truth. I actually was here officially, I thought to myself, and this was my business that I was involved in.

"What do you mean?"

"I'm a writer doing research on some local history. I've come up to St. Paul for the day and I've been doing some research. It was suggested I check with you. Please, it shouldn't take long," I pleaded.

"You'll have to come back tomorrow during regular business hours," she said again through the glass.

"That would be difficult. I'm just in town for today and then I'm leaving the Twin Cities to head home."

"Where did you say you were from?" she asked.

"I didn't." I said. I had committed to my tall tale now I had to follow through with my tale. With each new word out of my mouth I was moving into a fictional realm. I had to make sure I was convincing enough. I guess I was now a writer. If I was going to convince her, I had to convince myself. Anyone who has ever written something is a writer. I was researching local history even though it was for my own purposes. Yes, I could pull this off. "I'm a writer with the New Ulm Gazette," I said. "I'm looking for some background on a farm that was sold around the turn of the century and how it might be tied to a prominent local family in New Ulm. Can I come in and explain?" Pretty good I thought to myself. The more I spoke, the more I was even beginning to believe myself.

"I don't know. Can't you come back when we're open? It is getting late," she said.

"I did come all this way. I'd hate to drive back up another day. It really shouldn't take long. You can kick me out whenever you need to go. I just need a half hour or so. It would mean the world to me," I pleaded using my most charming voice.

She hesitated for a quick moment and I knew I had her.

"Oh, OK," she said, "Please keep it short. I normally don't do this, but given your circumstances. . . ." She turned the lock in the door and pulled it open.

"Come on in," she said. "I only let you in because you look like my son."

"Thank you. Thank you so much," I said.

"So what exactly are you looking for?" she said trying to move things along.

"Well," I said, "as I said, I'm looking for some information you might have on the Magogson farm. It was a farm for many years just west of the city before it was bought and swallowed up by the growing city. It was turned into a development, added as a part of the city by a developer right after the turn of the century. We're looking to see if there was a connection the Magogsons up here in the cities might have had to the Magogsons in New Ulm," I lied. Now I couldn't stop. It didn't matter what I said. The important part was that I continued to weave a believable tale. And so, I just kept going. Father Tom would have been shaking his head if he could hear me now.

"I'm putting together a set of articles for the 150th anniversary of New Ulm. Getting this information would be of great interest to our community. I'm competing with another writer for the paper to see who can come up with the most unusual connections and information New Ulm has with the rest of the state. Hopefully, I'll find a connection here."

I hesitated for a minute. How much further could I go?

"Would you have any information like that? I mean on the Magogson farm. Anything at all?"

"It all depends. We don't keep records like copies of deeds or official documents. We have had letters and other artifacts donated to us by different people over the years. We collect things that are off the public grid. The farm was located in Ramsey County here?" she added.

"Yes. According to the land records it was."

"Let me think. It seems to me there was some old correspondence, letters and notes that had been in old boxes that we were just now starting to catalog for a new display on early Minnesota in Ramsey County. We were trying to tie in the contribution of women to the growth of St Paul. The name Magogson doesn't ring a bell though. Anything else that you have that might help?" she asked trying to remember.

"Well, the name of the subdivision was Apple Orchard. The development company was Apple Orchard Development Corp. I think the original developer was Cornelius Rademacher. He owned the company. At least that's what appeared on the deed."

"Hmm, that sort of rings a bell, not Rademacher, but Apple Orchard. We just categorized some letters and notes from an attorney, a woman by the name of Candace St. Simmons, some attorney from out East. We got some funds from a private benefactor. Rare these days to get funds for anything. We just started cataloging everything. I can let you take a look. It will have to be quick though, I can't stay longer than another forty-five minutes.

Even though you're a reporter, mind you, you can't leave with any of the documents. I'll have to check your bag before you leave. We've had problems in the past with people walking off with artifacts. Strange couple of men came in last year, in fact. Said they were searching for a long lost relative. Actually it turns out they were with the Georgia Sons of the Confederacy. They were looking to get back some Georgia Civil War era battle flags that they felt belonged to their group. Said they were taken by those damn Yankees all those years ago. My thought is that our people fought and died for the right to bring those battle mementos back here and here they should stay. That's just my personal opinion. Now there's correspondence going back and forth between the governor of Georgia and the governor of Minnesota. The governor of Georgia says it belongs to the state of Georgia. It all happened 150 years ago and they're fighting it out like it all happened yesterday. Now that's living history for you." She shifted her feet and I could tell she was trying to shift her thoughts as well. "Now let me think, where did I put those recently catalogued items." She thought for a moment and then said, "Follow me."

I had the urge to tell her the truth. That I was just a nosy neighbor who was doing some strictly personal background research on the history of my neighborhood; that I wasn't writing an historical piece or trying to solve a city mystery. No, I was just a personal snoop. How would that help anyone at this point? I was trying to track down what my neighborhood was like before it was divided up into a residential neighborhood. That was true. No, I had a legitimate purpose to be here, plus it seemed like she really was enjoying trying to help me.

We headed beyond the small entry area. The space opened up into a broader hallway leading to the back of the house and a wide stairway that angled off to the right. She started to climb the stairs.

"These stairs give you a workout every time you go up them," she said slowly moving up them; and I followed.

"I think the package is still on the desk in the archive room. That's a fancy name for where we go through everything as we try to catalogue it. It's nothing more than a back office. We really don't have any elaborate electronic systems like the large museums. Can't afford it. No, it's all done by hand, by volunteers. Wish we had better funding. Really, this is run more like a family treasure trove than a real museum. Oh, I'm not saying everyone that works here or volunteers isn't committed. I just wish we had better resources to maintain all this state history. Our members though truly appreciate our dedication."

As she reached the top of the stairs, she led me into a room straight ahead of her. Boxes sat haphazardly on the three desks that took up most of the room. Along the edges of the room leaned framed pictures propped here and there.

"As you can see, this is a work in progress. Slow progress," she added. "Now let me see, which desk did I last see that packet?" She shuffled around the contents on two desks. Upon reaching the third she lifted some loose papers that sat on a cardboard box and then lifted the cardboard box as well. Underneath it was a worn brown leather folder tied loosely with a string. She pulled it out. "I believe there might be some information in here that might be helpful to you. I can't guarantee it though. I didn't catalogue many of the contents. I was just the one who found it up in the attic, filed away in an old trunk. See the name on the front of the folder? That's why I think it might be helpful."

I looked down as she held it up. It was worn at different areas along the edges of the folder where hands might have carried it at one time. It was made of thick leather that appeared smooth and polished. And there on the front, engraved in fancy lettering were the words "Candace St. Simmons, Esq., and directly underneath was the Latin phrase *"Crede quod habes, et habes"* and the date "1890".

"1890. Is that how old it is? And what does that Latin phrase mean?" I asked. I was beginning to think that sometime in my life I should have taken a course or two of Latin. Who would have thought that anyone would need to understand a dead language during their lifetime? Not me for one.

"Yes, I believe it is that old. At least the folder was made then. Based on the dates of the contents, they are from ten years later or so. I'm guessing she may have received it as a gift or something like that. The Latin means 'Believe that you have it and you do'. It was probably some reference to the fact that she would be successful as an attorney. It was probably wishing her luck in her career. I'm guessing she needed all the support she could get back then. There weren't many women attorneys back then. It was a man's world. Most men wouldn't be open to seeing her achieve her goals as an attorney. That's just a guess on my part. It was true there weren't many women attorneys back then. In fact, most states didn't see their first woman attorney until well after the civil war. It was even more unusual to have a woman attorney here in Minnesota, even into the beginning of the 1900's. That is why this find is so unique. It gives some background on a woman attorney in the early days of this city. Interesting indeed. Well anyway, I'll let you have a look through. Forty-five minutes tops, then I have to lock up."

She moved some papers off the corner of one desk, pulled a chair up and said, "Here, you can sit here. I'll check back with you before I lock up," and with that she moved out of the room and turned down the hallway. I could hear her footsteps grow quieter as she moved to another part of the building.

I sat down in the chair, pulled the string to loosen the simple knot and then opened the leather folder. Inside, were a number of envelopes and some neatly folded sheets of paper as well as some legal looking documents that weren't folded, and small leather bound book. I pulled the contents out of the leather case and laid them on the table.

I began to examine the contents.

Before long I could hear her footsteps growing louder coming down the corridor. In a moment she stood in the entryway to the room.

"I'm sorry but I've got to lock up now. Hope you found what you were after."

"Yes and no. Interesting, really fascinating. Where did the historical society come across that leather satchel and its contents?"

"I'm not 100% sure, but we found a note with the leather case . . . let me see if I can find that note . . . I think we put it with the notes we make when we catalogue things." She walked over to a shelf on the side of the room and pulled down a large three ring binder. Opening it, she pulled out a slip of paper.

"This was tucked inside the leather case when I found it in our treasure room, or should I say our attic." She handed me a worn slip of paper.

It wasn't just a simple note it was a receipt of some sort. On the top it read,

"St. Paul Police Department. Release of Evidence."

It looked official. Then in handwriting below, in hard to read scribbling, it read:

"Personal effects of Ms. Candace St. Simmons: one leather binder with papers, one brooch, suitcase with contents, one lady's overcoat." and was signed "Sergeant McAndrews". The date was: December 30, 1892.

"What does this mean? I asked"

"Seems to me, from what I can figure out it was a release of the personal effects of Ms. St. Simmons, the attorney who owned this leather brief case."

"Well, what happened to her?" I asked.

"I'm not sure. We don't know. We've just finished cataloguing the contents."

"Do you have her other belongings?'

"Not that I'm aware of. This was the only item linked to her that we've found so far. I'm not even sure how we came across it. Like I said, it had been sitting in the attic for quite some time. It could have even been there when the Ramsey's donated this house to the historical society back in the 60's. I don't know."

"The Ramsey house?" I asked.

"Yes. Alexander Ramsey. He was an attorney, judge, mayor of St. Paul and well, then governor of Minnesota. His family donated this house to The Historical Society back in the sixties along with many belongings, artifacts, memoirs and the like. He was the second governor of Minnesota. He was very involved in the growth of Minnesota as a young state."

"Well that is interesting," I said.

"I thought any good reporter would know his history about the state. Especially if he is researching and writing articles of historical significance," she noted.

"No, I was referring to the interesting fact of finding the leather case in this house and the possible connection to Alexander Ramsey. A great find indeed." I said trying to give as much praise as I could to her, while deflecting my lack of knowledge of the history of our state. That seemed to put her at ease again.

"Tell you what. I can't do it today, but I can do some checking and see if I can come up with anything on our Ms. St. Simmons. Give me your number and I can call you if I find out anything."

"Tell you what, I said, what if I swing by next week. I'll be in the neighborhood again, then. If I need any additional information that comes to mind, I can make notes in the meantime and bring by my additional questions. Then, I can talk to you about any additional information you come across. Plus, I owe you for all you help. I know of a great bakery I'll pick up something and bring it by. What day works?" I didn't want her knowing any more about me than she had to. I had already made up a story to get the information so far. I didn't want anything to come back to haunt me. It was best that she didn't have any hard information on me.

"You'd bring up bakery all the way from New Ulm for me? Well, next Wednesday would work. Anytime in the afternoon."

"It'd be my pleasure," I said. Not telling her that it would be from a bakery in St. Paul. I made a mental note to myself to remove any references to the St Paul bakery when I brought it in to her next week. Driving 100 miles down to New Ulm just to get some bakery wasn't going to happen.

She walked me down the stairs, after briefly making sure I hadn't grabbed any notes, paperwork or civil war battle flags and ushered me out the front door. I turned back and there she stood behind the door waving through the glass as she locked it.

I now had more questions to be answered. I was getting excited, this simple investigation was getting more complex. It would require more of my time; and time I had.

Chapter 8

Reading the Other Documents in the Folder

As I walked back to my car the contents of the portfolio drifted through my mind. To me it was like opening up a time capsule. I could only imagine, sitting unopened for more than a hundred years, waiting for me to come across it. Sure the lady who had catalogued it had opened it, but I was the first to find its connection to something. I had stumbled across this piece to a bigger puzzle of a mystery that was yet to be solved. It was a mystery that I alone was aware needed solving. I knew it. I was on to something of importance. I could feel it. My job search would have to wait.

Forty-five minutes had been barely enough time to rifle through the contents and briefly look at the items. I hoped I hadn't missed anything important in there. I had quickly gone over all of the contents in the order they were placed in the folder. Then, I took more time and went back over every item, looking at each item more closely. But even now the different contents, the documents, the note began to blur together. I wasn't sure if I was keeping them all clear in my mind. Too bad I couldn't make copies. Maybe I could have, I just didn't ask. Let me think. I closed my eyes for a moment and tried to go through the contents in my mind.

The first thing I had come across was a copy of the deed that I had found recorded in the county records earlier in the day. It appeared to be identical to the recorded deed, except for the fact that the one in the case wasn't signed. That really wasn't unusual. Usually, more than one copy would have been drafted. It may have been a copy for the attorney's records. It was in her case. Maybe she had kept a copy to cover her butt. Or, maybe it was meant to be passed on to her client. Either way, from what I could remember looking at the recorded deed, they were identical. I should have compared it to the recorded deed, I just didn't have time. Trying to cut corners and now I wasn't sure.

I guess I'd have to see where some of the other pieces of information took me. Then if I still had concerns about the deed, I would have to go down to the county and look at it again; and this time I would have to make a copy.

Next, there were some loose odds and ends. Mainly receipts for things the attorney had purchased while she was in St Paul. I probably wouldn't be able to match those old handwritten receipts to anything else I came across. One was for Sam's Livery Stable; another was for the gift shop in the Ryan Hotel; and still another for the Endicott Building Hat Shop. So she did get out to do a little shopping. She wasn't just all business after all. And then, there was a receipt for the Wild Steer Restaurant. I turned it over, there was no date anywhere on it. I looked closer, the only things scribbled on the receipt was what was ordered to eat and the cost of each item, with a total at the bottom. That must've been a St. Paul Restaurant back then. It was probably located downtown. Who would know for certain? These items were truly just a pile of loose odds and ends. If they were current clues I might be able to follow up on them. But, seeing how dated they were, they were just little pieces of history. None of those items were out of the ordinary. Probably, she was keeping track of her expenses to charge her client while she was working here in St. Paul. It was hard to say what, if anything could be learned from any of those items. It would probably be difficult, if not impossible, to track down any leads from those scattered bits of information. Something a bit more curious and unique was an old fashioned calling card that I located in the bottom of the case, after I had dumped out all of the contents . The name on the card was Julius O. Holm. Below his name it just read: Painter St. Paul, Minnesota. That information at least I had written down. I would see if that name came up anywhere else. Then, there was an interesting letter to

Rademacher that referenced the deed. I wasn't sure how this tied in, but it really started me thinking. It was hand-written on Ryan Hotel stationary in a most precise penmanship. I remembered marveling at the smooth strokes of the letters. Her writing showed a refined, classy style. It made me really want to meet her in person. Who was she? What was she like? She must have been pretty self assured to get involved in a profession that back then, was dominated by men. In fact, most people wouldn't have even thought of hiring a woman attorney. Why would she have been hired? Of all people, why would she have been hired for this matter? I tried to recall in my mind what the letter said:

October 10, 1892

Re: The Magogson Farm Matter

Mr. Rademacher:

So far I have been unable to procure the necessary signatures for the transfer of the Magogson farm. As discussed I offered them a life estate in their homestead so that they could remain in their home for as long as they wish. Also, I discussed with them an option to allow them to farm the adjacent farm land even after the sale of the farm land for a limited amount of time. I assume that additional offer is acceptable as well. Even with that offer, Mr. Magogson was not open to discuss the sale of the land any further. I understand your concerns regarding the urgency to move forward with the purchase. I can be reached at the Ryan Hotel where I have arranged accommodations while in the process of completing this business. You can leave a note for me at the front desk if I am not in. I do have some additional ideas on how to complete the purchase.

I think it may be easier to work with Mrs. Magogson. I would like to have my backup plan in place before going back out to the farm. I was able to arrange for a stableman, Sam Proudfoot to take me out to the farm. I'm sure he would be willing to take me out to the farm again as needed. I await your response.

Miss. Candace St Simmons, Esq.

Interesting, I thought to myself. So at this point in time when the letter was written, she hadn't gotten the Magogsons to sell yet. No signed deed. When did that occur? Maybe she was never involved with the signing of the deed. That seemed more likely. But then who was responsible for wrapping up the sale of the farm. And what did she discuss with Rademacher? Also, why was this letter still in her possession? Hadn't it ever been sent to Rademacher? The letter didn't appear to be a copy. It looked like it was an original. The ink on the paper showed signs of smudges here and there. All of these were more questions to be answered if I was to solve the growing mystery. On the plus side, I now had the name of the person who drove her out to the farm, "Proudfoot". There was the receipt for Sam's Livery Stable. That must have been for the trip out to the farm. Why else would she have gone to a livery stable? I don't know why, but that name "Proudfoot" rang a bell for some reason. Couldn't be could it? Where had I heard that name before? Yes, the Indian I ran into downtown. Didn't he say his name was Proudfoot. Maybe that was a common Native American name. I don't know.

Most curious of all was the small leather notebook. That definitely looked promising. Maybe it held more answers.

For a moment I stopped and just stood there. I tried to picture what she might of looked like, this attorney. I really couldn't come up with a picture of her face, but I could see her in a white blouse buttoned up the front all the way to her chin, a long skirt that stopped above the ankles to reveal black pointed shiny boots, and a simple bonnet. That was all I could picture.

Chapter 9
Reading the Diary

I unlocked my car door and hopped in the driver's seat. I paused for a moment and then pulled my pant leg up and reached down into my sock and pulled out the small bound diary. I just couldn't resist. I knew it was wrong. Father Tom would have a field day with this one, as well. I just didn't have enough time in there and I had to get more information. It would have killed me to wait for a whole week to find out. Anyway, I'd return it next week once I had finished reading it. The Historical Society wouldn't even miss it. There was no harm, no harm at all, I thought to myself.

I held the leather bound book in my hands. I hesitated for a moment, moving it back and forth in my hands. The fact that I had removed it from The Historical Society without permission heightened my excitement. I couldn't believe how the building anticipation made my thoughts race. Then carefully I opened it up. Throwing back the cover, I opened it and there was a stale smell of dust. Even though it was dry, it smelled old. I thought to myself that I was the first person to open it since Candace penned the words I was about to read in its pages. I flipped the pages. The pages were filled with simple scribbled writing in what appeared to be pencil. It was almost in short hand, nothing like the carefully written letter I had seen in The Historical Society. No, it seemed that this writing was more of a personal nature. It was probably written for her eyes only. In places, the pencil was more worn than others, almost indiscernible. As I suspected it was a journal or diary of some kind. I began to read the first entry.

September 30, 1892

Even though I know I need to focus on this trip because it is business, I can't help but be a little overwhelmed at what I am undertaking. Here, I am traveling halfway across the country to handle my first real assignment. I think I am up to the task, but I still have my doubts. Here I sit in my seat looking out the window in the train station, the Grand Central Depot, thinking I still have the option of getting off. I could just stay here in New York. I could find another client, something easier right here in the city. No I am up for this challenge. Sure it is well out of my liking. St. Paul isn't the Wild West, but it certainly isn't New York. No, this is a grand experience I am undertaking. The train is leaving the station.

October 1, 1892

I arrived by train last night in St. Paul. I hope that I am up to the task and that I have made the right choice in coming out here. This town is nothing like the organized bustle of New York. The smell of horse manure is everywhere. I can't get it out of my head. The smell of the river is the only thing that masks it from time to time. That smell is a mixture of sewage and debris. Flooding can occur, but I have been told not to worry, that that only occurs in the spring.

A pleasant coachman was willing to take me to The Ryan, I almost fell asleep going the few blocks to The Ryan. The pamphlet that I had seen before making arrangements to stay there touted it as a place of grace and elegance rising more than 6 stories in the heart of downtown St. Paul. The problem was, it is the first and only building to rise more than 6 stories above the skyline of a growing downtown St. Paul. It doesn't compare with other hotels I am familiar with in New York. It will have to do, it is the best thing available in St. Paul. As the carriage pulled up, gas lights lit the front doorway. Yes The Ryan does have charm. Standing in front of the entryway it looked taller than its seven stories. The multiple towers and ornamental metal spikes add certain delicateness to the brick face that angled in and out the length of the block. I hope my initial curiosity lasts for as long as my business makes it necessary for me to remain here.

October 2, 1892

The downtown is a bustling place of shops and wholesale mercantile shipping areas. Sitting on the Mississippi, the city was where the last tentacles of civilization had reached before the wide expanses of the west opened up. St. Paul is a boom town. It appears to be growing in leaps and bounds. There is much energy, like the business districts of New York, only on a much smaller scale. I Talked to a gentleman I met in the hotel lobby, a Mr. Holm, Julius Holm. He was really an interesting person. He wasn't your normal well dressed sophisticated gentleman. No, he was rather down to earth. Actually I think he was overseeing some painters at the Ryan. He wouldn't admit it, but during our conversation the hotel manger talked to him a couple of times, asking about how progress was coming. Mr. Holm seemed to be a wealth of information and talked in detail about how St Paul was not only a destination, but a hub, serving the travelers who reached here as a jumping off point for all points north and west. He also pointed out that it was a destination for Easterners headed here to forget their past, so they could start over. I assured him that wasn't the case with me. I wasn't here to start a new life, I was here on business. He still seemed fixated on the fact that Easterners were all just displaced immigrants, unable to take root and prosper in New York or the other main cities and so they came to use the hard scrabble lessons they had learned, but in a more "friendly" environment. From what I had seen of the downtown area maybe he was right, it was just that: a strange mix of people, people looking for a second chance maybe. He wouldn't discuss his occupation but did say that he was a distinguished painter in St. Paul. I asked him what works he had completed. He tried to evade my question. He did say he was working on a scenic masterpiece of St. Paul covering a great event that had recently occurred in the city, "The Lake Gervais Cyclone". In actuality, he told me the Lake Gervais Cyclone was a Tornado that swept through St. Paul in 1890. Mr. Holm said he was hard at work on his masterpiece and that shortly it would be hanging in a prominent spot in the lobby of the Ryan Hotel. I don't know if it was my look of disbelief on how important it was to do a painting of a tornado, but he made a point of calming my fears, stating that the chances of another tornado coming through St Paul were very slim. Yes, St. Paul is interesting. I don't know what to think of it.

I thumbed forward in the journal and a letter fell out of the journal. There tucked into the journal were some sheets of paper. I opened them up. It looked official and was on letterhead. Letterhead from what appeared to be a law firm from back east in New York. I began to read through it. It was addressed to Miss. Candace St. Simons, Esq. As I read through it, a section caught my eye.

"As a favor to your father we would like you to handle a delicate matter for us. It will require you to travel to Minnesota. We are in the process of completing land purchases around St. Paul for further development. At this time, the true ultimate purchasers of the land wish to remain anonymous. We have set up a Minnesota corporation as the vehicle to initially hold the title to the land purchases. We have retained as a partner in St. Paul, Mr. Cornelius Rademacher, to assist in the final purchase of some remaining parcels. Specifically, we are concerned about his completion of the purchase of a parcel of land known as the Magogson farm. We would like to retain your services to resolve the purchase and then obtain from Mr. Rademacher the full details of the total purchase of the other various parcels. We are willing to pay fully for your travel expenses and lodging while in St. Paul and . . . ."

The letter continued on to a second and third sheet. It appeared to be just more details and background on the land to be purchased. So that was why she was the one chosen to handle this legal matter. One more question answered. As to the rest of the details n the letter, I would get back to that later. Right now I wanted to get back to the journal entries.

So, it seemed she was an attorney from back East and a curiosity in the city just like so many others new to the town.

I flipped forward a couple of pages and started reading another journal entry.

October 4, 1892

I believe staying at The Ryan was the right choice. It sits right in the center of downtown St. Paul with easy access to shops and businesses that I might need to avail of their services.

New to town, I didn't know where to go to get the service of a driver with a horse and buggy. The coachman at the hotel was nice enough to point me in the direction of a livery stable on the edge of downtown that might be able to assist me. He apologized, that the coach service the hotel offered only went as far as the top of Ramsey Hill and that was when the weather wasn't too inclement. It's finally sunk in that I've been hired by a land speculator, or land developer if that's what you want to call them. I couldn't help but wonder if the true purchaser was a railroad. That would make sense. Moving west to the Midwest they would look for parcel or tracts of land adjacent to growing cities, land that would connect their tracts to a new growing city. Then, with money from deep pocket investors they would give large sums for farmsteads and then subdivide them into lots for settlers moving west who were looking for homes just beyond the city limits after they had subdivided off the strip of land for their track right of way. Not that it makes any difference. I've taken the job and I will follow it through to completion regardless of who my true client is.

October 5, 1892

Today I went further than I had gone in my previous walks, checking out downtown. The clerk at The Ryan had told me about some interesting shops in the new Endicott building. Of course, the offerings didn't compare to the different fashions back in New York. I did find a simple hat in one of the shops. I don't want to stand out as an East coast dandy and so I purchased it to wear when I head out on official business. Finally, making my way to the edge of downtown I came across the livery stable recommended by the coachman . . . .

As I continued through the reading of the journal entries, I began to drift off in my mind and imagine her movements as she moved about the streets of St. Paul. I pictured her in long dress and broad brimmed hat with a floral arrangement on top cocked sideways, carrying her leather case trying to look businesslike, but really unsure of where she was going and more unsure of her surroundings. I pictured her young pretty face pale with thick brown hair that she tried to hide tucked up underneath that broad hat. Did she have an accent? Maybe that thick New York twang? Maybe she was able to hide it to blend in more. Maybe she just wore simple clothes and a colorless bonnet carrying her case as she went about town handling whatever business it was that she needed to do. No, I settled on her as most likely a fish out of water. A New Yorker no longer protected by the big city. Sophisticated enough to miss the refinements New York had to offer. I still wasn't sure if she was just book smart or street smart as well. I would have to work on that in my mind.

I pictured her walking along the downtown streets from the hotel trying to mingle with the locals, but looking out of place in fine East coast fashions. Maybe she took a detour down a side street. I could feel the warm sun still sitting high in the sky even on the fall cool day. It was probably dry. She wouldn't have had to avoid muddy stretches in the street, but maybe the occasional horse dropping. The combination of animals and city living would have mixed together incompatible odors. There was grease and cooking smells from local apartments and restaurants, animal waste and the overall smell of a bustling city in motion.

A few more steps, just blocks from her hotel she would have come across the livery stable. Things were quickly changing in St.

Paul. It would only be a few short years from now and any remaining horses in the area would be outside the city limits and horseless carriages would be the new mode of transportation. But for now, horse and buggy transportation was the safest bet.

She walked through the doorway and standing before her, looking like he had been waiting for her, was an Indian with broad shoulders, a black rounded top hat with a broad brim and what appeared to be an eagle feather angled backward. He was in dirty jeans and a tan leather vest that hung against his body.

"Hello," she said. "Do you know where I can rent a coach or a buggy with a driver to run an errand for a few hours?"

"Ma'am, I'm sorry but this ain't the place. This is a livery stable, as you can see by the sign." Looking above she could see a hand carved wooden sign that said "Livery" with an outline of a horse's head and what looked like half of a wagon wheel.

"We repair coaches and shod horses. We're not in the stagecoach business."

"Oh is that so, a coachman over at the Ryan Hotel suggested that's something you might do," she said.

"You mean Windy? Skinny guy that walks with a limp? Has a permanent smile on his face?" He asked keeping his stern serious look in place.

"Yes. He said you could help me. 'Sam', he said, 'would help me out.' Those were his exact words."

"He gets me into more messes. Where are you looking to go," he said trying not to sound too interested.

"I have business out at the Magogson farmstead. I understand it is it not too far from here."

"It's less than a half day's ride from here, without a break or to water and feed the horse on the way. It's already well into the afternoon. You wouldn't want to be out on the road after dark. You planning on staying there the night? It's not the most welcoming place to stay the night."

"No. I wasn't planning on it. I just need some papers signed and then I would be heading back. Do you know where I can find someone to take me?" she asked backing down a little from directly asking him.

"Like I said I wouldn't want to be on the road after dark. Its right past the city limits. Tell you what; I could take you tomorrow morning after I've finished up here. Then I could take you. Cost would be four bucks. Take it or leave it. I don't think you'll find anyone to take you out there tonight, but there are some other livery stables further down that way." He pointed down the block beyond a worn picket fence.

"I think I might take you up on that. I really need to get this taken care of as soon as possible. I'm really getting paid for how quickly I can carry out the task."

"Why, are they relatives of yours?" he asked in a direct manner.

"Oh no, nothing like that. I'm an attorney. I have some business at the request of my client. That's why I need to head out there. I probably shouldn't have told you that. Anyway thank you though for your help. If I can't find anyone else I'll be back in the morning. Good day," she said and she turned and walked out.

She slid forward on a patch of horse dropping but quickly caught her balance and tried to regain her composure.

The Indian watched her go until she was out of his line of view. The Indian turned slowly back around and the feather in the band on the side of his hat fell forward onto the ground. Looking down, he thought to himself, "Not a good omen. I hope that is the last I see of her. She probably means well but she doesn't know what she is getting herself into."

The lady made her way back through the streets the way she had come. Three crows seemed to follow her, sometimes swooping down. She thought that maybe they were playfully eyeing her hat.

Chapter 10
The Trip to the Farm

The next day rolled around and strolling through the doorway of the stable was that familiar face from yesterday. Today she again carried her worn brown leather case in her hand, this time it was just a little more full of papers, and her attire was much more conservative. She was dressed for a buggy ride, with a bonnet tied down with a piece of light colored cloth. Her hair was tucked back up and under so all you could see was the lower outline of her jaw line. She was even more businesslike than the day before. He was pretty sure she was using it to hide her nervous energy.

"Well, does the offer still stand?" she said trying to get his attention before he had even turned to face her.

He was slowly brushing down a horse, his brush carefully moving down and back, down and back with his other hand trailing close behind. At first she didn't think he had heard her. But then after the third brush stroke, without turning around he said, "I really didn't expect you back. I thought you'd find someone else to take you yesterday. You seemed pretty motivated to get going." He spoke more for her benefit than for himself. He knew in his mind that no one else would have been willing to take her out that late in the day. It would have meant staying overnight on the road or out at the farm. Few people wanted to do either. Why do that when if you left first thing in the morning you could get back to the city by nightfall. No, he was just trying to see how she'd respond to his comment. Size her up a bit he thought.

"No," she replied. Actually she hadn't really checked with anyone else. She could be stubborn, but she also realized when some things made sense even when they weren't her idea. No, traveling out on the road, after dark, with someone she didn't know all that well, in an open air buggy, surrounded by wild nature that was closing in at every moment, didn't seem like the best odds. No, she figured tomorrow was another day, a better day to travel.

He waited for her to go into more detail, but there was just a moment of silence. She was a more difficult read than he had first thought. Maybe she was just nervous, maybe there was more going on underneath that tight bonnet.

"Yes, I told you yesterday I would. I'm a man of my word and I keep it. Let me get the carriage ready. It'll take me fifteen minutes or so to get it set up for us to leave. You can sit and wait over there. He said pointing to a small, worn wooden bench.

"Now we're just going out there for you to get some papers signed?" He quickly added.

"Yes. That's it," she said moving over towards the bench. She sat down and quietly waited, watching him as he went about his business of readying the carriage. It was a square black gig, a simple two wheeled carriage. There wasn't any protection from rain or wind, but she thought that wouldn't be necessary. The sun shone brightly and the weather didn't look like it would be changing anytime soon. Plus, the Indian felt no pain in his left knee. The pain usually came on right before there would be a change in weather, usually a storm.

As the Indian led a horse out to hook up to the carriage, he yelled words back towards the rear of the stable, words she didn't understand. Out came a young boy about nine or ten.

"You'll have to keep an eye on things while I'm gone. I'll be back before dark if things go well. I know you can to do it. Make sure the horses are watered and give Mr. Phalen's horses some extra oats."

Mr. Phalen was one of his best customers and he expected Sam to give his horses extra attention. Plus, one of the horses seemed to be a little under the weather. He didn't want a horse up and dying on him while it was under his care. No. That would be bad for business. It was hard enough getting business. Many people around town still held a grudge, a prejudice against Indians. It wasn't too many years ago when any Indian, if he wasn't shot on sight, would have been offered a chance to head out west to be placed on a reservation. It was a chance he luckily had been able to pass up. No, he had remained in St. Paul. He had grown up around horses all his life. He didn't remember much of his childhood. He had worked as a stable hand at Fort Snelling. The fort sat well outside the city a good half day's ride from the city. It was placed where it was at the meeting of the Minnesota and Mississippi rivers. Sitting high up on the bluff it overlooked the river valleys for miles. Sam couldn't remember how he came about to start working at the fort, but he somehow was taken in because that's where he worked for a number of years. The work was hard and there were plenty of horses to be cared for on a daily basis. They need to fed, watered, bed down at night. But he had a warm place to stay and food to eat. Plus, as he got older they even paid him a small sum each month. It was that money that he had turned into savings which he used to start up his Livery stable business. No, all things considered he was luckier than most Indians. Hopefully his luck would continue to hold out. With that last thought, he turned back to the lady.

"You were wise not to travel out yesterday late in the day," the Indian said to her. "You know it just isn't safe to be out on the road after dark. If your horse throws a shoe or your carriage breaks down then you're stuck where you are. You never know what wild animals you might come across. People who have become stranded out on the road at night have been found the next day, their bodies almost unrecognizable. It's hard to say what animal or animals killed the people. Most people would believe it was probably a bear. Who really knows? I'm not trying to scare you, just trying to make people respect nature," he continued.

He was trying to scare her a little though. Instilling a little fear in travelers who weren't familiar with traveling in open country in an open carriage was the best way he had found to keep them quiet and make sure they did what they were told throughout the trip. That would definitely make the all day trip just a little easier for him to handle. He felt a little bit bad about what he had said when he saw the anxious look on her face. He decided to tone it down a bit.

"Actually it's all about respect. Not many people take the time to respect their surroundings. It is really awareness. Let me finish getting the carriage hooked up and we'll be on our way. I know the area like this," he said showing her the back of his hand. "You don't have anything to worry about. Just make sure to stay close to me and obey my instructions should anything happen. You'll do just fine," he finished.

Finally the carriage was readied. The lone horse stood still seemingly unaware that shortly he would be the sole source of motion for a carriage and two passengers.

"Have you ever ridden in a carriage?" he asked.

"Yes. Yes of course. Plenty of carriages in New York," she said trying to assure him.

"This carriage is a little trickier. He grabbed hold of harness attached to the horse. "It only has two wheels so it's balanced in the front by the horse and we add weight in the back to stabilize it. Plus it's different out on the open road, lots of stones and uneven ruts. It will be a bumpy ride all the way out there. It's nothing like the paved brick street of New York. That I'm sure." He moved back towards the carriage. "Here let me help you up. Place your foot on this metal step and I'll help you up."

At first she thought she would tell him she could do it on her own. But, then she moved forward, grabbed his hand and accepted his offer to help her up. Why start their trip off on the wrong foot?

They started out on the road moving slowly. Carriages, pedestrians, and all types of wagons loaded with hay, barrels, timber and crates moved back and forth all around them. It felt like being in a sea of waves rolling back and forth with the concern that at any moment a carriage, cart or wagon might get out of control and chaos would ensue. The Indian kept a calm focus staying attentive to the horse. The lady sat rigid one hand gripping the edge of her seat and the other folded over the leather case in her lap. She could feel the wheels moving along over the solid ground and wondered how much different the ride would be once they got out of the city.

At first, businesses lined the cobblestone street and people were scurrying here and there amid the noise of a city in motion. Slowly, fewer buildings lined the road. The chaotic noise fell away to a dusty dirt road where neat houses faced the street from time to time, and trees and shrubs lined the roadway. She was focused on the errand she was running. She had come out here from the East, she thought to herself, looking to make a name. But she was finding out that it was not that easy. Here she was, out on a lonely dusty road. She began to think how this city and the task at hand might just swallow her up before she could finish what she had come to do. She finally took a deep breath and decided to start a conversation seeing as her companion seemed content to complete the journey without saying a word.

"Do you come out this way often?" she asked.

"No," he said content with just the one word.

"Hmm, are you familiar with this road then," she said hoping she could get a little more out of him.

"Yes," he said

"Don't you say more than one word at a time?" she said turning and looking at him.

He continued to stare straight ahead.

"Words don't mean you're wise. You don't need to use a lot of words at times. Sometimes it's wise to just use a few," he added.

"That is true, I suppose," she agreed. "But sometimes using a few extra words might help make an idea clearer for someone asking questions. Especially if they aren't familiar with their surroundings," she added admitting that maybe she was in a situation totally unfamiliar to her.

"I think you and your people always want more from us. There are some things you just can't take from us. That is the truth. Well, you can't always take what's in our mind. No. That we can keep to ourselves. Nothing you can do about that. I learned that the more I was forced to listen to the words from the teachers at the fort." With that he gave the reins a little jingle trying to pick up the horse's pace.

"No. I was just asking a question. I didn't mean to offend you. Just figuring out what this trip all entails," she said staring ahead.

"Oh I'm not offended. It'd take much more than your words to offend me. I'm just not much of a talker. But, it sounds like you wish to hear me speak. I'm content to just sit back quietly for the trip. But you're paying for it. So if that's what you would like then who am I to say no," he said. Then he continued on. "This road takes us by the fort, Fort Snelling. That's why they call it the Old Fort Road. Not as well traveled as it used to be, but it's probably the quickest way to where we're headed."

She just nodded and continued to listen.

"Do you believe in good and evil?" he asked changing the topic. The question caught her off guard, but she recovered quickly.

"Oh I believe people do good and bad things. I don't think there's this ongoing battle between good and evil like so many religious expert would have us believe. No, I think people are people. Some do good and some do evil," she added.

"You know there is a story that dates back to the beginning of our people. The Dakota people, my people, believe in an evil spirit as well as a good one. Those two spirits are just two of many spirits found within the Great Spirit. We do not consider these spirits necessarily opposed to each other; man is not faced with an ongoing struggle between good and evil like the white man believes. No, men are not tempted to do wrong by this evil spirit; it is a man's own heart that is bad which makes a man do evil things. There are many things that remain a mystery. Maybe the answers to those mysteries we weren't meant to solve," he said.

"It does sound like your people believe in a god then though just like we do," she added trying to find some common ground.

"No, ours is no god. It is a Great Spirit. It would be impossible to put a limit to the number of spirits the Dakota believe in; every object in nature is full of these spirits, they are all around us and define who we are and what happens to us. For example, we believe death can occur for many reasons. It may be caused by the powers of any number of spirits or it could be caused by the Great Spirit; but most frequently a death can be caused by a spell having been cast upon a man by his enemy," he said growing more serious.

"Do you believe that? That someone can die simply from a curse?"

"What I believe and what actually is true are two different things. Who am I to say what actually the case is. Many strange things occur that we cannot explain. Why isn't my people's explanation of why things occur any better or worse than the White man's explanation? Don't you also worry about your own death? We also believe that death can be the work of the Thunderbird. The Thunderbird only seeks revenge on someone who had done some evil, though. Who knows? In any event, whenever a death happens, even along this road, it's assumed that the person who died was deserving of it in some way. No, for the most part, death isn't random and over time evil doesn't just go unpunished. Evil has a way of being found out," he said.

"Hmm, that story was more than I anticipated. Why would you tell me that?" she asked.

"You wanted a story it seems, and that is what came to my mind," he added.

At that moment the carriage hit a root or stone in the road. Immediately one of the wheels started to make a sound. The Indian pulled up the reigns to stop the horse. He tried to hide a worried look, but Candace saw the concern on his face.

"I hope it isn't something major," she said worrisomely.

"That's why we left early in the day," he said forcefully. "I'll take a look." With that he tied the reigns to the seat of the carriage and jumped down.

"Stay put," he said looking up at her. She glanced around. Going through her mind were the words "they were really just written off as two deaths. Cause unknown. Most likely due to wild animal scavenging after their carriage broke down". Quickly, he came back from examining the wheel.

"It's just a wooden spoke that came loose. It should just take just a minute. But you'll have to get down out of the carriage while I fix it. He reached his hand forward to help her down.

She was too nervous to sit down. Afraid of what small animals or snakes might be lurking about. And so she paced back and forth alongside the carriage waiting for the repairs to be made. From time to time the peaceful quiet was broken by far off chatter and animal sounds. She wasn't sure what they could be. She only listened intently to make sure that they weren't drawing closer.

Finally, the Indian gave her the word that the wheel was fixed. In a few minutes they were on their way again. It was not quickly enough for Candace. She now sat nervously thinking she heard a new noise coming from the wheel with every rotation it made

Chapter 11

The Indian's Tale - Trip to the Farm

They continued onward on their journey to the farm. The sun now stood high in the sky. The warmth was refreshing on their faces, even in this autumn time, the brightness blinded. Both occupants of the carriage kept their eyes down and on the dirt path trying to shield their eyes from the sun's rays. The initial anticipation had changed into a quite relaxation as the trip wore on.

The horse plodded along slowly as though it knew the route. Maybe it didn't so much know the route as knowing to stay on the path. It was a difficult journey, but the surefooted horse stayed in the center of the path, a path well worn in most places, but overgrown with tall grass in others. Still, the horse with its blinders kept its head straight and maintained an even pace. Except for the even paced sound of the horse's hoofs as they touched down on the trail and the creak of the buggy wheels turning, there was simple silence: silence broken by the occasional cawing of birds in the distance. After the carriage breakdown, the two travelers were initially lost in thought. After about a half an hour the attorney broke the silence.

"I don't understand why you changed your mind and agreed to take me out to the farm. Yesterday when I first met you, you didn't seem all that interested in taking me out here. It seemed like you were too busy and weren't interested in driving me out here. What changed your mind?" she asked.

"Oh, I don't know, maybe it was just the money," he said turning to look at her with a serious looking smile. "Or maybe it was a change of heart; then again maybe you're just a little too pushy," he answered.

"No, I can't believe that. I know I couldn't persuade you if you didn't want to come," she countered.

"Maybe today was different than yesterday. Maybe I wasn't interested in a little too much adventure yesterday. Maybe today is a better day to take the trip. You can't always rush into things if the timing isn't right. Everything has a way of happening when it's supposed to."

He looked up towards the sun, squinting, trying to gauge how late in the day it really was.

"Today is a better day and so far we're making good time, all things considered. You've never taken this trip. This trip takes a little bit longer than you'd think. It appears to be a quite simple process. But, really you need to be prepared. Going when the weather is in our favor and leaving at the right time of the day that makes the trip go so much easier. Then you need to be prepared for those unforeseen things, like the wheel earlier. If we had left yesterday, we'd be camping somewhere along this trail at nightfall. We wouldn't have made it out to the farm by the end of the day," he added.

"No, I really would like to thank you for taking the time. I don't know how else I would have gotten out here on such short notice. When we talked yesterday you had mentioned that you had concerns going out to the farm. You really didn't make it clear what those concerns were all about. Do you care to explain at all?"

"It wasn't that I was as concerned about going out to the farm as it was traveling along this road especially as the days get shorter. If you have a run in with any trouble along the way, you're really stuck on this path throughout the night with nobody around to help. That was more of my concern, just plain and simple. And, it's not the farm I don't like as much as those on the farm. You must learn to understand patience. You are still young. You don't understand how patience can serve you well. I still don't understand why you were in such a hurry to get up here yesterday? What difference does one day make?"

"I'm sorry; I can't go into details except that time is of the essence. The person that hired me really wants to get this business taken care of as soon as possible. Business that I have with the farm's owner, Mr. Magogson; and I thought the quicker we made it out there, the quicker we could get this taken care of."

"Being injured or dead doesn't get anything moving along quicker," he added turning to look at her.

"I understand, but really I have a limited amount of time to get this taken care of . . .”

"Before what?" he asked cutting her off.

"Before someone else reaches an agreement with the Magogsons," she said getting a little worked up in the process.

"White men talk too much about what may or may not happen. You should really take time to take in that which is around you. Sometimes taking in the nature around you helps to cleanse the mind. You have to realize you are only part of one big spirit that oversees us all. Why worry yourself. If it is meant to happen it will. We shall be to the farm shortly."

"Thanks for your advice," she said not really believing it. "It sounds like you do know a little about the owner of the farm, Mr. Magogson. Have you ever met the man?"

"No. But my people have. More than they'd care to." To them, he's Matchitechew," the end of the word trailing off his tongue with emphasis.

"What do you mean "Matchitechew"?" she asked.

"It means he has an evil heart. His evil heart makes that place evil."

"How do you know? What makes him evil?"

"Let me tell you a story about our people and Matchitechew, the one who made that place evil. Originally, that whole area was a sacred place to my people. That whole area that I talk about was the creek that ran by where the farm house now sits, the oak that still stands next to the creek, the animals and birds that inhabited there, the tall grasses and reeds that grew up all around. The oak was a big part of what made that spot sacred. But, it wasn't just the massive oak. It was the spirit energy of the hill, the creek behind it and the oak standing tall against the elements. That oak had been both created and preserved by the great sky spirits. People knew it was sacred. It had gone undisturbed for many generations. That tree grew, it had never caught fire, it was special in the eyes of the Great Sky Spirit. That in itself was a source of great magic and power for our people. For generations it stood tall, created by the spirits as a sign of strength and peace for our people. The spirits were alive in that great oak, the stream that flowed by it, and the land surrounding it.

Then the white man came. Over time, he drew closer to our sacred place. And yet we still continued to preserve it. We prayed to the Great Spirit that he would keep the white man within the confines of his cities and those few farms that he began to occupy. But somehow, the Great Spirit didn't hear our pleas. Finally Matchitechew chose our sacred location for his farm. What did the Great Spirit want us to do? My people tried to maintain a simple peace with them. At that time we didn't know the evil that lived in their hearts. My people took great care to preserve the sacred goodness of the place. It was the center of a special meeting place for our people, a sacred location. No harm had ever come to anyone while they were on that sacred ground. My people wanted to keep it that way and so they thought Matchitechew would too.

It was special. It was where my people came from time to time to talk to the spirits to get advice and understand what direction they should go to find plentiful game and where to set up a good winter camp. The spirits would talk through the medicine man who would interpret for the rest of the tribe. Even though the white man had obtained this land by "legal deed", my people still considered it their land. No white man could keep them away from their sacred spot. Even after the farmer built his homestead and started to farm the land, at different times throughout the year, my people would come back to the spot under the oak tree and stay from dawn til dusk working through their rituals. Sometimes they would light a fire, sometimes they would sit silently in a circle and sometimes the medicine man would weave in and out in animated motion for hours on end until he would drop to the ground. The Magogsons had an understanding with the tribe. The tribe would drop off a freshly killed animal pelt as payment for their access to the spot. This would entitle them to remain the day. By dusk they were always gone. That was all my people wanted, to preserve the gifts of the Great Spirit."

"It sounds like it worked out fine for Magogson, his family, and your people," she interrupted.

"Yes for many years it did. All that ended one day. As long ago as my people can remember, the "ancient tree", as it was called, was a sacred place. It wasn't just the tree alone, it was the fact that the tree sat on a hill that overlooked the entire plain around it and sat beside a creek that was fed by clear spring water from mother earth. No, the ancient tree held sacred powers. It was a place where tribe members could go and seek out advice from our great ancestors. If a larger branch fell off from the tree in a storm or heavy wind my people would take that as a sign from the Great Spirit and use the wood to make a new staff for the medicine man. A staff that would help him see answers to questions that the tribe members asked from the great ancestors. No, it wasn't like what happens so many times today when forests are cleared or animals slaughtered, not because they are needed by someone for food or shelter. No, they are destroyed simply because that white man has the power to destroy. My people conserved. They used only what they needed, knowing that the spirits provided these resources, but provided them to us as long as we used them wisely.

We should only take what is needed. You don't destroy nature, you live with it. You only take pieces that you will actually use. You don't waste pieces of the Great Spirit. Today they take down the entire tree they kill the entire herd. It is all so much waste.

No, occasionally my people would cut off a branch. It would have to be the right size and shape. It was handpicked. The medicine man would pick it and make it into a flute to play music to welcome the spirits. Every year, in the fall, my people would gather up acorns in a large basket and roast them beside a fire built under the great tree. Then they would be distributed to the tribe members and each would eat from the fruit of the tree and gain strength from our ancestors through the life that came forth from the tree and in turn from mother earth. No, it was a very sacred place for our people as long as our forefathers roamed the great plain. It brought us good luck for the harvest, and helped us make sure we would have a successful hunt.

For generations, it was a thing of wonder; it was the tree of knowledge. Sitting by the water's edge, the creek's flowing waters passed on its spirit life to the great tree. It was where my people for generations met and decided the outcome of many a dispute; it was also where our medicine man worked his magic to make sick tribe members well; and where our young warriors and squaws were tied together in what you would call bonds of matrimony. In the eyes of my people it always has been a joyful place. One held in high favor with the spirits. We never associated it with anything evil, until the occurrence of that event now so many years ago. It was that event, brought on by the Matchitechew that changed forever that peaceful spot."

"It sounds like that place was very symbolic for your people," she said trying to understand its meaning.

"It wasn't just symbolic; it was also a place of sanctuary. If another tribe had a dispute with our tribe, we would call a council under the large tree. The medicine men from both tribes would hold a ceremony at the tree from sunup until sundown. Then, depending on the shadow of the tree branches that could be seen with the setting sun, the outcome of the dispute would be decided. Members of both tribes were welcome to attend throughout the day. The decision at the end of the day was however final and could not be appealed. It was through the great tree that the ancestors spoke to us. But that was many moons ago. Now, it is a place to be feared. It is not good to go there after dark. That is why I asked that we start out early in the day so we could be back by sun down. Too much has happened there."

"What did happen there?" she asked assuming he would continue on with the story.

"That is not a story for me or my people to tell. That is a story for Matchitechew to tell. Evil should explain its own evil."

"Are you saying that place is evil?" she asked.

"No, it's not as simple as that. To our people there continues to be much strength in the oak tree. But, the white man has brought with him his own powerful spirits, spirits that change and try to control my people's power and the powers of the Great Sky Spirit. That place contains and embodies great spirits and the strength of the powers attached to those spirits. The balance and power of those spirits have been changed by the white man's spirits; and not for the better. Your people in many ways have twisted our beliefs and changed them. It starts with little things and over time big changes occur. Did you know that your game of "tag" originally came from my people? It was played by our children. "Tree tag" as it was called. Those that touched the oak tree were considered safe from harm. Also, my people would "knock on an oak tree to assure a positive outcome or event. Those were just simple ways, symbols of respect. Your people don't know the true meaning and power of the spirits. They only make the spirits angrier. But the spirits are not to be ignored. They eventually must be made to be at peace again."

"Hmm, I certainly wouldn't ignore them. I know that for a fact," she added in a drab tone, hoping he would stop talking about this topic or stop talking altogether.

"You may not believe in the traditions of our people and what I have said. But think about it. What if we are right? Why wouldn't you be willing to show some respect to our way of doing things? White men are very close minded. They don't want to look at things other than through their narrow sight. Maybe you, along with the other white men might want to take less of a chance at angering any spirits. Why seek out trouble when you don't have to? Even your religions rely on prayer and talk with your god. My people and you white men aren't all that different, maybe," he added.

She felt she had to respond after that last comment.

"I think you just have more rituals that tie you to the nature around you, because you needed to rely on the nature around you to survive. We, on the other hand, try to remove ourselves as far as we can from nature. We try to get closer to our God. We want to be just like our God even with all our shortcomings. We work hard to be more Godlike. Maybe that is the difference between our two peoples. It's just my thought, nothing more," she said hoping to reduce the possibility of a heated discussion.

"Don't you think that there is a right and wrong way to do things? Our traditions tell us to harvest in a certain manner. For example, acorns should be harvested in the light of day while the wood and leaves are harvested by the light of the moon. When done harvesting, we pour water on the roots of the tree in thanks. Oak bark helps relieve indigestion but it needs to be removed from the tree in small strips and from smaller branches that won't harm the tree. All these steps have a larger purpose of preserving nature, preserving the ancient spirits of our forefathers and of the Great Sky Spirit that lives in that tree. It's all tied together in many layers. If you destroy one layer you risk destroying other layers. Before you know it, much has unraveled. I sense, no matter what I say, you will find disagreement. Maybe it is time for me to stop talking."

Deciding she wasn't going to win this argument, she tried to wrap up this topic of discussion with a quick summary.

"You might be right. Maybe it's best to treat gods or should I say spirits with respect even if they aren't your own spirits." In the end though, she wasn't sure what she was agreeing to.

With that, the conversation ended. They both turned their heads forward and up focusing on the path in front of them and a line of trees in the near distance. Along the tree line in the distance, a flock of crows flew fast towards a distant tree. As they flew they emitted a shrill screech as if calling back and forth to one another, warning of something approaching. The two passengers could only wonder whether the birds were calling out a warning to them or a warning that they were approaching. The birds' distance didn't give them much cause to worry; instead they focused their attention and their eyes on the roadway, thinking about how close they were to getting to the farm, each one for distinctly different reasons.

Chapter 12
Meeting the Farmer

Coming around a bend in the road, they happened upon a hill that rose up in front of them. Neither of them had spoken for quite some time.

"Are we almost there?" she asked.

"Yes, it is just over the hill up ahead. Remember what I told you. Show respect for the spirits and be wary of the Matchitechew. I don't care to know any more about the business that brings you here. But be on your guard while you are here. There are many things you don't understand about this place. The less time we spend here and the less involved you get with this place the better off it will be for both of us. It is much later in the day than I had hoped it would be. I fear we will be forced to stay overnight in this place. Hopefully, there is enough good spirit still dwelling in this place to protect both of us." With that he stopped talking as the carriage rose to the top of the hill.

There, tucked in a small valley below lay the farm, with corn fields rising up behind into the distance. And there, tucked behind the house, sturdy, full, and broad, was the large oak. It was everything she had imagined it would be based on the Indian's description. It dwarfed the plain white of the farmstead that appeared almost one dimensional next to the vibrant colors of the oak.

They began their descent down the hill and came to a split rail fence that ran off in both directions from the road. As they crossed the plane of the fence, they could see what looked like a scarecrow to their left. It had the usual worn hat and clothes that scarecrows normally do, but around the front of the scarecrow's chest, black feathers ruffled as the wind blew.

As they drew closer, both of them realized almost at the same time that the feathers were attached to the carcasses of blackbirds. A whole bunch hung around the neck of the scarecrow. The bird's bodies were lifeless except for the ruffling of the feathers. A few feet behind were a couple dozen wooden poles about four feet high. Topping out the poles were blackbirds impaled heads tilted downward, their black eyes staring in unison: a lifeless flock. The Indian stopped the carriage for a moment.

"See, was I not right?" He said not expecting a response. She remained silent.

Quickly, they continued down the narrow road and pulled up to the house. The Indian quickly jumped down. He came around to the other side of the carriage and offered his hand to help the lady down out of the carriage. The lady still held her briefcase tightly in the other hand.

"Thank you," she said.

"Just helping the lady. All in a day's work," he added.

Just as they got down, an old man pushed open the front door and walked out on the front porch. His skin was leathery and redder than the Indian's. He was covered in a pair of worn overalls and was using a red kerchief to wipe his brow.

"You two lost?" he asked. "You probably want to go back down that road and take a left instead of the right you took at that row of bushes. "

"No, we're not lost we came out to see you," the lady stated.

"I can't see why a damn Injun and woman would take the trouble to come all the way out here to see me. You snake oil salesmen then?" he said with a hint of annoyance.

"No, we aren't peddlers. And actually, it's just me that came out here to see you. My driver here was kind enough to drive me out to your farm," the lady said stepping forward hand outstretched. "I'm Candace St. Simmons," she said. She almost lost her nerve, but then quickly added at the end, "I'm an attorney."

He made no motion towards her to shake her hand he only continued on talking.

"What are you selling? You've got to be selling something. No matter what you're selling I don't want it. Not interested. I've got everything I need," he stated cutting her off.

"No, I'm a lawyer not a salesperson. I'm here with an offer. I represent the owner of the Apple Orchard Development Company. Can I come in and sit down and talk to you about a business proposal?" she said.

"Lawyer, you said? Worse yet. Business proposal? Well I'm not too keen on any sort of new business proposal at my age especially from no damn lawyer." But then he seemed to gather himself and stop for a moment. He slowly looked her over still wiping his face with his red handkerchief. Then he had a change of heart.

"Looks like you're a little dusty from the ride out. I guess the least I can do is let you clean up inside. No guarantees; and I'm definitely not interested in discussing it on an empty stomach. Tell you what, you join us for dinner, I'll get something to eat for your Injun there and the horse and I'll listen to your proposal. Can't say I'll agree to it, but I will listen."

He stared at her more intently, without saying anything. The moment of silence lasting a little too long, made everyone uncomfortable. Then he turned to the Indian and in a more serious tone said, "The barn's over there," and pointed off in the direction of a small building that looked more like a shed.

Turning back to Candace, he said, "I'm not going to stand here much longer, what do you say, it's starting to get dark. Isn't always safe on the road after dark." He tried to add some factual urgency to staying.

The Indian just glared at the farmer and then looked back at Candace and said "I don't like it; I'd like to be on the move as soon as possible. I want to make sure that wheel gets checked out as soon as possible. The longer we wait the bigger the problem it might create," he added

"Tell you what," the farmer added changing his tone ever so slightly, "you and your Injun friend talk it over and let me know what you decide. Let me bring out a fresh glass of water. That might help you decide."

He went into the house.

Candace spoke up. "You did say it didn't make sense being out on the road after dark. I'll tell you what I think: his bark is worse than his bite. I'll give you an extra three dollars for your trouble if you agree to stay the night. Is that a deal?" she asked.

"A dead man can't spend extra money," he said, "But it is getting dark. I'll put the horse in the barn and check the wheel." With that, he turned and grabbed hold of the reins to the horse and led the horse and carriage off towards the barn.

She found herself standing on the front porch all alone in silence. Shifting her weight, she could hear the floorboards shift beneath her. Finally, Magogson pushed the door open and came out holding two worn clay cups. "The cups aren't much to look at but the water's cold and fresh. Here you go," he said handing one of the cups to her. "So what did you decide? I hope your Injun friend didn't decide to just up and leave you stranded out here."

"No, he took the horse over to the barn. And yes, I will take you up on your offer."

"Fine. Just fine. Come on in the wife is just getting the food out. I asked her to add another plate. Come on in off the dusty porch."

She followed him inside. The dusty air followed her inside and mingled with the staleness trapped with the walls of the house. The setting of the sun made the house appear darker then the porch. Shadows were beginning to grow in the corners, long and broken as they began to creep across the surfaces. She stepped into a large sitting room. The furniture was sparse. A rocking chair stood in one corner and simple wooden chairs were set around a handmade, low wood table. An old oval rug sat in the middle of the room covering the worn, wooden floorboards. The walls were blank except for a picture on the far wall that she couldn't quite make out.

"Kitchen's back here," he said, motioning her towards the back of the house. As she walked back, she could feel a thin layer of dust under her feet which allowed her feet to move smoothly across the wooden floor. Even before she entered the kitchen, she could smell a wide range of aromas, but nothing that she could pick out as distinctly familiar.

"We didn't expect company, so it's nothing fancy," he said. "Come here into the kitchen." He led her through a simple square doorway into the kitchen. A solid table was set with three plates. A woman of slight build was staring at the two of them, a plate in hand with what looked like some type of chicken dish on it.

"Here sit down over here," he said showing her to a chair at the table.

Quietly the woman began to speak, "You must have had a long ride. Do you want to freshen up a bit? There's a jug of water and a bowl over there." She motioned to the end of the wood counter where there sat a large jug, a low broad bowl and a small towel.

"I think she's more worried about getting something to eat than cleaning up, woman." the man said raising his voice to the woman.

The woman put the plate on the table and turned back around to the stove without saying a word.

"It's hard to say what I need first," Candace said. "Maybe a little water on my face might get some of the dirt from the road off of me. Thank you for the offer," she said looking in the direction of the woman.

"Don't use all of the water, it's all we've got til I bring in more from the well tomorrow," the farmer said, talking down a little bit to both women. Candace walked over and poured some water into the bowl, just enough to cover the bottom. Then gently laying the towel in she let it soak up the water and then applied the towel to her face and then the back of her neck. Out of the corner of her eye she noticed the farmer standing and staring at her. She quickly finished up.

"You can just leave the towel and bowl there. The wife will take care of it won't you dear?" he said the last word trailing off his tongue in a low drawl.

Candace moved to her seat at the table and sat down. The farmer was already seated. Throughout the meal, Candace and the farmer sat and ate with the wife moving back and forth serving them and removing plates as they finished. Few words were spoken, the main conversation being that the farmer warned Candace to look out for pellets in the main course, as when hunting pheasant, you were never assured of a head shot. More often than not the body could be riddled with the pellets. And so he told her to "chew lightly." Candace kept her eyes on her plate, trying to focus on finishing her dinner. The only time she looked up, she noticed an accumulation of dirt in the corner of the kitchen with what looked to be a dead mouse in the middle of the pile and the farmer's lingering grin focused on her a little too intently. She did everything she could to force down her dinner.

Chapter 13
The Farmer Tells the History of the Farm

"Great view out here," the farmer said as he came out on the porch holding a pipe in his one hand. Candace had been out on the porch for awhile after dinner. She had offered to help the wife clean up, but thankfully the wife had waved her off, telling her that maybe some fresh air would be better for her. She was just hoping she could keep down what little food she had eaten. She had almost reached the point where she was starting to relax when he joined her out on the porch.

"Those Injuns call it the Hunter's Moon. It's the first full moon closest to the end of summer. I really don't care about all that mumbo jumbo others tie to it, I just like the view and the extra light it gives me for harvesting," he said, looking off the side of the porch down past the oak tree to the large orange orb sitting high in the sky.

"That oak tree is pretty amazing, too," she said. "It must have been here for quite some time."

"Been here for as long as I've been alive and was here before I settled this farmstead. Nah, I certainly didn't have a hand in planting it. But if you ask me, all it's good for is attracting lightning and all those little birds and critters that like to feast on its acorns. Other than that, eventually it will bring a tidy sum for its wood when I get around to chopping it down. That is, if it don't burn down before then. That's if it doesn't rot out first. Just my luck just like everything else on this farm," he said.

"It is peaceful out here, you sure can get lost in the vastness of this whole area. No one around for miles. I can see why you chose to settle here. It'd be hard to move from here," she said.

"I guess I don't have a choice. Ain't that why you came out here anyway, to get me to move? You just want my John Hancock turning over this farm and the land on it to some developer so they can get more city folk out here. I don't know what right you have coming out here to ask me to sell in the first place," he stated getting a little worked up in the process.

"I haven't even brought that up yet. Why don't we take a moment to relax, let our dinner settle? You can finish your pipe. And then we can discuss that matter. How does that sound?" she said trying to get him in a better mood. It seemed to work. He quickly changed the topic.

"You know when I first came out here there was nothing but that old oak tree and the stream that ran down yonder. I think I just plum ran out of steam that's how I wound up here. I used to always say that I was just resting here awhile, before I headed out west. I came up on one of the riverboats out of New Orleans. A little money in my pocket and not enough common sense to be worried that it wouldn't all work out in the end, bought a couple of horses and a wagon and some provisions. I was supposed to leave with a wagon train heading west. But I arrived a few days late. By the time I was ready to hit the trail, the wagon train had already three plus days' lead on me. I headed off anyway, figuring I would catch up to them along the trail. But a number of miles out just beyond Fort Snelling I ran into an attachment of troops moving back along the trail. It seems the Sioux were on the warpath, a small uprising led to a number of settlers being killed. They told me they couldn't guarantee my safety along the trail especially at night. So I tagged along with them back to Fort Snelling. Stayed there until things settled down. By then, I had lost the desire to continue west. Actually, I never really lost the desire, I just had a case of no money and the realization set in that I wouldn't make it much further.

So instead of heading west, I headed north an hour or so and came upon this very spot. I used to tell everyone it was the oak tree that spoke to me. It was just like the great oak of Sherwood Forest which I was told about in my childhood back in Scotland. I always said that the great oak was the start of my new Sherwood Forest. But you know, the funny thing is, no new oaks have grown since I settled this farm, not that we didn't try. Many a sapling would sprout up. At first we'd try to tend them. Water them and such. But no sapling would make it through the first winter. Leaves just wouldn't sprout come spring. No, it's just that one oak standing tall until lightning strikes.

You know, you could walk down to that tree tonight pick up a couple of acorns and if you put them on the windowsill, by morning you'll be kept safe under the protection of the low country faeries until the next full moon," He let out a broad deep laugh. "That is, if you believe all that nonsense. Maybe I used to, but not anymore. No, I don't know that I believe in it. Too much happens in life. I just don't know," he stopped for a moment and then changed his tone.

"You know, the more time goes by, I think about it, the more I'm attached to this land. It's an extension of me. My relatives are buried on this land. See down there, along that wooden fence," he pointed down across the road to a low wooden fence, "follow that fence down to a small pile of stones and there in a little corner of grass land are my kin, or what's left of them. Some of them gave their lives to keep this farm, even murdered. That's probably where I'll be buried once I die. It's all about the proper burial to allow you to peacefully move on to the next world. Or, so they say. I'm not one to be hung up on all that religious crap. Religion is more for the living than for those that have died. The dead are just dead. Nah, you don't think about religion after you're dead. But where you're buried is where your roots are. Nah, now my roots are here. Can't very well move off once you've put down your roots."

"Murdered?" she asked. She was still hanging on the first part of his comment.

"Yes, murdered. Let me tell you about it. Don't really talk about it anymore. Not many people want to still hear about it. At least that's what people in these parts will say. They keep to themselves when this topic comes up. But the old timers, like me, well, they know what happened here. And so it's up to me to tell the story to keep the history of this place alive. If I don't do it, no one else will. That's for sure. It happened down by that creek just below the oak tree," he said pointing down below the house.

Chapter 14
The Farmer's Tales

Before he had another chance to speak, she spoke excitedly, "What was that noise, coming from the house?"

"Oh, nothing. You know how old farm houses creak and moan."

"No, I distinctly heard something. Sounded like a lady crying somewhere. It was muffled. But it sounded like it came from somewhere in the house."

"I didn't hear anything. The only woman in the house is my wife and I just checked on her a few minutes ago and she was sleeping soundly. Anyway, care for a drink out here on the porch, before I continue with my story? I always find the night air really soothes the mind right before bed time. I'm sorry you two had a problem with your carriage on the road today. You could have been back in the city comfortable, safe and warm in your own beds. But I guess I shouldn't have said safe. You are definitely just as safe out here as in the city, maybe even safer, without those thieving street tramps and carpetbaggers all about."

"How did you know we had trouble with the carriage?" she asked.

"Oh, just a lucky guess on my part. I know those Injuns aren't crazy about coming out here to begin with. He would have left early in the day. This place spooks them. No, when you arrived this late in the day, something had to have happened on the ride out," he said.

"Oh, you're right, nothing too upsetting though" she said. "This fresh air has helped." ignoring his reference to carpetbaggers.

After she spoke she remembered, that it was his wife who had suggested the fresh air. She hoped her comment would go unnoticed.

"Where's the Injun?" he added, "Got to keep an eye on that one."

"Oh, he chose to stay in the barn with his horse. Says he feels more at ease with the animals. Something about this farm. He just doesn't feel comfortable out here. I don't know why," she said.

"Oh, I'll tell you why. I think it's just all a bunch of superstitious junk."

"What do you mean?" she asked.

"Did he tell you anything on the ride out here? Whenever they bring anyone out this way, which isn't all that often, they usually have a way of talking their passenger's ear off. They say Injuns are pretty quiet, but then a lot of them like to tell stories. Just lookin at him I'm guessin he probably talked your ear off the whole way, about my people this and my people that. Usually people come out here then with their minds already made up that we're evil people and that we don't care about their people and just want to take their land. Well they speak bullshit pure and simple. Sorry for my use of profanity in the presence of a lady, but that's the only way I can describe it.

Nothing good comes out of their mouths. I don't know why I even let them step foot on my land. He stays in the barn because he thinks the horse will help him ward off any bad spirits or at least let him know if an evil spirit is creeping up on him. No, he's more comfortable with animals than people. If it weren't for the nice people he brings out here from time to time, present company included, I'd shoot him on site." He made a particular point to look her in the eyes and moved his head slowly up and down. She didn't know if he was doing it on purpose for effect or if he did it subconsciously and was unaware. But that moment made her feel creepy and afraid. It was the first time she was really nervous about her safety since she'd been out West here. The moment passed and Magogson moved on.

"Nah, he's just a troublemaker like all of 'em," the farmer finished up, his face turning a little red as his voice raised at the end.

"He did talk about the story of the oak tree. How it was a sacred presence to the Indians in this area. But he added that everything changes over time. For whatever reason, he seemed to be afraid about coming out here. He didn't go into any details." She left out the Indian's comments about letting the evil man talk about the evil.

"In fact, he wanted to leave no later than mid-morning from town so we could be back to town before the sun went down. He wasn't too happy when the buggy broke down and it set us back long enough that we had to stay the night. I also got the distinct feeling that he didn't care much for you," she added.

"Figures as much. We don't understand them. I don't really care to understand them and I know they don't try to understand us. They always pretend they have some perfect bond with nature. That they understand the spirits that surround them, that they know what it is to be one with nature. It's a bunch a bunk. Planting crops, building a house, raising a family, all with own two hands and no help, that's being one with nature. Nature doesn't want to be one with you; it wants to kick your ass if you let it. Nah you have to protect your own back side if you know what I mean or you'll wind up frozen to death one cold morning in the middle of winter because you didn't chop enough fire wood. That's nature for ya. It's the old, blame us, the white folk on that," the farmer added.

"I'm sure he didn't tell you the whole story. What really happened out here? His people aren't all that innocent in any chain of events. Like nature, they'll just kick your ass if you give them half a chance. Tell you what, le'me fix you that drink, and I'll fill in the details he probably left out. Have you ever had an Irish coffee? I'm not Irish, but I came across it in a little bar in St. Paul, when I went into town to pick up some seed one day. Those Micks sure know their way around a liquor bottle. I normally wouldn't offer it to a lady. But on a cool night, it really sets the mind right. Plus, I want you to last through my story if you're willing to listen. It won't be but just a minute and I'll be back out with them. In the meantime just enjoy the night air.

"Sure, I guess. I'll be right here. Wouldn't your wife want to join us?"

"My wife? She's not much into conversation. Likes to get to bed early. I don't think she'll be joining us. Here's a blanket for you," he said tossing her a horse hair blanket. At first, she cringed, seeing what looked like bristly mottled hair lined by a leather backing definitely in the outline of some creature. But when it touched her hands and she felt the warming softness of the hair. Her fear subsided. She grabbed hold tightly of the blanket and stepped a little further out on the porch. "Take good care of Ginny," he said opening the door.

"Ginny?"

"Yes. Ginny is the name of the horse that blanket comes from. She was like a member of the family. We didn't kill her to make the blanket if that is what you're thinking, she died and so to keep her in our memory, we made a blanket out of her hide. Anyway, I'll be back out on the porch shortly. Enjoy the night air."

She headed over to the edge of the porch and put her hands on the railing. From the porch, she could see the full moon lit up behind the skeletal outline of the large oak tree. She had to wonder if the story the Indian had told was true and what details were left out. She guessed she would find out shortly. She knew she needed to focus while she was out here at the farm. She had come for one thing only. But, she found herself getting lost in the Indian's story. It kept running back and forth in her mind.

Finally, she heard the creaking of the footsteps which moved closer and then the porch door swung open. The farmer turned towards her with two well worn mugs in hand.

"Here you go. Irish coffee, just as I promised."

He handed her one of the mugs and set the other mug down on the table between her chair and another empty chair. Neither chair matched, but they appeared to be handmade, crafted by someone who had a little bit of a skill at woodworking, but not enough that you couldn't help but notice the imperfections in the rungs of the back of the chair and the misshapen outlines of the seats. He sat in the other chair and grabbed into his front pocket underneath his wool overcoat.

"Mind if I continue with my smoke? It's one of life's few simple pleasures, that and an occasional drink." He didn't wait for her response. He pulled his pipe out of his front pocket along with a small pouch of tobacco out of his overcoat pocket, assuming already that she would say yes.

"Sure, go ahead," she said.

"Well, I did promise you a story. Not a story, but the facts as I recall them."

"Well what are the facts?" she asked, "as you recall them."

"Let me see. You know I've owned this farm from the beginning. Came here with $50 in my pocket from working on the railroad out East. Just me and the wife. Back then they weren't offering free land like out West, but it was cheap anyways. I was able to lay claim to 80 acres and filed my deed for less than the money to my name. We had thought about continuing west but we came up the big river from New Orleans and we had had enough of traveling. Plus, it was spring time and the feeling was we were ready to plant our roots. St. Paul was just a dead end river town back then. Mostly, it was a destination for trappers and wilderness men heading further up into the north woods looking for beaver and mink and whatever other pelts were popular with those dandies back East. Or, many of the men came to join up with the logging companies that were growing rapidly to harvest the old growth trees that spread across the state. Aren't many old growth trees left now days. Heck that old oak out back is the closest thing we have to an old growth forest. I don't even know how old that tree is. Anyways, we bought a wagon and some supplies and headed out from St. Paul. This location was a day's ride west. We had fresh water from the creek, shade from that the tree out back and land that wasn't as hard scrabble as most areas round here. I just set up our homestead right here. House didn't come 'til later. The first house on this spot was just a one room cabin. It got us through the first two winters. The kids came quickly after that, the oldest Abaddon, and then the twins. The Minnesota Territory was just about to become a state; it was pretty rough back then. Everything you see here I built. I turned this untamed land into a family farm. It's our sweat that made it what it is. We own it. We take pride in that. Those Injuns might argue that it was theirs. But they didn't put any sweat into it. They wandered back and forth and never set up roots. They were just nomadic people doing as they wished. Na we own it. It's ours." he said beginning to raise his voice.

"Just how many kids did you have?" She broke in realizing he was starting to get himself worked up, was stuck on that one detail about Indians, and hadn't really told her much more than he had told her earlier.

"We had three, only one left now. I guess that's what he probably told you. I suppose you already know what this story is all about. People still continue to talk about it. Just can't move on. Try to get over it, but it's just not something that you can do. You know early on in life, you have this whole unplowed field of life ahead you. You have an idea of what your life will be like. But truthfully, you can never know what to expect. Nah, it just comes at you and comes at you. Most of it you don't have anything to do with bringing on. They say the good Lord doesn't give you more than you can deal with. Yah know, at times out here, it's been more than we could manage. We're still here though. Through everything, we're still here. I don't know if I'd do it all over again. I don't know if I'd do things differently. The bottom line is you just survive out here. We survived. It is our land; it is what we made of it. No one can take that away. No one."

"So you just have the one child. Is the child a boy or girl?" She added urging him on, hoping that the question would keep him moving on to the actual story.

"Yep, just have the one son. He's scatter minded that one. Can't focus to save is soul. Always rambling on about what he's going to do, what he's going to accomplish, but then he can't even get the daily chores done. Always concerned about some pipe dream that will make him rich. Nah, its hard work that makes you rich. He just doesn't understand that. I have to watch him every moment, keep him on track or he begins to wander. He's more energy than he's worth. I think the woman is too easy on him. Nah, he needs to be kept in line at all times. Sometimes a little healthy encouragement is what is needed if you know what I mean."

"No, what do you mean?" I asked.

"You know spare the rod spoil the child. I think I haven't spared him. He just has to learn. I've worked too hard to let him ruin what I've worked so hard to build. This farm is my doing. I made it."

"You were going to tell me a story?" she said trying to bring him back on track again.

"Yep. I am telling you the story. You know things would have been a lot different if the twins were still around. They knew how to get things done. I wouldn't have to deal with that one now if they were still around. Let me tell you . . ."

Chapter 15
Death of the Two Boys

"It really was all about those Injuns. When we first settled this land, cleared it for farming and finally built this house, and the porch you're sitting on now, those Injuns would still always come around. Looking for handouts they were. Always thought that by leaving some little trinket, some beads they got from a trapper, a bear claw necklace or whatever, that they could help themselves to chickens or chicken eggs. Nah, we had to set some rules early on. That is exactly what I did. Oh, they made it seem like they never understood. But they did. They just always wanted something for nothing. They had this idea that they owned the land, that they could come and go as they pleased. Nope, it wasn't theirs anymore it was mine.

We finally reached an agreement. Only way for them to leave us alone for the most part, was to let them have access to that old oak tree out back. That was really why they kept coming back. Should have chopped that tree down long ago. Only thing that kept those Injuns coming back. They always thought that the tree had special powers; it was a place where they could get in touch with the spirits, their spirits. Well, they just didn't understand that their spirits no longer had a place on my land. I couldn't get them to stay off the land, so I let them come back.

That one day, those Injuns were there. The whole lot of them, the local tribe. Sure enough, they had been carrying on their dancing and chanting and who knows what else throughout the day. It was like that when they showed up. They would put on some sort of ceremony. They needed to draw out the spirits, make sure they were still there and willing to talk, I suppose. You know, if you don't talk to them just right, only certain members of the tribe could, the medicine man was really the only one, and you might just tick them off. Then, you're stuck with the consequences: evil spirits in your backyard." He looked at me and paused. She believed he was trying to get her nervous and anxious, for what reason she wasn't sure other than he liked making people uncomfortable. He continued on.

"As sunset came, they had packed up and gone, leaving some small animal bones, a trinket and twig tied in an oval with criss-crossing sinew, like a dream catcher, at the base of the big oak. Then I found a beaver pelt by the back door. We had this unwritten agreement they could stay the day at the oak tree and complete whatever ceremonies they needed to at the cost of one pelt, but then they would have to be gone by nightfall. I didn't want them hanging around, but like I said it was the only way we could limit how many times they came through our farm. For them, one beaver pelt was hard to come by.

That day, my twins had spent the morning doing chores. They were inseparable, into everything, couldn't keep them on task to save their souls. They were good kids, just full of energy like boys are. They had rushed throughout the morning to get their chores done. It started with collecting eggs from the hen house. That was girls work, but we didn't have any girls and so it was their job to handle. I remember it was a Saturday. Saturday it was understood, was the one day that once they finished their chores they could have the rest of the day to do what boys do. On this particular day they were planning to head along the creek and look for frogs or what other critters they might find. Usually it entailed tracking small animals through the field or looking for minnows or frogs down by the creek. They had seen fox tracks a week ago and would see if they could locate where the fox might be living. They knew they just had to get their tasks done and quickly, if they hoped to have part of the day left on their own. After collecting the eggs, they laid down some fresh hay in the barn for the cows. I didn't see them after that, not alive at least. They were concerned that I might add some additional tasks. If I had added some extra chores, yah know that might just have saved their lives.

It was after dusk I began calling for them from the porch of the farm house. Those two boys had been off since early in the day after finishing their chores. At first, I thought because it was their first free day in quite some time and like most boys their age they were off looking for adventure, they were going to make it last as long as possible. There was no answer. I checked with my wife and son, Abaddon. Neither one had seen the boys since the morning. It got darker and later and still the boys didn't show up. We all searched around the farm, checking all the out buildings. We wanted to check throughout the farm and along the creek, but with no moon to show us the way, we could only look so far. We decided to give up the search til morning when, with the aid of light, we could get some of our neighbors to help as well. After a sleepless night, with the break of dawn, I sent Abaddon by horseback to the neighbor's house two miles over on the other side of the stream past the oak tree. It was Abaddon who found the boys. I still remember that moment. He had only been gone for a few minutes. I thought he had forgotten something. He was always doing that. He was riding the horse hard when he pulled up screaming and babbling. At first I couldn't get it out of him. He kept yelling "Save them, save them. They're down by the creek." I hopped up in front of him on the horse and we rode the horse back down to the creek.

I pulled up the horse as we rode past the oak tree. I looked at the charred remains of the fire that had burned the day before. Then I looked at the trunk of the tree. In the dirt in front, were some animal bones laid out in a pattern and at the top of the bone pile, was what appeared to be the skeleton of a dog's head. It was then that I noticed, perched silently in the great oak were more than a dozen crows, sitting motionless. At first it seemed as if they were dead. But then I noticed a little movement. Nothing else caught my eye.

So we hoped back on the horse and headed off along the edge of the creek. It was only then that the crows began a noisy chatter as if they were telling us to go and not come back. As I rode on, Abaddon pointed wildly to lead me to the place where the two boys lay. There they were a short distance further on.

They were leaning over the edge of the creek as if they were still in search of frogs or minnows. They looked peaceful, neither of them had been aware of the evil that must have quickly over taken them. I jumped off the horse. It was then, as I got closer, I could sense that they were lifeless. The color of their skin was a dull grey and their position appeared unnatural. I grabbed the nearest body and pulled him back. He was heavy and flopped back. I looked into what used to be his face and realized what had killed him. His face had been opened up by a number of blows which appeared to be made by an axe of some sort. I laid him down a little farther back from the creek and then pulled back the other lifeless body. He was in the same condition. I looked around. Back aways there were some footprints, moccasin tracks. I looked around the bodies, but the horses' tracks and our tracks were all that I could see. Pressed into the mud closer to the creek, were four crow feathers. I listened; the only sound that broke the silence was the random croaking of frogs a little off in the distance and the nearby sound of crickets. I looked back and down at the two bodies. In one of their hands something multicolored caught my eye. I pried open his hand and out fell a beaded necklace held together with a sinew strand with seven multicolored feathers. I knew where it had come from. I shook Abaddon to his senses. I told him to get on the horse and ride on to the neighbors across the creek. I needed to run back to the house to tell my wife and grab my gun. I told him that he shouldn't stop for anything. He needed to warn the neighbors and warn them quickly. He listened to me, but his eyes were blank. I wasn't sure if he was in shock, but then he spoke to me these words slowly "We musn't spare the rod and spoil the child. We musn't spare the rod and spoil the child." I thought he wasn't tracking. I thought he had lost what little brains he had left; so I shook him again to his senses, helped him up on the horse and sent him on his way. I had to, I couldn't be in two places at once."

"Then what happened? Who killed them?" She asked.

"You know who it was, them Injuns, it was. And they paid for their crimes they did. That was the end of it. I'd rather not discuss anymore. Let's just say an eye for an eye and leave it at that. Justice has a way of catching up with you it's just a matter of time. In this case, justice was swift.

"How do you go on after that?"

"I don't know that you do. Sure you go on. But things are different from that point on. You can't look at things the same. In fact, I don't like talking about it. I try to move on, change is good sometimes. Can't live sometimes without change." He took a draw off his pipe and then a sip of his drink and then he looked over at her.

"I don't know that there are any words I can use to express the sadness I feel for you and your family," she said. She wasn't sure if he was listening. He was already staring off into the distance and she couldn't tell where his mind had wandered off. Then he spoke.

"Strange thing about those murders, after that fall, after the hanging, a huge flock of blackbirds, settled in the oak tree. Every year about that time they would come through, probably on some migration or just looking for a free handout with the crops ready to be harvested and all. But they had never settled in the big oak. No, that was the first time I ever remember them doing that. Anyway, they settled in one day, and in the morning they were gone. To this day they haven't come back since. They're gone. After that, flocks of birds never came back to settle in that tree. Almost knew something about the tree had changed. Like it had lost its good luck charm. I don't know." With that he stopped and changed the topic altogether.

"Now what's your real business coming out here Miss. St. Simmons," he said looking at me intently and waiting for an answer.

Chapter 16
The Attorney's Proposition

"That is awful. I can't imagine having to go through something like that. Nothing would seem to be that important after what happened. It's just awful."

"Yes. Yes it is. But it can't be undone. It's in the past. Can't change that now. It's what we do with today. That is important. What do you want to talk about today? I'm tired of the past and I know my future is limited. You don't live forever. So that brings me back to the question of why you are here."

"Yes, I did come to talk to you. That is definitely why I am here. We can go over what I want to talk to you about, why I came all this way out here. But, are you sure another time wouldn't be better?" she added seeming to lose her motivation a little.

"I said I'd give you some time to explain to me your proposal once we had dinner and settled in," he added. "This is as good as it gets. End of the day, relaxed with a pipe and a drink. No, there really isn't a better time to discuss," he said taking another puff off of his pipe. "Give me your best pitch. Then I'll decide if it makes sense. If I say no, then no hard feelings. I'll fix you a nice breakfast in the morning and you can be on your way after that. Is that a deal?" He asked.

"Let me think where the easiest place to start is, we'll take it from there. But I'm not going to agree to give up that easily," she said. "As I tried to tell you earlier before dinner, I've been retained by a developer. He is looking to purchase your land from you, all of it. He's willing to offer you a fair price. In return he will allow you to stay on the homestead and stay in your house for as long as you live," she said.

"What does he really get out of it then if I'm allowed to stay? You mean I can continue to farm?" He asked.

"No, you'd have a place to live in the house, but as to the rest of the land, that would be divided up to be sold in smaller parcels, lots are what we refer to them as. New houses would be built on those lots. You know it's just a matter of time; the city will be moving out and around you. You're going to be city folk shortly, whether you want to or not."

"What would I want with city folk? I'm not interested in being some city folk much less living with them."

"Maybe now is the perfect time to decide. I really don't mean to change the topic. But I do want to make it clear how sorry I am for your loss. Sometimes, when there's a personal loss, we don't realize that change is the right thing for us. It seems like it's been a tough time building this farm and keeping it going. It's even harder when you take into account everything that has happened to you and your family. What do you see going on with the farm once you retire?" she said trying to get him to focus on the bigger picture.

"Don't see myself retiring. I've worked too hard building up this farm. It was really nothing but open grass land when I first got here. No, I can't see myself retiring. I'll stay right here even when I'm in a pine box. I can't see anything else happening," he added. Then he just sat back and thought for a moment.

"What I just told you, that is the business that brought me out here, that I wanted to discuss with you. But, really it's about something more for you," she said trying to keep his interest.

"What's that?" he asked.

"What I really wanted to discuss with you, is to show you how this is a way to provide for your retirement. A way to give you security in your old age. Aren't you concerned about your retirement? Aren't you interested in hearing the details? I would think you would at least like to hear the details," she said, as she shifted gears into her attorney mode."

"No, I don't need more details. My mind was made up the minute I saw your carriage come over that hill."

"It was? Then why did you keep us here. Why didn't you just stop us and tell us to be on our way?" She asked becoming confused and a little angry.

"Oh, I thought you'd get around to the business you wanted to discuss when you decided the time was right. We don't get many visitors out here and you are quite easy on the eyes. No, I didn't mind postponing any conversation we might have to have about business. No, I was content with the small talk. Nothing wrong with that when you finally get a visitor. Most people either come out here trying to sell me seed or a new fangled piece of equipment. You didn't look like an implement salesman. Last year, some guy came out telling me he had a system that could find better drinking water for my family and my livestock. Said for just $50 he'd show me where to locate the new well. It was guaranteed. Said he'd even come back next spring to check and if it wasn't improving life on the farm, he'd hand me back the $50 with interest."

"What did you do?" she asked.

"You know what I did. I talked him down to $15, just toying with him. Then I told him I had a deal for him."

"What was it?"

"I said now you have five minutes to get off my property. I'm going to get my shotgun and if you're still on my property after the five minutes, I'm going to unload both barrels filled with rock salt into your behind. Now get. I've never seen a man move so fast. He hopped on his horse, almost fell off the other side and then rode hard never looking back. No, I usually know what people are looking for. You, now with you I wasn't sure. I was willing to wait, to size you up for awhile. No, nothing at all came to mind right away," he said.

"No. I suppose now is just as good a time as any to re-explain the details." she said, trying to ignore the fact that she had already given him her offer and he had turned her down.

"I'd ask that you hear me out fully, before you make a hasty jump to any conclusions," then she hesitated for a moment and began again in earnest, hoping different words would help to better relay the offer she was proposing. "I've been hired to deliver you a proposition. A man has hired me, actually a company. They want to see if you'd be interested in selling this farm. They are willing to make you a reasonable offer and if you sold the property they'd allow you to stay in your house as long as you like."

"Again, what's the catch?" he said stringing her along in a non-committal tone.

"There is no catch. You know eventually the city is going to catch up to this area. It's growing in leaps and bounds. City people will need more space. I'm not saying that is going to necessarily happen overnight. No, you'll have time to still enjoy this land. The farms around here are going to be gone shortly. That's the bottom line. You can make sure you're taken care of when that change happens. I'm prepared to offer you a fair deal like I said."

"So, again I ask, will we be able to still farm this land?"

"Yes. You could farm it until we started dividing it into lots for a subdivision. I don't know how long that would take. But yes, you could farm in the meantime. You'd continue up until the time we needed to start building houses. Until then you would have the ability to continue farming. What do you think of the offer?"

"As I said, not interested."

"Don't you want to hear the price that's being offered? Don't you want to at least consider it? The chance to sell, especially at this price might not always be an option. The landscape could change quickly. We're really taking a gamble with this offer, at this price. I can leave the deed to have you look it over or have anyone you want look it over. It's all proper, with the language in it allowing you to remain on the property as long as you live. It just needs to be signed by you and your wife and then we'll get you paid, however you'd like."

"Not interested. This is my farm. I worked to build it with these two hands and my own sweat. No, I'm not going to give this up. It belongs to me, it's mine. Those city folk don't deserve it. They don't understand what it takes to work the land, to tame it. Heck, if it weren't for us farmers, those city people would starve. No, this land isn't for sale. No, land can't just be bought and sold to the highest bidder. A true owner of the land understands what needs to be done to own it, to maintain it. I do. Some rich city folk wouldn't appreciate what I can appreciate about the land. No, too much effort has gone into this farm to let it all be taken away, dismantled as if it really didn't matter at all. No, that isn't an option. At least not while I have a say in the matter and I do. I think we're done here. I've enjoyed your company, but I think that is at an end. Because I'm nice, I'll ask that you leave first light of day and make sure you take that Injun squaw with you. No, I think we've had enough discussion tonight. You can find your way to the room in back of the kitchen. The wife already made it up for you. Good night."

He turned, and leaning over the side rail of the porch, tapped out what was left in the bottom of his pipe, then grabbing the two mugs he opened the door and headed in with the parting words as the door closed.

"Hope Ginny keeps you warm tonight."

Chapter 17

The Attorney Thinks About Her Situation

My daydream was interrupted by the sound of someone tapping on my car window.

"Sir, can you roll down your window," the man said. Standing next to my car was a uniformed officer.

I rolled down the window. "How can I help you officer?" I said.

"Could you pull out your car registration and license, please?" he asked in a firm manner.

"Why, what's the problem?"

"We've had a number of break-ins in the neighborhood recently. I noticed you had been sitting in the car here quite awhile. This was my second time going past you."

"No. I understand officer," I said feeling a little perturbed. What was this city coming to that I couldn't sit in my car on a public street? I opened the glove compartment, pulled out my registration and then leaned forward to grab my wallet out of my back pocket. The angle that I could see in the rear view mirror changed and I was looking into my face. The growth on my face was more than a day old. I could see a dried crease of drool on the side of my mouth. My hair was a little long and unkempt. I realized I was two to three weeks past the need for a haircut. I noticed semicircular bags under my eyes that I hadn't noticed before. And there were crow's feet spreading out from the edges of each eye. A few age spots dotted my face here and there and I even noticed a few grey hairs mixed into my sideburns.

"Sir, Is there a problem? Do you have your license and registration?" the officer spoke breaking my train of thought.

"Yes. Here they are," I said, handing him my license and registration. All of a sudden I felt weary. The adventures of the day had all come to this culmination. And it made me realize, I was just growing older, not moving in a direction, just growing older. The police officer walked back to his car. Then for a moment panic set in. I looked over to the passenger seat and there slid over, hanging slightly over the edge of the seat was the journal. Yes, I must have nodded off, but the journal was secure. The officer finally walked back up to the side of my car.

"Everything appears to be in order, Mr. Stogh. You can be on your way. Next time you may want to take a nap somewhere else. Just a thought. Have a nice day."

I thought for a second. I was starting to get angry. Angry at what I wasn't sure. Maybe I was angry that someone had challenged my right to be here, angry at myself, angry at my situation. I didn't know. I didn't care. I just knew I was weary. Before heading on my way, I decided to take one more look at the journal. I turned over the journal which was open to where I had left off and turned to the next page.

October 7 1892

After my conversation with the farmer, I sat out on the porch, hoping by the time I went in the house he would be sound asleep. I could feel the autumn chill enter the night air. Even sitting under that heavy blanket the cold had a way of seeping in. For awhile, my mind drifted off. Maybe he was right. Why did the city people have any more right to the land than he did? He had been here, him and his family the first settlers to lay down roots. But, how did he appreciate it or deserve it more than anyone else? The Native Americans were here before he ever knew what this land even looked like, what about them? Who appreciated it more? No, land wasn't really fully utilized by any one person, it was there always there, the people, they were the ones just passing through. No, people never owned the land; they just borrowed it from time to time, hopefully leaving it in good condition for the next borrower to come along. I began to wonder whether I had made a mistake coming out here. Looking up into the sky, I was amazed at the night sky filled with stars, stars that never appeared over the city of New York at night. Were they real or just scenery that went with this wide open landscape? I felt a little nervous, no neighbors to hear through the walls next to me, no sound of horses and wagons, pedestrians, and the controlled chaos of the city to calm me. I was all alone in a vast expanse with nothing to limit what came and went. I thought for a while longer and began to grow tired. I didn't hear any movement inside the house so I picked up the blanket and headed inside for bed. Thoughts of what I would tell my client and how I might still close this sale began to fill my mind. I was exhausted, but not yet ready for sleep. It was a restlessness, an uncertainty of what to do next. I was stuck out here in the middle of nowhere. It really made me uneasy. I thought about heading out to the barn. No, that would create more problems with the farmer and I didn't know how my Indian friend would react to me heading out to talk to him this late at night. No, I was stuck with just me right now. I'd have to figure out a way to calm myself down on my own. Back in New York, I could stoke up the fire, grab a book and sit by the front room window in that overstuffed high backed chair that my father so loved. I was the only one who he'd let sit in it. From there I could wrap myself up in a wool afghan and look at the street below as carriages moved by, lit here and there by the new electric street lights that were slowly going up throughout the city. One street light sat below our apartment on the other side of the street. I'd play a game waiting for pedestrians or carriages to pass through its illuminating light. Then I would try to imagine who it was. Or in the case of a carriage, see if I could see who might be sitting inside. I could go on for hours just sitting back, comfortable knowing there was no place I needed to be. I was safe and secure, yet part of the bustling city outside my window at the same time. I missed those comforts, now more than ever.

I can't get the initial sight of the scarecrow and the impaled blackbirds when I arrived at the farm. I knew it was a harsh existence out here and that in order to survive you had to protect your crops at all costs. I had heard about that practice out East. There were stories about the farmers placing dead birds out in their fields. They thought it would keep the other birds away from the crops. Maybe it was the smell of death that was supposed to keep other living things away. Maybe it was simply a warning that we killed your friends and this is what we have in store for you if stick around. Anyway, it really wasn't a welcoming sight. There had to be better ways to deal with unwanted creatures. At the moment, I'm just not sure what those might be.

Chapter 18
The Farmer's Wife Tells a Story

I thought about continuing to read the journal where I was presently parked, but then it occurred to me that the police officer might circle around to see if I had taken his advice and gone on my way. My curiosity was piqued though. I needed to continue on. I didn't want to head home. Where to go now? I thought about it quickly. Yes, I could grab a burger at The Four Leaf Clover. They had great burgers, even a better side of fries, and this time of day it would be quiet. I could get a quick bite, grab a beer and sit back in a rear booth to read the journal in peace and quiet. I could barely wait as I drove over to The Clover. It had been around four years since I last visited; and it was on my way home. Why had I waited so long to go back? I clutched the journal and headed to the door of the pub. As I entered it took a few seconds for my eyes to adjust to the darkness. It was a bar with the darkness and stale air to go with it. I walked past the waitress standing near the door and pointed to a rear booth.

"Can I grab that booth, in the back and get a menu? Oh, and I'll take a bottle of beer. Any kind will do, just surprise me."

She nodded and moved back over to the bar.

I slid into the booth angling myself in the corner. I don't know why I felt the need for a beer, Maybe it was the mystery of the journal or the excitement of the reading. I hadn't had anything to drink in a long time. But a beer, no that wasn't really drinking. Plus, I was just having one with dinner. Nothing wrong with that. I started into the journal where I had left off.

October 8, 1892

When I awoke, a dim light surrounded me. It was barely starting to become light outside. It was that brief time between night and day when the hope for a new day hasn't appeared quite yet and you're still trying to make sense of the dreams from the night before. I hadn't slept well. My thoughts hung on my discussion with the farmer the night before. There were a number of different things about that conversation that were going through my mind. I didn't know what to think of his story about the death of his two sons; I kept going over in my mind how I had presented the land deal to him. I kept wondering if there was a better way to present it to him, a way in which he would have said "yes". I didn't know. Maybe I should have waited and presented it to him at a better time. But what time would have been better? And I didn't like the way the conversation ended. As my mind cleared, I looked over to the door to my room, a couple feet from the bed I lay on. It was still there where I had placed it. I had pushed the lone wooden chair in front of my door before I fell into a fitful sleep, hoping that if someone did try to enter the room that the noise from the movement of the chair would wake me. I'm not sure who or what I was afraid of, only that I felt more comfortable with it there. What was I thinking? The dark of night must have gotten the best of me. Now, with first light, any fears that I had the night before vanished.

I sat up in bed, turning to the night stand beside my bed to grab my hair clips to put my hair up. They were sitting there where I left them, but laying crossed next to them were two black feathers. Just two black feathers. I quickly turned back to check the chair at the door. It hadn't moved. I looked back at the nightstand. The feathers were still there. I looked down in front of the nightstand and there on the floor were four more feathers. I looked around the room. Nothing else was unusual. There was no other way to enter the room except a window along the far wall. I got out of bed and went to the window.

I looked out the lone window which faced back towards the rear of the house. Overnight, it had evidently rained. I could see that the damp ground was covered by an icy coating of frost. It was a warning by nature that winter was on its way. It was way too soon, as usual.

I stared further out into the field beyond and could only make out the large form of the oak tree, a shadowy figure against the gray twilight sky slowly giving way to the morning light. Colors were yet to come alive. Everything was just different shades of grey. I could hear the cawing of many crows off in the distance towards the great tree. I looked down at the ground in front of the window. There was nothing but frost on the ground. There was nothing to show that someone had been at the window. Then I leaned down to look at the ground below the window. There, breaking up the layer of frost were some bird tracks, distinct bird tracks. How, I thought, how did those feathers get here? I looked up. The window latch was securely fastened.

I could hear movement in the kitchen on the other side of the door. Those feathers must have been there all along. That was the only possibility. I turned away from the window. I grabbed my hair clips and tried to make myself look as presentable as possible. There was no water to wash up with. I was stuck with presenting myself in this condition with whoever was on the other side of the door. I pulled the chair back from the door and pulled the handle. I was hit by the smell of brewing coffee and bacon sizzling in the frying pan. The old woman had her back to me. . . .

My mind began to drift as I put the journal down for a moment and thought back to that moment. . .

"Hello," Candace said as she entered the room. The farmer's wife turned.

"How did you sleep?"

"Oh, it was sleep I guess. Not home though. Thank you. Thank you for the hospitality," I said.

"You can sit in that far chair. My husband said he wanted you two out by sun up. I guess it's a little later than that. He gets ornery sometimes. But you can't travel all day on an empty stomach. Sit yourself down. Here's some coffee."

Candace moved towards the chair. The farmer's wife turned and moved towards Candace. She looked more worn than the farmer. Her straggly grey hair was pulled back tightly along the side of her face and wrinkles crisscrossed her face. One eye stared at Candace and the other lingered to the side, a little puffy and bruised.

"What happened to you?" Candace asked

"Oh, the eye? I tripped into the bed post last night. I'm not as sure-footed as I used to be," she said as she shuffled over to put a cup of coffee in front of me as I sat down.

"Have you seen my driver this morning?" Candace asked.

"He came to the door earlier to check on getting some hay and water for the horse. He's probably getting the horse and buggy ready. After you get done eating, I'll give you something to take out to him. Sorry, but we can't have an Injun in the house. There'd be hell to pay if the mister found out."

"Hmm, OK. Yes I noticed he can get a little agitated depending on the topic." Candace said. Regretting the words the minute they came out of her mouth.

"Here, let me get your plate together." the farmer's wife said in a worn voice choosing to ignore Candace's last comment. The farmer's wife grabbed hold of a plate, stabbed a couple of slices of thick bacon, spooned in some chunks of browned potatoes, added two overdone eggs and then placed a thick slice of homemade bread with half-melted butter on it on top of everything.

"Here you go. It's all we got. Eat up and then I'm sorry you'll have to be on your way."

All of a sudden I heard some clanging of glasses over by the bar and I was brought out of my daydream. I paused for a moment to think. I picked up the journal again and began to read where I had left off.

October 8, 1892 cont.

I had a lengthy conversation with the farmer's wife, at least longer than I expected. As I write I'm trying to recall the details.

"Where's your husband?" I asked her. I could smell the stale grease and smoke from the kitchen. It hung on her.

I wondered if she was ever outside to breathe fresh air or was she stuck inside doing chores. Her apron hung over her with spots of flour and other food stains from meals past. She attempted to brush back one side of her hair as it fell down only working it more loose from her hair pins.

"Oh, he was up early. Out mending a fence somewhere. I don't know what you were talking about last night but he was all riled up. Took me a good twenty half hour to calm him down last night. Even carried over til this morning. I'm surprised you didn't hear us out here this morning."

"I must have been more tired than I thought. That ride yesterday was longer than I had imagined and we have the same thing today. I hope without a breakdown. We did talk last night. I'm so sorry. He told me all about the loss of your two boys."

"It's not like it was yesterday. Happened so long ago. The world has changed a lot since then. Oh, I still grieve from time to time. That won't change anything. Just biding my time now. Each day is the same as any other."

"I don't think I would have been able to forget. That would be difficult," I said trying to console her without knowing what to say.

"Yes, that event really changed everything. After it, we couldn't hire any help out here on the farm. People just wanted to steer clear of this place, I guess. It just didn't hold good memories. We had to work it alone with just my older boy and his wife. She was an Injun you know, tough as nails, but then she up and dies. Hangs herself in that oak tree out back and after everything we done for her. No, just too many bad memories stuck here."

Before she continued I broke in.

"What do you mean Indian wife? Your husband didn't say anything about that. She died out back? I stopped talking. My mind raced. What happened here? What is this all about? "All I knew was

that your two boys had died under mysterious circumstances and that it turned out it was the Indians to blame." I said getting concerned about what I had gotten myself into even if I was just wading through their unfortunate past. For me, I was living this experience for the first time. Each thing I was told was more unsettling than the last.

She continued, "For my husband, what he told you was the most important part of the story and for him the only part of the story worth mentioning. He blamed the Injuns for our sons' deaths, still does. Justice was served, end of story. But there's more to it than just that."

"What do you mean?" I asked wondering if she was willing to talk about it and not sure if I wanted to hear, but curious about what she had to say.

"Sure the boys were killed. . ." she started in.

I cut her off. "I guess I understand. Not to be nosey, but I can understand why you and your husband don't have a real tolerance for Indians."

"Oh we always tolerated them; we just didn't care for them. Anyway, it was my son who took a liking to her, for his wife. Plus, she was all alone when he met her."

"What do you mean all alone?"

"Didn't my husband explain that last night?"

"No, we got side tracked in our conversation and then it started getting late."

"To be honest, that's where the rest of the story begins. My husband found the bodies of our two precious little boys down by the creek. Well, he come running back full tilt and outa breath. He was swearing something fierce, went straight for his shotgun and swore he was going to kill them all, kill all of them Injuns. I tried to sit him down for a second. And when I asked him if he had found the boys, he just stared at me with a blank stare in his eyes. Kept saying he needed to make it right, an eye for an eye. I was beside myself, thinking the worst. It was then that a number of men on horseback rode up. They were from the next town over. They said they were

here to warn us that an Indian uprising had started throughout the area and that some fellow homesteaders on the other side of the town had been killed. They said the army was sending out a detachment from Fort Snelling, but they didn't know how quickly they would arrive. They told us we should stay where we were and to secure our house, if possible. It was then that my husband told them what had happened to our two boys. He was beside himself. Well, next thing I know he's saddled up a horse and takes off with the men to show them where our boys were.

Without a horse, I was forced to run after them, trailing far behind them as I ran down to the creek not knowing what I'd find. When I finally caught up to my husband, he was all by himself with just the two bodies. He was sitting there just looking at them not moving. I'd never seen him like that and hope I never do again. I wound up consoling him when inside my heart was breaking more than his. Together we sat and rocked each other for what seemed like hours. In reality it was probably more like three quarters hour. Finally, we realized we didn't know where Abaddon was. I asked, and my husband told me he had sent him off to the neighbors to get help. Losing another family member just wasn't an option to us. So we hopped on that one horse and headed off in the direction of the neighbor farm. When we came close to the farm, we came across the god awful site. It was like the end of humanity. It seemed like bodies everywhere, it was a whole extended family of Injuns shot down where they stood, where they were camped down for the night. Every one of them shot through the head and the heart and scalped and left to rot. Young, old, everyone, or so we thought. And there, there sitting beside a small shrub was Abaddon with what looked like a burlap sack. As we drew closer we realized what it was. She was the sole survivor. He had found her hiding down aways behind some brush. She was pretty crazed. I don't know what Abaddon saw or what she saw. It took them both months to finally say anything to us about what happened."

"That's just awful."

"No, now that wasn't the half of it. Turns out it was our neighbors, the men that came to warn us that did it. They wanted to teach those Injuns a lesson, make sure they paid for what they had done. Thought that if they killed that group of Injuns it would give the rest a sign, a warning not to come back. They were sure the rest would stay away. To make sure, they added another warning.

When we finally worked our way back to the farmhouse along the creek we came across the oak tree. There, hanging in the tree were a number of young Injuns, mutilated, swaying in the branches with the scalps of the others tied around the trees trunk. It was an awful sight. And to think it was done by our own people. Our own neighbors."

"That's terrible. Why would your neighbors ostracize you then?"

"Ostrocize?"

"Why did your neighbors not want to deal with you after that? You were the ones who had lost family members."

"Before it was all over, a number of farms lost family members to the Injuns. It wasn't as bad up here as it was in southern Minnesota. Hundreds lost their lives further south. The army did finally come out and restore order. They rounded up many able bodied Injuns and gave them a speedy trial and hung them for their troubles. That put an end to the Sioux Uprising. But my husband kept opening his mouth. I think he resented the fact that he wasn't there to get his pound of flesh, instead it was his neighbors. Well, he resented them for it and they resented him for not being thankful that they had avenged his sons' deaths. I don't know where it began. Over time we had less and less use for their help. Sort of shut ourselves off. I suppose it didn't help with Abaddon and the Injun girl."

"That is terrible. And the Indian girl, so you took her in?"

"We couldn't just leave her there. Brought her up to our house. Let her stay in the barn. After time my son took a liking to her. We never let them two officially get married but they was as good as husband and wife, even had a ceremony here at the farm for the boy's sake. We didn't approve of it, you can understand why. But

we really didn't have much say in the matter. That didn't sit kindly with the neighbors round here.

It was never spoken about who killed that Injun family but you could tell when you talked to those neighbors which ones had a hand in it. I think Abaddon and that Injun girl knew too. They mainly kept to themselves. They had an interesting bond. Prejudices are almost impossible to overcome, though. They wanted to get rid of those Injuns and here we are letting one breed with our son, both witnesses to a coldblooded killing, warranted or not. No, it didn't go over well after that. We kept to ourselves after that. Couldn't get any help in the area just the four of us working the farm. How does she up and repay us for us taken her in? She keeps trying to run away. I don't know where she expected to go. The rest of the Injuns in these parts had already been shipped off to reservations out west. But how would she know it? She was probably trying to get back to her people. Finally, we find her hanging in that tree down by the creek the old oak tree just swaying back and forth there one morning. Can't imagine why."

"Where's your son now? Does he still live with you?" I asked.

"Oh, Abaddon? Don't know where he is right now. He comes and goes, currently he's gone."

"Abaddon? You named him that. It's an unusual name."

"Yes, we named him Abaddon. I used to care when he came and went. It's just too hard with everything that has happened in my life. I don't blame him for any of it. Maybe if things had just happened a little differently. That boy always was a little strange. Maybe he was an omen of things to come from the day he was born. We had struggled through a couple years of locusts. Right before he arrived. They nearly wiped us out. It's hard enough to make a go of it, without those types of things happening. I don't know why but as a joke to get past or get over the problems we was facing we named him Abaddon. Came across the name in an article in the paper. King of the locusts it said, Abaddon. Sort of fitting at the time. Locusts didn't come back after that, after he was born. But as he grew, we

realized he was a little off in the head, though. I used to have to stroke his head every night just for him to fall asleep. Good worker, but never was much for conversation. After his wife passed away, I went to look for him one morning and he was just gone. He lost his mind and just took off shortly after that. It must of broke his heart to just see her hanging there like that. Now, it's just me and my husband. Just the two of us. But, he does come back here from time to time when he needs something. I don't know. We haven't seen him in months. Kind of comes and goes as he pleases. Not really sure where he goes when he isn't here. Tried to get him to stay, but he just won't. So, eat up. Your food's getting cold.

Chapter 19

The Trip Back from the Farm

"Here's your beer. Are you going to order anything?" she asked. The voice caught me off guard. I looked up from the journal and there standing beside my booth was the waitress, with form fitting t-shirt and a pair of tight jeans.

"Oh, yeah. I'll take a cheeseburger basket with fried onions." I said putting my head back down into the journal.

"Must be a good book," she said pointing to the journal, "I've been watching you read that for a few minutes now."

"Oh, I'm reading this book for a friend. He wanted me to review it. He's trying to become an author. Don't tell anyone but it's not that great," I said.

"Could a fooled me," she said. She sort of nodded her head a little sideways without saying anything else and moved on to the next table.

I sat there for a moment, and partially closed the journal and thought about the last journal entry I had read . . .

The frost still blanketed the ground, not willing to yield that quickly. At least not until the morning sun was higher in the sky. With some cakes and a thick slice of bacon wrapped in paper, I walked out to the barn in search of my ride home. The chill hit me. A damp cold quickly seeped in and around my outer clothes and crept up my spine. It seemed much colder than the night before when we arrived here. I hesitated and looked back for a moment. My footprints left distinctive marks in the frost covered ground, not complete imprints but just enough to show that I had been there. Soon those footsteps would disappear altogether once the sun warmed the ground. Hopefully, that warm sun would make the ride back easier. The wind at our back would also make the ride easier. I looked back past the house towards the oak tree. It sat serene and motionless, a mixture of green and red. The leaves were changing quickly with the onset of late fall. It was still alive but about to go dormant, shedding its full plumage to reveal its bare skeleton. I thought about the farmer's wife's story and could almost see an object swaying in the tree. It looked like the outline of a body. I refocused my eyes and a chill ran up my spine for a quick moment. Then the outline of the body was nothing more than a thick patch of red leaves.

I was hoping I would have another chance to get that deed signed. I thought I'd let him cool off a bit. Think about it for awhile and then readdress him about the issue. I knew I didn't have much time to get the matter resolved. I wondered, I don't think the timing was right just yet. Those two didn't really know me. They were just getting to know who I was. Maybe this couldn't be done so quickly. Not all in one visit.

My clients back East made it clear that this matter should be resolved as quickly as possible. There was who knows how many other potential developers lurking around waiting to pounce on the opportunity to buy up land around St. Paul, this land included. It was no longer valuable for its farmland; it was now more valuable for the sales potential as individual city lots, lots to become part of a growing city. The value of the land was in the lots that it could be subdivided into smaller parcels of land: parcels that families would buy to put up their home; families that didn't farm but earned their living in the city. Things were changing quickly. It was only a matter of time before more people lived in the city than on farms. Maybe St. Paul would grow to be bigger than New York. Who knew? The city was growing by leaps and bounds from what people were saying. Everyone was moving west, always looking for new opportunities, a better chance to make a life for themselves and their families.

Am I crazy to want to go back to New York? It is what I know, it is who I know there. It is where I feel comfortable in the uniform chaos. It's a composite of people in motion, a level of noise and motion that never stopped. St. Paul wasn't even close to reaching that fevered pitch. Sure, St. Paul was trying. It was just a long way off from reaching the charmed sophistication of a true city. It was trying to develop, trying to gain that complexity, but it didn't have all the pieces to get there quite yet. Maybe it was a few years away, maybe more. Sure, I like the unusual characters, but for me it will have to be a place I can say I visited, not a final destination for now.

Sorry, I got off track. My thoughts about St. Paul really didn't have anything to do with business at hand. I know I need to focus on what I'm here for, that is all. I know this won't be the last trip out here to the farm. But for now I have to reassess how I might be able to complete my task. It will just take a little more time. When I reached the barn, my driver was next to the horse which was already hitched to the buggy.

"Here you go," I said, "Breakfast," handing the wax paper package to him. "Sorry you weren't able to join us for breakfast."

"I'm not sorry. I know when I'm not welcome. Didn't I warn you in advance? You didn't believe me. Now you understand their true character, assuming you had time to talk to them."

"Yes, I did have time to talk to them. I think everyone has opinions, some more misguided than others. That is what I've learned."

"Who do you think is misguided?"

"Maybe misguided isn't the right word. Each of us is molded by what happens to us in our lives. Like a sponge we soak up things, the interactions we have with the world around us. Depending on what we soak up, that defines who we become as we grow older. No, everyone has their own unique view of the world, right or wrong. That's all I'm saying."

"I think you are missing the true picture. Man is but a small piece of the world, or the universe as you call it. There is a force that

flows throughout the universe. My people call it Wakan Tanka. People either choose to try to understand this guiding force and grow to become better people or they shut their eyes and never see the goodness that the force has to offer. There is no difference between the natural world that you think we live in and the supernatural world and the spirit world because it is all one big universe. Who knows where one begins and the other ends? Not me. I'm just a small piece of it. No, people like them think they understand the world around them, that they are bigger than it. In the end, it just swallows them up. It will swallow us up just as well if we aren't careful. It is time for us to go. Staying at this place too long can be dangerous to your spirit. It doesn't happen all at once, but if you stay here too long the evil that holds its grip on this place has a way of tagging along with you when you leave. It's best for us to leave now."

"I think you're being overly superstitious," I added.

"It doesn't have anything to do with superstition; it has everything to do about being smart. Don't challenge spirits, especially evil ones. Let me ask you this. Do you walk up to a coiled rattlesnake when it is sitting ready to strike?"

"A rattlesnake? Well, no. But what does that have to do with this place?"

"Everything. You walk away from the rattlesnake before it bites you and leaves its venom in you. Just like this place, you don't want to leave with the venom inside you. It is then difficult, if not impossible to remove it; and worst case it kills you. No, let's go."

As his words trailed off I looked down and noticed a ring of black feathers stretching in uniform intervals around the horse and buggy."

"What are those feathers doing there?" I asked pointing to one of the feathers lying on the ground."

"They are for our protection. They are crow feathers. They help ward off evil spirits here and on our trip back to the city. It is none of your concern."

"Yes, it is. Those same types of feathers were on the nightstand by my bed this morning when I woke up. Were you in my room last night?"

"I was here in the barn all night. I made sure to keep us protected from this evil place. The evil here is powerful, but the good spirits are powerful too. Maybe there is still hope that evil will be left here when we leave. Just be thankful that you are being watched over. Don't question how it came to happen. Just be thankful that The Great Spirit decided to watch over you. As I just said, the universe is a much bigger place than either you or I can understand."

For the most part, our ride back to the city was uneventful, except for a few moments in our discussion when he again brought up his concerns about the evil spirits. His outlook improved when we'd see crows from time to time. He would say:

"See those crows? They are good luck. They bring great protection to us. They guide the living but more importantly they guide the souls of the dead so that they might find the great spirits of our forefathers. They may be playful at times, but they are true messengers, messengers of the good spirits. No, never fear the crow, they are our friends even though they make a noisy sound." As he finished talking, he suddenly stopped the carriage. I looked over at him and his face grew pale.

"What is it? Why did you stop?"

"Look!" he said pointing a ways down the dirt road.

At first I couldn't make it out. I wasn't sure if it was alive or dead. Then, as I focused a little more I realized what it was. It was a large wood owl picking at the freshly killed carcass of a large black crow. In relationship to the owl it appeared small, but as crows go, it was large. The owl sat there claws grasping the lifeless form while it slowly pecked here and there working on the soft spots.

"We are too late," he said shaking his head slowly.

"Too late to save the bird," I thought. No nature is cruel and yes, it wasn't a pretty ugly sight.

"We are too late to save ourselves," he continued. "This is a very bad omen. Seeing an owl is bad, but seeing it during the day is much worse. Plus, it is eating a crow. We must go around. We cannot travel across its path."

With that, he turned the buggy off the road. Then, he stopped and pulled out a leather pouch that sat on the end of a leather necklace. I hadn't noticed it before, probably because he kept it tucked in under his shirt. He opened the small pouch and pulled out a large feather that had been tucked inside."

"What's that?" I asked.

"It's an eagle feather. It might protect me from the evil. I hope it can. Maybe it is too late." He held on to the feather tightly in his one hand and with the other he dug down into the leather pouch and pulled out a mixture of dry herbs. He said a number of words that I didn't understand and then looking up towards the sky, he tossed the herb mixture in the air. Then he grabbed tightly a hold of the reins of the buggy and started cutting across open brush making a wide loop from the road. I thought to myself for a moment that maybe I should have brought an eagle feather with me as well. After awhile, when I thought for sure we were lost, he made an abrupt turn and we were back on the road heading towards the city. The whole way back he barely spoke a couple of words and appeared truly shaken. He continually held the feather and the reins tightly. He wasn't the relaxed man I had grown accustomed to earlier in the trip.

"You really must have changed your mind about that book, you haven't touched your burger and your beer is still half full." Her silence pulled me out of my lost train of thought. She was right I had forgotten all about my cheeseburger.

"Wow, I guess you might be right," I said looking up at her.

"What's the book about anyway?" she asked.

"I'm sorry, I can't tell you. When it gets published, I'll get you an autographed copy. Deal?"

"Deal," she said. "Can I get you anything else?"

"No, just the tab. Thanks," I said watching her as she turned and walked back towards the bar on the far side of the room.

Chapter 20

Dinner with My Wife

I rushed home, hoping I wouldn't find my wife sitting at the kitchen table with "the look" on her face and two plates of cold food sitting out; or even worse, a single plate of cold food to make a point and her in the process of finishing off what was left on her plate. I shouldn't have let the time get away from me like that. My cell phone was dead. It wasn't until I got in the car that I realized what time it was.

When I opened the door I tried to sound upbeat and cheery. The best way to put her off guard if there was going to be a problem, was to keep the conversation moving.

"Hi honey. I'm home. Sorry I'm late. Where are you? Is dinner ready?" I figured by throwing out a few questions she would have to switch gears and at least answer one of them.

"Where have you been? It's almost 6:30. We were supposed to have a quiet dinner tonight. This was the only night this week when I didn't have to work late. You knew that. Where have you been?" Her voice was loud and clear even though it came from the kitchen one room over from where I entered the house. And then I realized she was better at the question game than I was. She was more focused and persistent.

"I'm sorry, time just got away from me. I spent the day on my job search except for a quick review of the county records on the history of our house."

"It didn't take you all day to look up the county records on our house."

"Well, you wanted me to be thorough."

"No, I said get me the Reader's Digest version. I mainly wanted to get you out of the house."

"Well, actually I spent some time looking up that old house across the street and then took a quick trip to The Historical Society."

"Are you getting fixated on the history of that old house? I thought you'd just do a quick search of the land records, and that would be the end of it. That's what you told me."

"Well, yes that was my intent. But you know, I, well, I thought about it a little bit more and I just had some more nagging questions. So I just swung by to ask a few questions at The Historical Society. That was it. And, it's not like I spent the whole day chasing down information on that old house. No, I'm done with the search."

"I hope you are. You told me you'd be focused on looking for a job. That's what you said. Honestly, you need to figure out your priorities. Plus, how long ago was it that we talked about doing that search on the houses, and you finally get to it today. I thought you had moved on to focus on looking for a job."

At that moment I turned the corner into the kitchen and realized a half a second too late that my version of the story was unraveling.

"So you were out looking or interviewing for jobs in those clothes. I don't buy it. What were you doing all day?"

I had to think fast. "You know a job search isn't all about personal contact. I was down at The County Employment Center. I was using their computers most of the day."

"Oh, and the computer here doesn't work?" she asked not letting me off that easily.

"Well, no it works. But they also have a loose folder listing of the most recent job offerings that aren't put in the system yet. That's why I went down, to look those over and I also had some questions for the staff," I continued on.

"Well, maybe you should have been going down there on a regular basis if that's the case," she added. "Your dinner's still warming in the oven, at least the chicken. The rest of the food: potatoes, broccoli, and rolls are in the fridge. You can warm them up in the microwave. I just finished with my dinner."

"Sorry for being so late. Want to join me?" I worked my way across the kitchen to the sink where she was standing. "Why don't you just sit with me while I eat?"

I came up behind her and grabbed her hand gently in an affectionate grasp turning her around to face me. "Come on, you can pretend you haven't eaten yet." As my words trailed off she cut me off.

"Have you been drinking? Is that liquor on your breath?"

"No, what makes you think that? No. It must just be bad breath from something I snacked on earlier in the day or that power drink I had a half an hour ago. No, I haven't been drinking," I said.

"You better not be. You promised no more drinking. Remember what happened the last time. It started slowly and then before you knew what was happening things got out of control. No, I won't put up with it another time around. I've got some work to do. Enjoy your dinner."

I backed away from her and opened the refrigerator door. The cool air felt refreshing and for a moment I wished I could just stand there with my head inside.

Chapter 21
My Return to the Historical Society

Wednesday rolled around and I found myself heading back to the historical society. I had a busy week, at least from my perspective. I had sent out a few resumes followed up on some job leads and checked in with some old work acquaintances. It was just enough to show my wife that I was staying busy. But that was just what I was doing to tread water. The real excitement I had been anticipating was happening today. I had gone back and forth in my mind over the various facts and details that I had already come across about the old house down the street. I knew there was more and today I might just wrap up the mystery. My mind wandered in all different directions and I found it difficult to stay focused. I hadn't been this excited about anything in a long time. At the last minute I remembered to swing by the bakery. I decided on their mixed fruit tart: nothing too expensive, but something that would stand out a little and show my appreciation for allowing me in last week. I made sure I took off the label with the name of the bakery on it. Luckily, they had a plain white bag to put it in.

I also had the diary with me. I hoped it was an easy transition to just put it back in the portfolio. I started to fixate on how I would get it back in the portfolio without her catching on. I shouldn't have taken it, I know. Just a simple compulsion. Those moments of indiscretion always got me in trouble. They always came back to haunt me. They never worked out like I planned. Maybe this time would be different. I thought for a moment. I paused. No, it was the correct decision not the right decision, the correct decision. It was worth it. I had gotten some good information. Reading through the diary I had come through some interesting entries. Actually, it was more of a journal than a diary. The difference in my mind being that a journal holds some theme or some purpose in the entries. A diary is just a useless stream of consciousness babble that has no cohesive purpose throughout. No, this was definitely a journal. It was a record of her experiences while here in St. Paul, especially as they related to the business that brought her here. At times, she was pretty detailed. Other times you could feel that she was rushed and was hoping to get back to write it all down. Life is like that. For the moments that you are really alive, it's moving at you so fast that you don't recall, you don't have time to write it down because you're too busy taking it all in. It's like going on a roller coaster ride. It's a few minutes of sheer terror. You're so focused on the ride, on the moment that everything around you falls away in a blur. Then, when it's over, all you can remember is that it was simply awesome, something extraordinary. I paused and then my mind wandered back to the journal.

I thought about the entries that were dated right after the attorney's trip to the Magogson farm. It seemed to me that the trip hadn't really gone as planned. She hadn't gotten the deed signed and Magogson really seemed like a difficult person to deal with. I didn't see her getting that resolved anytime soon. There were only a few entries after the trip and then the remaining pages in the journal were blank. I had some specific questions before reading the entries, like when did she finally get the deed signed, and did she wind up going back out to the farm. After reading those additional entries, I had even more questions swirling around in my mind. The first entry after the trip was dated October 10, 1892. It read:

I'll be meeting with Rademacher tomorrow. I say developer rather than client, because I believe my true client is the person who hired me back East. I shall make sure to keep my eye on him. The concerns raised by my client are whether he is handling the affairs of the company in an appropriate manner. I shall not let him manipulate my assessment of the situation. It should be interesting. We have only corresponded by letter and telegraph. I have yet to meet him. What I picture him looking like in my mind and what he actually looks like should be interesting.

I still haven't been able to get the business taken care of that I came here for. Men take me for granted. They believe that I can't handle them on an equal footing. However, I think they will find that my persistence has a way of working through to the finish. While my work here isn't quite wrapped up, I am getting close and I will be happy to head back to New York when I'm done. While I've learned a lot I miss the hustle and bustle of the big city. Everyone here is just a little rough around the edges although they all want to believe that they are the ultimate in sophistication. I guess everyone has a perception of who they are and where they fit in the world. I'm always amazed at the over exaggerated importance most people have of themselves. But maybe it all about self worth; maybe one can't be too self absorbed.

I couldn't help but think that she really was a person who liked to think through things. I wondered though whether it was time wasted. It was inaction on her part. She could have been getting everything resolved rather than spending time writing in a journal. I just couldn't see myself doing that. But, if she hadn't, there wouldn't have been any record, no record at all of her thoughts. It seemed personal, but nonetheless I needed to keep going to understand what happened. I continued on to the last entry.

The last entry was also dated October 10, 1892, it read:

Rademacher left a note. He wants to meet me tonight at 5 pm instead at the Wild Steer Restaurant. I'm not concerned about meeting him in a public place. It's right around the corner from the hotel. I wonder why he moved the meeting up. I'll find out soon enough. After tonight, I'm sure I will be much closer to resolving this matter. Wish me luck.

That was the last entry. I flipped through the remaining pages of the journal but they were all blank. Why were there no more entries? What little I now knew of Candace, it appeared that I would not learn anything more. Still, I was hopeful, maybe my friend at The Historical Society had found out some more information.

I pulled up to The Historical Society. With tart in hand and journal in sock, I headed up to the front door. It was locked. I rang the front door. In a couple of seconds, I heard the clicking of shoe soles heading towards the front door. The curtain pulled back and the lady from last week looked seriously at me , and then turned back the lock in the door. As the door opened I leaned forward into the entryway and at the same time said, "Hi."

"Did you bring it?" she asked me in a fairly monotone demanding voice.

"Yes, just as I promised," holding out the tart which was covered up in a white box with a red ribbon. I had pulled it out of the white paper bag at the last minute, thinking the ribbon would be a little more special presentation wise. "I brought you a tart."

"No, you know what I'm talking about, the item you removed from here last week. Do you have it with you or do I have to contact the police."

I could feel the smile on my face slowly evaporate. Still I tried to keep up the upbeat sound in my voice as I spoke.

"Yes, I have it, but there must be some sort of misunderstanding. Yes, I took it but it was by accident. I must have folded it up in my binder that I was using to take notes. It was definitely unintentional. I didn't realize until I got home that I had it. I would have called, but I didn't think it would be a big deal what with me coming back today and all. Plus, I knew I couldn't get back up to St. Paul until today. I am truly sorry. I can assure you that that is not how I do business. I didn't get to be a reporter for all these years by doing things like that. I would hope you can accept my sincerest apology."

She paused for a moment and I wasn't sure if my lie had won her over.

Finally with a sigh, she said, "All right, I accept your apology. But from now on I'll have to remain in the room if you're examining anything here. I'm the steward of the society. People depend on me to take great care in maintaining every artifact owned by the society. I don't take kindly to being taken advantage of."

"I am deeply sorry. Please accept my humble apology and accept my peace offering," I handed her the box with the tart in it. Hoping I wasn't laying it on too thick.

"And the diary? Where is that?" she asked.

"Here in my binder where I left it. Can you grab my coat for a moment, so I can pull it out of the binder? I don't want it to become damaged in any way." Luckily my coat was currently draped over my arm. I clumsily dropped my binder and the coat on top of it. "Sorry, how clumsy of me." I bent down with the binder on the floor and the coat covering my lower part of my pants, I quickly pulled the diary out of my sock underneath my coat and let it fall to the floor. Then I picked up my coat and then picked up my binder and the journal. "I normally don't drop things and I've been taking good care of the journal." I handed her both my coat and the journal.

"Thank you," she said. "I really do hope I can trust you."

"Be assured you can."

We began walking toward the back of the building, not up the stairs as before, but down the first floor hall and in to an office on the right. She broke the silence.

"I assume you read the diary."

"Yes I did." Before I could continue on she cut in.

"And?"

I continued, "After reading it, it seemed to be more of a journal, focused on her reason for being here in St. Paul. It answered a few questions, but raised some more questions. The entries in the journal abruptly stop in mid October 1892. Were you able to find out anything?"

A crease grew across her closed mouth which slowly began to open. "I don't know why, but yes, I did go ahead and look up some information on our attorney friend. You know, I'm still not sure I trust you."

"Well, what did you find? And thank you for looking." I ignored her trust comment hoping that if we could slowly change the topic we could get past the issue of my little indiscretion. How stupid of me. I was lucky she was still willing to talk and work with me.

Chapter 22
The Indian Takes the Rap

She continued on.

"Yes, I spoke with a friend of mine over at The Pioneer Press. You might know her seeing as you are both in the newspaper business. Her name is Sandra Swenson."

"Name sort of sounds familiar," I lied knowing in my mind I had no clue who it was because I wasn't a real reporter. No, I was just a wannabe reporter/private detective, who had too much time on his hands, my mind wandering as I continued my response. "But I'm not sure. I just don't get up to the cities that often. Swenson, I'll have to think about that, maybe it will come to me."

"So," a little excitement grew in her voice, "she was able to look at some old records from the paper. What my friend found was pretty interesting. She had to really do some digging. The Pioneer Press wasn't around back in 1892. However, The Pioneer Press purchased the paper that was around back then; they've kept, well actually converted, all of the published papers from The St. Paul Daily Globe onto microfiche. That was the paper that was around in St. Paul back then."

"Well, did she find anything?" I asked. I tried to keep her moving on while admitting to myself that her excitement was now wearing off on to me.

"Yes. It's over here." She walked around her desk and pulled a blank manila envelope towards her. Opening it, she pulled out a piece of paper. I could see that the piece of paper was a copy of an old newspaper article. This was the article she found in the paper archives:

> **"Attorney Found Dead**
>
> *A New York attorney on business here in this fair city was found dead in an alley off 6th and Robert in downtown St. Paul. Miss. Candace St. Simmons, Esq. had been residing at the Ryan Hotel for almost a fortnight while handling business for a local real estate developer. The cause of her death is under investigation. It appeared that Miss. St. Simmons met her untimely demise due to a fall in which she struck her head. At this time it has not been determined whether she met with foul play. Turn to the pages of this publication for updates as they develop."*

"Well, that is quite interesting," I said looking over the short article to see if I could read any more information between the lines. The article was just too short. Just as I was starting to put the piece of paper down, she added.

"And there's more. Here's the follow up article about her death."

She then handed me a second sheet of paper, another copy of a newspaper article. It read:

> **"Attorney's Death Ruled a Murder**
>
> *A New York attorney on business here in this fair city was found dead in an alley off 6th and Robert in downtown St. Paul three days ago. It has now been determined that she met with foul play. Miss. Candace St. Simmons, Esq. who had been residing at the Ryan Hotel for almost a fortnight while handling business for a local real estate developer was struck on the head by a horse bit from a horse bridle. An indentation of the bit was found in the back of her head. Suspects are being interviewed to determine who might have been involved in the grisly murder. It appears that Miss. St. Simmons was on her way to meet a client when an assailant or assailants attacked her. It is unclear whether the motive was robbery or whether it was*

just a case of depraved opportunity. More details can be found in the pages of this newspaper as the story develops."

"Wow, it gets more interesting," I added. "If it was a murder, as the article suggests, then there must be more."

"And yes, there is," she said.

"Here's the last article I was able to find," handing me a final sheet of paper. It read:

"Suspect Charged in Murder of New York Attorney

A suspect has been arrested in the gruesome murder of a New York attorney. Miss. Candace St. Simmons was found murdered in an alley behind the Ryan Hotel. People of interest were interviewed including her current client, who was the reason why she was here in St. Paul. It was determined that she was killed by a blow to the head by the metal bit from a bridle and died instantly. Information obtained from her client led police to interrogate the owner of a local livery stable. While the owner, Sam Proudfoot, still professes his innocence, the police found a bridle with blood and human hair on it hanging in his stable. Mr. Proudfoot had been hired by Miss. St. Simmons to convey her on business around the city. It appears that there may have been a disagreement with Miss. St. Simmons about payment and that an altercation between the accused and Miss. St. Simmons resulted in her death. We acknowledge that Mr. Cornelius Rademacher was helpful in providing the police with important information about the suspect, which ultimately led to Mr. Proudfoot's arrest."

"This is quite interesting," I said, "More information than I thought we would be able to find. Or should I say, thought you would find. I can't thank you enough."

"That might not be all," she said, "No that might actually just be the tip of the iceberg. There might actually be quite a bit more information on this whole matter. But the details probably wouldn't be in the newspaper. We would need to take a look down a little bit different path. It seems likely that if Sam Proudfoot was charged, then he was ultimately tried for the murder of Miss. St. Simmons. And what do you think that might mean to us?"

"What do you mean? Well, I'm not sure. You mean who was the judge? Oh, maybe Judge Ramsey presided over the case."

"No. You now, for a writer or journalist you really don't know much about Minnesota history. By 1892 Ramsey had already served as Governor of Minnesota and Secretary of War under President Rutherford B. Hayes, he hadn't been a judge for years. No. What I'm saying is there's probably additional information about the trial of Sam Proudfoot, records, correspondence, I don't really know. The fact that we have already found some records here in the house related to Ms St. Simmons murder, might suggest that there may be additional records here. I don't know what Ramsey's involvement would have been in this affair, but I don't think he would have presided over the murder trial. I'm not sure why Ms. St. Simmons effects were here in the house, though. Maybe they are tied to Alexander Ramsey in some way. It was his family that ultimately donated the house to The Historical Society. That is probably why that portfolio somehow got into the attic. Even though he was retired in 1892, Ramsey would have still been involved in St. Paul affairs; plus I don't know what type of business any of his family members were involved in at that time. Given his background though, he may have been interested in the murder case. That would definitely make sense."

"Well, do you think there might be more information on that murder trial? Like something that Alexander Ramsey would have written down or kept?" I asked.

"Not sure. He did keep some memoirs that were passed down with the house. We just haven't really gone through and cataloged it all. I'm not sure if the trial would have been a big enough sensation back then. An Indian on trial wasn't all that unique. Although the death of a woman attorney, from back East, now that may have been more of a matter of interest. I asked Ms. Swenson to see if she could find some more info on the trial in the paper's archives, but it seems that there was a fire at the paper some time ago and the records going forward from those articles I just showed you were destroyed. I'm not sure where else we could look."

"How about the Ramsey County District Court records?" I asked.

"No, I asked Sandy at The Pioneer Press. She didn't think the county records went back that far, at least in any detail."

"Well, are you sure you don't have any more records that haven't been reviewed, maybe up in the attic?" I asked.

"All I know is that we haven't come across it yet. If anything is up there. It has piqued my curiosity, though. We might be able to do some extra checking, go through some items in the attic and see if we find anything else. I can't promise anything though."

"Well, thank for everything so far. This is really turning into a mystery, isn't it?" I said standing up trying hard to contain my excitement.

"Yes. It really is a mystery. Her voice rose to a higher pitch revealing a level of excitement as well, that I hadn't noticed before. It is actually quite interesting. I'm not sure in the end though, that we'll solve whatever it is we're ultimately looking for, or should say you're ultimately looking for. I've seen it all too often with historical artifacts that when the search is completed you're usually left with more questions than answers. But we'll see. Who knows?" she added.

"When do you want to meet next?" I asked cutting her off before she could continue on.

"I'm not sure how long it will take. Can I give you a call?" she said.

"Tell you what," I said. "Why don't I swing by next Wednesday again? I'll be in town again on some other business. If you don't have any new information then, no problem, I'll just be on my way. I really don't want to put you out more than I already have. I'll swing by early afternoon if that's OK."

"Sure that's fine with me. And, I'm getting interested in this too, so it's really no trouble. Then next Wednesday it is. Oh and it just came to mind, isn't this getting a little off your New Ulm Magogson connection?"

"Oh, no. Not really. It may in fact make for a more interesting story in the end. We'll see. Do you need to frisk me to make sure I haven't taken anything?" I said jokingly.

"No. I've had my eye on you the whole time."

I didn't know if she was serious, flirting, or a combination. The thought of an older woman putting the moves on me just didn't seem possible. I just kept serious and said "You don't have to worry about me."

With that, she walked me back down the hallway and out the front door.

I became lost in thought. My new friends were dying off as quickly as I was meeting them. Well, I really wasn't meeting them in the flesh, but it was as if I really knew them. Candace, my attorney friend was dead, I thought to myself. I wish I had gotten to know her better.

Chapter 23

My Meeting with the Notary's Granddaughter

It took a number of phone calls, but finally I was able to track down someone related to the notary, Mary Percy. It was her granddaughter Ann Percy. It's amazing St. Paul is like that. People don't move too far from where they grew up. Usually as adults they tend to stay in the same neighborhood. It's like a bunch of small towns within a big city. And you don't wander too far from your town.

At first she was hesitant about meeting with me. But when I explained my official background, and the importance of the information she might have, she agreed to see me. I was surprised she was willing to meet with me. I'm always amazed that people will let a complete stranger into their house. But if you use the right context and the people are lonely enough, I guess they just justify that the risk and reward are worth it: personal contact versus death at the hands of a potential serial killer.

On the phone, she seemed so distant, so quiet, barely audible on the other end. I hoped she even understood what I wanted to talk about and more importantly was lucid enough to talk about it.

I pulled up at the address. It was a small one story, clapboard house neatly painted white with light blue trim. A short metal railing was the only ornamental piece to the house. I assumed it had been placed there out of necessity and the fact that it actually looked nice was secondary. I walked up to the front door and noticed well worn curtains covered the inside of the windows to the side of the front door, making the house look worn. I rang the doorbell. It took a few moments, but finally the door slowly opened. Staring back at me was a frail, thin, short lady. Her boney hand pushed open the front door. Before I could introduce myself she said

"Won't you come in?" she softly spoke.

I stepped in and was struck by the smell of stale air. It was dark inside, the only light that came in from the outside filtered in around the edges of the drawn curtains. It felt a little claustrophobic, like a tomb with a person more dead than alive trapped within.

"Thank you." I said, "You know you shouldn't open the door to just anyone."

"Silly man. You're not just anyone. I know who you are. You're the man I talked to on the phone. I don't get much company these days. I knew you were coming over. Who else would you be? Plus, I've just about lived my life through to the end. I don't have much time left so does it really matter? Do you want some tea? I just brewed a pot?"

"Sure, that would be nice," I said. My eyes were still adjusting to the darkness of the room. In front of me was a well worn couch with arm covers that were worn as well. Behind the couch were tandem pictures of what I thought were old style pictures of Mary and Joseph, maybe Jesus, I couldn't be sure. On the table by the side of the couch were a few pictures in frames of what were probably some relatives. I still couldn't get past the staleness of the air. It felt as though cooking odors had mingled with dust and dirt hanging in the air. I could only imagine what I was breathing in.

"Do you want any sugar or cream in your tea?" she said, working her way back into the kitchen. "Sit down on the couch and I'll be right back in with the tea."

Cream and sugar, I thought. I'd had sugar with tea before, but not cream. "Yes, both I answered."

"Oh, so you're one of those sophisticated Brits, huh?" she said catching me off guard.

"Brits?" I questioned.

"Yes, they like their tea with cream or milk. I never acquired the taste though. I like mine straight up as they say. No sugar either."

"No. I'm not a Brit. I just like cream in my tea." I had never had cream in my tea before but I didn't want to get into a drawn out discussion about the tea. There I was, setting myself up for another misunderstanding.

I sat quietly for what seemed like hours.

"Can I help you at all," I yelled in the direction of the kitchen, finally growing impatient.

"No," she said I'll be out in a second.

A few minutes later she slowly emerged with a teapot and two cups on a tray along with a small plate with what looked like three small cookies. She set the tray on a low table in front of me and poured tea in both cups.

"I already added cream and sugar to your cup. I hope that's all right. If you want more let me know. Also, help yourself to a cookie."

I leaned forward and before I grabbed a cookie, I grabbed hold of my cup of tea. I glanced in the cup and could see the cream curdled on the top. I'd try to sip my way around it.

She moved over to the other side of the room which wasn't really that far, as the room was quite small. She slowly lowered herself into her chair steadying her cup of tea in her thin, long, boney fingers. Her dress hung on her and she wore a pair of slippers with no heels but had flesh tone socks that ran up to her mid calf. She really looked like a toothpick in a cotton bag.

"So young man, you wanted to talk to me about my grandmother. I don't know whether I can help you. She's been dead for so many years and I'm one foot in the grave myself. The memory isn't what it used to be."

"Yes. Your grandmother was a notary, right?"

"Well, that wasn't her job really. She was a teller at the First National Bank of St. Paul for a number of years, but I believe she was a notary as well. Why do you ask?"

"Well, I'm doing some background for an article on "St. Paul, the Early Days." And I ran into a question regarding a farm that was sold back over one hundred years ago."

"What type of article are you working on? I thought you said you were a reporter from New Ulm?"

"No. I said I was a reporter who used to work for the paper in New Ulm. Now I'm a freelance writer working on an historical piece for the St. Paul Weekly." Oh, I had to do a better job of getting my stories straight. What was I thinking?

"I've never heard of the St. Paul Weekly, but you know the eyesight isn't what it used to be I just usually listen to the TV, it's more like a radio. Can't really make out what's going on unless I'm close up. Eyes will go like that on a person when you're my age. Don't forget to try one of my cookies. I made them during the holidays."

I figured I might as well be polite so I leaned in and grabbed one of the cookies. I bit off a piece of the cookie. Immediately my mouth reacted. I don't know which year that holiday was in when she baked them, but the cookie was hard and had a distinct rancid taste. I set the rest of the cookie down next to my cup of tea and tried to wash the taste down with a sip of tea making sure not to sip up the curdled milk in the cup. Then I continued talking.

"Well, the St. Paul Weekly is a weekly magazine. It covers all types of different topics about St. Paul. I'm doing an article on the original farms that were situated where St. Paul is now located. I've been looking at old records and your grandmother's name came up as the notary on one of the deeds."

"It's the Magogson farm isn't it? She asked leaning now intently into me. Her eyes bulging a little in their sockets, a vein on the side of her head pulsing ever so slightly. Yes, she was alive.

"Yes, it is about the Magogson farm. How did you know that's what I would ask about?" I asked in return, leaning forward in the couch.

"Because young man, it has haunted me for all these years. And it's fitting that now that I'm getting close to meeting my maker that I would be forced to deal with this unfinished business."

"What unfinished business?'

"Allowing my grandmother's soul to rest in peace."

She grew serious, her face drew down long and firm.

"Let me tell you about my grandmother. She was a very beautiful woman. See that picture over there next to you on the table. That's her. My mother used to go on about stories about her"

I looked over: one photograph was of an older man and the other was a worn picture of a woman in black and white, with curly hair less than shoulder length. She had a firm glance that mingled with the shadows around the edges.

"That was my grandmother when she was 23, whole life ahead of her. She came to St. Paul on the train, just one small bag. She came from a well-to-do family back in a small town in Wisconsin. Turns out her father was a well known businessman in the town. To this day, there's a building that sits on Main Street with his name on the top. Anyway, he ran the general store. Oh yes, and he had remarried after his first wife died, my grandmother's mother that is. My grandmother didn't get along with her new stepmother and things took a turn when her father made it clear that he had picked out the proper gentleman for her to marry. Turns out, he was an older man; pretty much of a womanizer and a drunk but her father thought her marriage to him might improve his business ties. No sir, she would have none of it. I told him so to his face. What does he do? Says you've made your choice then. Says she is no longer his daughter. Gives her a dollar and tosses her out on the street. Anyway, she was pretty strong willed. Somehow she came up with enough money to hop on the train to St. Paul. Looked up some distant cousins to stay with for awhile and got a job in a woman's clothing store. So then, it turns out the cousins she stayed with had another boarder about her age, a young man. They started to get serious and finally got married after a brief courtship. And so, my mother was the result of that courtship and subsequent marriage. The marriage didn't last long though. He died of blood poisoning. Fell off a ladder while working and an infection set in from rusty nails in boards that he landed on."

"So she was a young widow, then. Oh, I'm so sorry," I added trying to keep her moving along.

"Yes, she was. After my grandfather died things really changed. My mom said her mom was always serious and determined. I think she was really trying to hide the fact that she was scared, afraid she couldn't or wouldn't be able to provide for her and my mom."

"What did she do?"

"Well, she kept working for the clothing store until she got on with the bank, The First National Bank of St. Paul. She started out as a clerk but eventually worked her way up to a teller. She would have been a great vice president or something some day. She had a good mind for numbers, very detailed oriented. But she also liked people. She could really hold a conversation, or so my mom said."

"Well, did she ever get to become a vice president or move up in the bank?" I asked, interrupting her.

"She never had a chance. Her life was cut short; I think it was around the turn of the century. My mom said she could always remember that day. She left mom home. My mom must of only been five or six at the time. She told her there was a sandwich and some milk on the table in the kitchen and that by the time she was done eating she would be back. Said she would be back in less than a half hour, but she never came back. My mom wound up waiting for hours, poor little girl. She finally went next door to the neighbors. They never found my grandma. They interviewed my mom, but she was little help. Scared to death and all alone. Finally my mom was sent to live with her cousins."

"Wow. That's awful. How does that have anything to do with putting your grandma's soul to rest though?"

"You need to be patient young man. I'm not finished yet. I'm getting there. When my mom turned 21 she received a packet from an attorney in St. Paul. It was addressed to my mom. Inside the envelope was a smaller envelope and a letter. The letter was addressed to my mom. "You may find it strange, but to this day I remember what the letter said. It read:

"Enclosed is an envelope which was entrusted to me by Miss. Mary Percy, to be held for you until you turn twenty-one years of age. Seeing as you have reached the age of twenty-one, I am forwarding this letter to you. There are no charges or fees associated with this letter. I am sorry that I will not be able to be of further assistance as I am not aware of the contents of the envelope. It was entrusted to me with strict instructions not to open the letter, but only to forward it to you unopened.
Sincerely,
Robert P. Sands, Esq."

"Well, what was in the envelope and how did the attorney come across it?"

"I'm getting to that." she said a little annoyed. Then she switched back to her quiet tone of voice. "I thought it odd, but my mother only told me about this letter about a week before she died. I think she wanted to clear her conscience, too. She made me promise not to disclose it to anyone. But, now that all these years have passed, I think it is best that it comes out. Anyway, inside the envelope was a last statement by my grandma. The letter stated:

"If you are reading this letter, you must now be twenty-one years old. I hope you have grown up to be a fine young lady. Also, by now you must know that I am deceased. This may seem like an odd way to contact you one last time, but I feel compelled to set the record straight. Know this: that I loved you dearly and worried night and day that you would be safe and happy. I only wanted what was best for you. When you try to do that, you have to make hard decisions at

times. In trying to protect you, I believe I put myself in harm's way and ultimately paid for it with my life. Please do not think less of me, but I want to give you some peace of mind about why I did what I did. Trying to make ends meet, I took risks that ultimately harmed people. Even though I had a full time job at the bank, times were tough. You were a handful, but a happy handful. But to get to the point, I was a notary. It was one of those tasks that the bank required of me. One day a bank customer asked me to falsely witness someone's signature. They said the people were dead and that it was their wish that the deed be signed. They were dead now and the signed deed couldn't be found. That man pressured me, said that I was only providing customer service and doing what needed to be done. He put on his charm. After a few days I caved into his demands. The money was too tempting and his persuasiveness too much. The minute I signed it I regretted it. I only did it once but it was enough to regret for the rest of my life. I am telling you this so you do not make the same mistake. Actually, it is not a mistake. Mistakes happen throughout life. No, this was a lapse in judgment, a moment when you should know better, but make the wrong decision. Now I must find a way to right this wrong. Yes, there are people negatively affected that need to be made whole. I must do what I can. If you are reading this letter then you know that I have failed. But know this, I have and will always love you and I miss you my little one who's now all grown up. The signatures I notarized without them being present were Marcellus and Eleanor Magogson. Beware of charming gentleman with hidden motives. Stay true to your convictions. Don't stray from doing what's right and always dream big.

  Your Mom,
  Mary

P.S. Beware of retribution because it comes from many places. Perceived wrongs are just as real as wrongs truly done."

"Well, that is quite interesting. But what does it all mean?"

"I asked my mother the same thing. She kept saying she was too young to remember."

Do you think your grandmother was murdered?"

"Not sure. But does someone leave a little child and not come back? I always thought she met with foul play when my mother first told me about her. I think this letter just confirms it. She was evidently trying to resolve or clear up what she had done, right her wrongs and I think she was killed because of it."

"Then who was responsible?"

"That I can't say. She doesn't mention any names. We can only infer from the letter who it might have been. Maybe the dapper Dan who talked her into signing the deed or some heir or relative of the Magogsons. That isn't much to go on, though."

"No, it certainly isn't"

"I've wanted to tell someone that story for all these years. Now, that's the story, I've passed it on. Now it's your turn to solve it, young man. I'm just the messenger. I wish you good luck."

"Wait, wasn't there anything else that came up."

"No, as I said nothing else that my mom was aware of or if she was, she never passed it on to me. No, I just tried to live my life. So, if you're done with your tea I'll walk you to the door. All of a sudden I'm getting quite tired. It's getting time for my afternoon nap. You're welcome to take an extra cookie if you'd like. Aren't they delicious?"

Chapter 24

I Reach an Impasse

What was I going to do now? I was at an impasse. I was getting too caught up in this whole mess of a mystery, if that was what you wanted to call it. Maybe I just needed to get back on track, get back to the job search. Settle into finding a job that would fill my week with constructive tasks and a welcome paycheck. But what if, what if my quest here was all about figuring out a mystery that needed to be solved? Yes, but solved for who and why did it need to be solved. Maybe it was just enough that I was interested, interested in all these long forgotten people, people that once walked this same location. Why shouldn't I take an interest in this? Weren't they really a piece of my world, one step removed? If I kept going, I could pull these disjointed pieces together and tie them up in a cohesive manner. I could make them part of my world. I could in a way breathe life into them, bring meaning to their stories. And I could put that sanctimonious ass Braddock in his place. I'd let him know the true history of him and his house. I'd figure it out. But I needed more pieces to the puzzle.

Think. Think. That frail old lady I had just talked to was hard of hearing; I couldn't tell if she understood me. So her grandmother went out one day and never came back. No one knew if it was foul play. But it seems that she was in the process of resolving something when she disappeared. Maybe I should look up that attorney: Sands. No, he was probably long dead. Plus, he said he didn't have any additional information. Where should I turn now? Maybe I was looking at this all wrong. I needed some more facts.

Maybe I needed to figure out when some of these people died. That would give me a time frame on what to look for and possible places to look. Let me see, I now knew when Ann Percy, the notary died and for the most part how she was involved. I had lesser information on Cornelius Rademacher and Abaddon Magogson and maybe even his parents. Those were the loose ends I needed to check into. But really, I was getting out of my zone. I only knew how to look up deeds and get historical society people to look up info for me. Now I needed to check on the death records.

I knew the internet was good for surfing for fun facts like the Nathan's hot dog eating champ in 2007, Joey Chestnut of course who bested Takeru Kobayashi. But I wondered if I might actually be able to find out some important information. I typed in St. Paul death records. A site offered them for a fee and another and then another. No, I needed free information. Finally, near the bottom of the screen. There it was "...records.org". Yes if a website ended in "org" it had to be the real deal. I clicked on the address. It took me to an actual website that offered a fill in the blank screen to search for deaths in St. Paul starting from 1863. I hoped the records showed up. I typed in Cornelius Rademacher. I didn't have a date of death so I just pressed enter. Up popped the record. I clicked on it, but it wasn't a copy of the actual death certificate, it was a form. I looked at the date of death and it said September 1, 1899; location of death in St. Paul. Otherwise there wasn't any additional information other than a microfilm reference number. I wrote that down.

Next, I typed in Abaddon Magogson. Again, I had no date of death, but pressed the enter key. Up popped the record. My eyes scrolled down the screen: date of death September 1, 1899. The same date, it couldn't be a coincidence. I looked at location and again it said "St. Paul". And again I wrote down the microfilm reference number. Couldn't be a coincidence.

I had to view the actual death certificates if I could. I went back to searching online and pulled up the official Ramsey County site. After some browsing, I found what I was looking for. It looked like I could order a copy online, just ten dollars per record. I put in the info and pulled out my credit card. It would arrive in five business days, or so it said. Now I had a hunch. I went to the website for "Coroner Reports." Wow, it looked like I could order an autopsy report! I punched in "Rademacher" and the year, nothing. I punched in "Magogson". It was there. It was dated September 1, 1899. Wasn't the internet a beautiful thing? Oh no, wait, there on the screen were the words "you must have a tangible interest in the subject". What did that mean? As I read further it meant that you were a sibling or other close relative, personal representative, licensed attorney, or the trustee of a trust involving the subject person. Oh wait, that's just to get a certified copy. I didn't need a certified copy. I just needed $13 and they'd send it to me. I put in my order for a copy. This would all be money well spent. I would soon have the additional facts I needed. I'd just have to wait to get them. In the meantime, were there any loose ends I could tie up while I was waiting? I surely didn't want to have to go back into the job search mode. I just wasn't ready. Plus, this was way more interesting. Let me think. I headed off to the kitchen for a cup of coffee and to clear my mind.

Chapter 25
Third Visit to the Historical Society

Well, Wednesday rolled around much quicker than I could've imagined. My new, fulltime private detective job was taking up much of my time. Whether I was collecting new information or simply thinking about it, the whole mystery began to consume me full time. Too bad I wasn't getting paid for it.

The more I waded into all of this, the more I also began to realize, that most, if not all of the suspects were long since dead. I was beginning to think more and more that I would have to fill in my own missing details. My wife said I was good at that. If we were at the same event, I'd always have a completely different view of what occurred. That lady at the Christmas party: she wasn't drunk, she was just expressive. That old man on the bus, he wasn't trying to pick up that young lady, he was just politely offering her the seat next to his. The list could go on and on. No, if I learned one thing from my wife, it was that there are usually as many different interpretations to an event as there are people at the event, and that what really happened is something different altogether. No, I would not make any judgments; I would stick to the facts. I'd keep my viewpoint out of this altogether. As to my wife, well that was a different matter. Based on our last conversation, I figured it was best to keep the facts from her until I had all the facts. Then I could get her viewpoint as well.

What I still didn't know is where this would all lead me and how Darrah Braddock and his wife figured into this whole mystery, if at all. Maybe they were just the current owners of a house filled with a twisted history. Sure, what I was finding was that the whole history of the farm was filled with numerous sad occurrences; but that didn't mean there was anything more to it. It didn't mean the land was haunted, evil or different from any other piece of land. Land was just land: nothing more, nothing less. Life was hard, life could be sad, it could be downright cruel. Maybe that was the lesson I was learning. But I had yet to find out whether all these different pieces would come together in the end. Maybe I was just looking at a bunch of different random acts that had occurred at the same location. I found myself hanging on that thought as I rang the doorbell to The Historical Society. The familiar steps grew louder and the lock flipped back. The door opened slightly and before looking at the person in front of me, I blurted out, "Were you able to find anything out?"

The response wasn't what I expected. "Did you have an appointment, sir?" was the question in response to my question; and the voice wasn't familiar but came from a much younger woman.

"Is the older lady here, I asked, I had scheduled a meeting with her today. We set it last week."

"No sir, there was nothing on her calendar I can assure you I checked."

"Well, just ask her. She can confirm our appointment."

"I'm afraid that won't be possible."

"What do you mean won't be possible? If I can only speak with her we can get this straightened out. I'm sure she would want to meet with me. Won't you at least let me in to talk to her and get this straightened out?"

"Sir, I'm sorry, but Anne passed away three days ago."

My jaw dropped. "How? where?" I thought to myself. All that came out of my mouth though was "I can't believe that. How?"

"She was working late up in the attic going over some old records stored there when a pile of boxes fell on her. Normally boxes falling on someone wouldn't kill them. She must have lost her balance just so, poor thing. We found her dead lying under a pile of papers and the boxes. It was awful. She was in a contorted manner as if she saw the boxes coming at her but couldn't move and stop them from falling on her." She took a deep breath and tried to regain her composure. Then she continued. "Odd thing was, I was the one who found her, and when I came up the stairs, there was a black crow sitting on top of the overturned shelf where the boxes had sat. We've had problems with critters in the attic before, but nothing that big. I have no idea how it got there. Then as I walked closer, it stood there motionless, as if it was stuffed. It was at that moment that I saw her body there. As I moved closer, the bird flew past me down the attic stairs, emitting a shrieking caw as it flew past. It was an awful sight. I still can't get it out of my mind. I rushed to her, but her body was cold; she had been dead for hours. I looked down and a pile of feathers partially obscured the heading of what was clutched in her hand."

"Feathers? What was in her hand?" I blurted out.

"The Official Transcript Record of the Murder Trial of Sam Proudfoot"

My jaw dropped. "Oh, that's awful." I couldn't help but think that it was me. I had a hand in that poor lady's death. If not for my request she wouldn't have been in the attic. It was my fault. Or, was it fate? I thought quickly. No, it wasn't my fault. She was just doing her job, nothing more than that. I just needed to move on and get back to the important things at hand. At the moment, I had a job to do. I gave the lady my most serious concerned look and said, "Do you think I might be able to look at the transcript?"

"What?" she asked.

"I mean that is awful what happened to Anne. When is her funeral? I need to know." I quickly realized my thoughtless comment and tried to change the focus of the conversation. I guess I really was that callous. A woman had died, and while trying to help me find some information. But realistically, the information couldn't be left behind in vain, that was for sure.

"No, what I was meaning to say is that I definitely need to attend that funeral. It is important for me to get some closure. We had worked closely together over the last few weeks. And I hate to even bring it up, but that Transcript was what she was looking for. She was finding it for me. I'm doing an article. I wouldn't even ask given the current situation, but my article is due within days. That was the last piece of information I needed to complete it. I'm really under the gun here to produce. I shouldn't even ask, but could I borrow it. I know Anne would have wanted me to see it."

She gave me a really strange look, which I took to mean that she was still trying to digest Anne's death and then said, "Well normally I wouldn't believe that story, but she had written down some notes on her desk about "Sam Proudfoot, Judge Ramsey, Cornelius Rademacher. I'm inclined to believe you. Plus, my dad was a newsman for forty years. I understand the pressure they're under. What did you say your name was and who do you work for?"

"I didn't. My name is Jim, Jim Daniels; I work for The Pioneer Press. You know your dad is a legend down at the paper. He's well-known that's for sure." I hope I wasn't laying it on too thick. For whatever reason, I still wanted as few people to know about what I was doing as possible. I don't know that it mattered: not telling people the truth I think it just made it easier. People always liked a little more substantial information to know who they were dealing with. I was just providing them with a little more excitement, something to talk to their friends about. I was making them happy. What was wrong with that? Nothing. Before I could say anything else she broke in.

"Yes, he worked over at the Minneapolis paper. I'm surprised they would know him."

"Oh, it's competitive courtesy. Anybody who's in the industry for that long is looked up to."

"Yes, but he wasn't a reporter, he was a printer, worked in the pressroom his whole life."

"Even those people were well-known. It was a challenge to typeset those papers day in and day out. Real old school. Did you know The Pioneer Press changed its typesetting process just to pick up on the changes your dad made?" I took a deep breath and paused. I couldn't go on any longer with a straight face or without blowing my cover which was evaporating in to thin air as I continued to speak.

Just as I was about to put my foot in my mouth again she broke in.

"He really was a great pressman. He's been gone for many years now, but I still think about him daily. That's amazing that he's such a legend. I never realized that. Tell you what; let me see if I can find that transcript. If it's easily available, I don't see any harm in letting you have a peek. You'll have to do it here though. Come on in, she said opening the door and waving me in, in one motion. Here, sit here and wait at this table. I'll see if I can find the transcript and bring it down to you."

I sat down and couldn't help thinking that maybe she was on the phone calling the police or better yet checking out my story with someone she knew at the paper. Just when I started to get uncomfortable, she came back carrying a bound multipage document.

"Here you go. Let me know when you're done," she said.

"Thank you so much for all your trouble. Say, before you go, can I ask you one question?"

"Sure, go ahead."

"Do you have anything here at the Historical Society on the Sioux or should I say Dakota uprising back in the 1860's? Why, what did you want to know?"

"Well, I just wanted some background on the whole event, for the research on my article. I don't want to trouble you though given the current situation."

"No. That's OK. Yes, in fact we do. We have some articles, letters, and other information that date back to that time period. That whole chapter in our state's history was pretty awful. The Sioux or I should say Dakota, that's what they like to be referred to as, rose up across the state, more than five hundred settlers were killed, and some figures even went as high as eight hundred. In the end, troops were brought in to re-establish the peace. Whole families were wiped out. The troops rounded up the Indians responsible and in

December, 1862 thirty-eight Dakota Indians were hung in a mass execution. It was the most people executed in one day in this country even to this day."

"Wow, I didn't expect that much information on the tip of your tongue. How do you know so much?"

"We just put together a small exhibit on it. It's down the hall if you would like to see it?"

"I think I would. Can I finish up with the Transcript first, though?"

"Yes, go right ahead. You can sit at this desk in the hall here." She turned and left, leaving me all alone. I sat for a moment looking at the Transcript trying not to let my anticipation get the best of me.

I started paging through the document. After the cover page, there was a blank page loosely inserted. Handwritten on that page were a number of words, phrases and incomplete sentences in two columns. It appeared to weigh the evidence at the trial. Were they notes by the Judge in the case, Alexander Ramsey or someone else? It wasn't signed or anything. I could only conclude that it must have been notes by someone written down during or shortly after the trial. The two columns read:

Pros	*Cons*
Bridle found in Stable	*Rademacher truthful?*
Miss St. Simmons never arrived at Wild Stag	*Native American bias*
Letter to Rademacher still in her possession never given to Rademacher	*Proudfoot and St. Simmons left on good terms*
Rademacher testimony	*Rademacher truthful?*
	Character witnesses for Sam
Feathers and native american charms found at murder site	*Native American Bias by jury*

I read through the Transcript. It appeared that the main piece of evidence was a bloody bridle found in the stable of Sam Proudfoot which matched the indentations in Candace's head. That was the only real piece of physical evidence. The other real evidence was really just the testimony of Cornelius Rademacher: he stated that he had waited for Candace St. Simmons at the Wild Stag and that she never arrived. It seemed, no one else saw the attorney at the Wild Stag either. Also, the deed, the one I found in her portfolio presumably, was still in the portfolio found on her possession in the alley. From that information, the prosecution raised the likelihood that the attorney never had a chance to meet with Rademacher, because she still had the draft of the deed in her possession. It was then that the blame turned to the Indian. Rademacher had said St. Simmons told him she had hired the Indian and that for some reason he was angry with her after they got back, maybe because it took longer to get back than was originally expected. There might have been an argument over payment. Mr. Rademacher testified that she was from out of town and wasn't aware she knew anyone else in town.

The defense tried to discredit the testimony of Rademacher at the trial. But in the end, Sam Proudfoot had no alibi for the night of the murder and he couldn't explain away the bloody bridle. The defense did present one piece of evidence: a simple note written by Rademacher that was found in the hotel room of Ms. St Simmons. It was written in a threatening tone:

Those East coast partners that you have in your pocket might not have a problem with you, but I do. I've put up enough money in this project to expect results. If you can't get results, you can get on the next train back East. You need to get moving. You need to get the sale of that farm wrapped up, or else.

Cornelius.

In the end though, Sam Proudfoot was convicted of first degree murder and sentenced to be hanged. For whatever reason, the Indian never took the stand. A number of people testified as character witnesses for him, probably his customers.

Finally, I came across another note. It was handwritten and appeared to be written by Alexander Ramsey. It read:

At the request of my good friend, Jim Brooks, I have reviewed all of the evidence over the course of this trial. While I disagree with the outcome of the jury's guilty verdict in this matter, I am unable to find any specific grounds to appeal or overrule their verdict. But, my conscience weighs heavy as I believe Sam Proudfoot did not kill Ms. St. Simmons. Instead, I believe Ms. St. Simmons may have met her untimely death at the hands of an assailant or assailants who will now not be brought to justice. I believe Ms. St. Simmons death had something to do with the legal matters she was handling for a Mr. Cornelius Rademacher. There is nothing I can do currently to change the outcome of this trial, but I will use my resources to make inquiries of Mr. Rademacher and his business dealings.

In the end, that was all there was. I was left with an old dusty manuscript, and notes from a long dead governor who had concerns about Sam's guilt and Mr. Rademacher's character. Nothing more.

I waited quietly for a few minutes until I heard the familiar footsteps and she finally reappeared from the front of the building.

"Thank you for letting me go over the Transcript. It was very helpful. Here you go," I said handing her back the Transcript.

"Now, I was wondering if you still had time to show me that exhibit you were talking about. The one about the Sioux, I mean the Dakota Uprising here in Minnesota?"

"Yes, I do. Follow me."

I was still trying to get past the fact that the historical society was housed in this old house. Most exhibits were set along the hallway interrupted here and there by numerous paintings that hung on the wall. It seemed as if there really wasn't a chronological order to anything, artifacts were placed here and there more out of convenience than purpose. I followed her to a room off what used to be the kitchen. There in the corner was a large bulletin board covered with pictures, letters and note cards with information printed on them. It was nicely done, but not fully professional. Along the top of the board it read, "Sioux Uprising of 1862".

Beginning to look through the bulletin board of information, I couldn't help but wonder if few things had really changed between 1862 and the Sam Proudfoot murder case in 1892. I don't think he had a chance going into it, whether he was guilty of not. I had heard somewhere that each of the trials for the Native Americans executed back in 1862 lasted roughly three minutes. From time to time, there was talk of posthumously overturning those convictions, but to date, nothing had been done. I hoped Sam Proudfoot's trial lasted a little longer.

"This is what we put together most recently on the Uprising of 1862, as it's referred to. I don't know if there will be anything of value here for you, but you're welcome to look."

"Thank you. One thing that may or may not be on your board and I hate to even ask, it might be too graphic to show or discuss, but how did the Native Americans kill the settlers?"

"No. That's alright. It is part of history. Now, you have to remember, the Native Americans, were trying to get the white settlers to leave, so they really didn't have a problem with how they killed the settlers. They really didn't spare anyone, men, women, or children. There was even an account of a woman having her fetus taken out of her and killed. Whether she was still alive when that happened, no one will probably ever know. They were pretty brutal in the killing. Remember, they were trying to protect their way of life. It was either them or the settlers."

"Specifically, do you know if they would disfigure the face of their victims?"

"No, not that I'm aware. They went for the shock value. They wanted anyone who came along to know that it was their loved ones that had died. They didn't have a problem removing scalps or severing the heads of victims from the bodies and displaying the heads on a pole or hanging them in a doorway. But their ultimate goal was to make any survivors in the area afraid to stay once they saw what had happened. The Native Americans wanted to make it clear to them that what had happened to some would happen to anyone else who remained in the area. No, the Native Americans wanted the survivors to know who had been killed and that they died painfully."

"That's enough. I think I understand the nature of the killings," I said cutting her off in her explanation.

"I can just let myself out after I take a look at this exhibit. Again, thank you."

"You're welcome. Just give a shout if you need me."

I turned to focus on the exhibit.

There was a picture of thirty-nine Indians in one picture. They looked solemn as they stood there. Two cavalry soldiers stood on either side of the large group, rifles in hand. The caption read:

"38 of the 39 indians who were executed at Mankato, MN on December 26, 1862. One was pardoned. Initially 303 were to hang but President Lincoln commuted sentences of 264."

I moved on to another picture. It showed Native Americans on a horse path in a prairie setting. It looked like an entire tribe loaded up for a long trek. The caption read:

"In April 1863, the rest of the Dakota were rounded up and sent to Nebraska and South Dakota and the United States Congress abolished their reservations in Minnesota."

Then, I saw another picture. Two people were lowering a plain wooden coffin into a grave. Other open graves could be seen next to the coffin being lowered. The caption read:

"Picture showing the initial burial of the executed Indians. They wouldn't have used the term Native Americans back then. This picture was circulated to show the humane burial of the executed Native Americans. Actually, they were buried in a mass grave, not before small pieces of skin where removed from each body and later sold as mementos of the event. A short time later however, their bodies were dug up and distributed to various doctors in the area for medical research."

I began to randomly look through the artifacts on the board. There were letters from settlers describing the aftermath. There was a letter from a cavalry officer on how they rounded up the Indians, and there were a number of other pictures. Then one picture caught my eye. I looked closely. Yes. It was a picture of the oak tree with the Magogson farm house in the background. There were men standing next to their horses, three to be exact, posing in the front of the picture. Behind them hung, not a few but seven Indians, ropes around their necks. They weren't all the same size, some appeared younger than others. The photo was grainy and it was difficult to make out the faces on anyone in the picture. The caption below the picture read:

"Death of Seven Indians, Location unknown, probably occurred during Uprising of 1862."

Chapter 26
Autopsy of Abaddon Magogson

I had been waiting now for days, for the coroner's report on the death of Abaddon. It doesn't get more nerve wracking than waiting day in and day out for something to arrive by mail, patience slowly fades, replaced by constant anxiety. It reminded me when I was a little kid and had ordered something from the back of a comic book. If I recall, it was a set of miniature plastic ships which were about one-tenth the size that I anticipated they would be. It wasn't just the disappointment when they arrived, it was also the fact that they took six to eight weeks to be delivered. Here it was just five business days and it still seemed like an eternity. It seems like when you wait for something, it doesn't arrive and then when you forget about it, even for a short time, all of a sudden it's here! And so it was this time. I wound up doing some odd jobs for the lady next door. It took most of the day and when I got home I checked the mail box. There it was, official as could be: two envelopes a small white one from the county and a large one from the county coroner's office. It took everything in my power to not just tear right into the envelopes.

Instead, I took a deep breath and handled them methodically. The first envelope I opened was the one from the county. I pulled out the two sheets inside. They both looked similar, identical if you didn't look more closely. The first one was the death certificate for Abaddon Magogson. I glanced through the form for some of the pieces of information that interested me. Going down the various boxes filled with information, I found one piece I was looking for: date of death, September 1, 1899. Next I found: age 60, estimated.

Ok, that's good. Now, where was the cause of death, I thought to myself. I scanned down the sheet. There it was "gunshot to the chest." There wasn't any more of a description than that. Let me see if there was place of death listed. Knowing my luck it probably would just say St. Paul. I looked down again. There it was, "Magogson Farm outside St. Paul off of the old Fort Road." No address was listed. They probably didn't have an address back then. Didn't need one. Reference to the farm was enough. So he was killed by a gunshot on his own farm. I looked down the form. There really wasn't anything more of interest.

I pulled out the other form from the envelope. At the top, like the other sheet, it read "Death Certificate". The name filled in was "Cornelius Rademacher". I scrolled down to the date of death; it read "September 1, 1899", with an age of 57 listed a little further down. I looked for cause of death. Odd. It said "Murder by stabbing." The other death certificate didn't say that. This specifically said "murder". I looked for the location of his death and it read "Magogson Farm outside St. Paul off of the old Fort Road." Both died on the same day, in the same place. But unless there was something left out on the death description for Abaddon, only one was murdered. How did the other one die then? I mean who killed both of them? Maybe the autopsy report would help answer those questions. Then I thought for a minute: before I put the two sheets of paper down and picked up the other packet, I looked back at both sheets to see if a next of kin was listed. On the Magogson death certificate it read Mary Lafond, cousin. Under Cornelius Rademacher it just read James McMasters, business acquaintance. I wrote those two names down on a piece of paper. Neither of those two names had come up previously. They might come in handy later.

Next, I tore open the other envelope. Inside was a multipage set of papers. The top page was just a receipt. I folded that page back, opening up the packet to the next page; it was some sort of cover sheet. The heading said "St. Paul Coroner, Autopsy Report of Abaddon Magogson, date of death September 1, 1899". I already knew that, nothing new there. Give me something new, I thought to myself. Handwritten on the cover sheet, after the typed heading, was the following information which looked like it had been added after the initial report was done:

"Age of person: Mid to late forties actual age uncertain, tried to verify with next of kin. No verification made.

Cause of Death: Single gunshot wound to the chest from a Smith and Wesson SW Model 10 38 special. Entered the abdominal cavity below the third rib. Bullet found lodged in lower section of lung. Slug verified as coming from a Smith and Wesson revolver."

Additional physical notes: Cuts on right hand from long curved knife, believed to be hunting knife. Broken arm, leg and ribs, all fully healed and unrelated to cause of death. Numerous healed over welts on back probably due to repeated whippings. Welts probably caused by buggy whip or other device. Whip marks healed over and unrelated to cause of death. Subject had five missing teeth and appeared to be malnourished with presence of lice and lice eggs on body as well as tapeworm in digestive system. Content of stomach included nuts, grass, and bread. It appeared that subject hadn't taken bath recently. Scrapings from nails only revealed dirt matter. Hands and feet were calloused. Body checked for other distinguishing features. None found except for missing middle finger on right hand past the first knuckle."

It ended at that. I couldn't read the signature at the bottom, but it must have been the signature of the coroner. Well, they knew the exact type and model of handgun. Without the gun how would they have known? They must have found the murder weapon. Who would have used a handgun back then? Farmers, might, but normally they would only own a shotgun or a rifle. I filed that thought in the back of my mind.

I turned the page. The next page had a full sketch of a human body front and back, just the outline. Notes were written on the sketches in various spots. One note I could make out was entry wound. It was right below the left upper chest. On the sketch from the back of the body I could make out a number of lines drawn in with the words raised welts, healed. It was hard to make out anything else on that page. I flipped to the next page. It was a handwritten listing of the contents found with the body:

> *Objects on or in possession of subject:*
> *1. Blue cloth shirt, grass stains and pieces of hay present along with clay like   material.*
> *2. One pair of overalls size 36 with various patches.*
> *3. One pair of worn brown leather shoes size 11.*
> *4. One thigh length blue wool coat.*
> *5. Ten cents in loose change.*
> *6. Other contents:*
> > *Handwritten letter in front right coat pocket, crumpled, that read:*
> *"I know what you did. You can't get away with it. You need to tell what happened or face me.*
> > *Abaddon"*

It didn't say who the letter was addressed to. I thought, they wouldn't have missed a fact like that. And if he had given it to someone, how did he get it back?

Next of kin was listed as Cousin Mary Lafond. Well, both the autopsy and death certificate were consistent with listing the next of kin. I had some more leads, but also a whole bunch of more questions. I thought there would be more information in the autopsy report, but it really appeared to be done as a formality. No detail. I wondered why that was the case. However, it was money well spent. The next question was, where did I look now?

Chapter 27

My Meeting with Eloise Lafond

I guess when you wish for something enough, it does come true. In a way all my talk about being a reporter from another part of the state was a perfect set up for me to go out state, out of the city that is. From my first few steps investigating this mess, I had wanted to see if there were relatives of the Magogsons somewhere, anywhere. I had done some checking. I checked through local white and yellow pages. The Magogson name no longer appeared anywhere locally. So I broadened my search a little. The internet has its positives and negatives: the positives are you can find anyone on the internet. The negatives are you can find anyone on the internet. This time around though, the internet didn't yield up the relative so easily. My initial internet research didn't pull up any relatives with the last name of Magogson. It wasn't until I reviewed the death certificates and autopsy reports that I had a name to connect to the Magogsons. I did some checking under the name Lafond. Of course the specific relative mentioned in the death certificate had long since passed away. I focused on the last name. I did some checking and found a pocket of Lafonds in Mankato. Eventually, I found out that Abaddon's cousin had a daughter who was still alive. And so I decided to take the road trip to Mankato to visit the youngest daughter of the distant cousin, Eloise Lafond.

The drive down to Mankato was one of those two hour intervals where when you finally arrive, you have no idea what you were thinking about the whole time and you don't remember taking in much of the scenery either. I finally arrived. The house sat on the edge of town. It looked like an original farm house that the city had slowly swallowed up. Rather than open fields, houses now surrounded it on either side. But there it sat, much older and worn than its neighbors. I hoped I had the right house. There was no address on the house, but a metal mailbox sat out at the edge of the drive with the name "Lafond " in black letters on it. I turned the car into the driveway and felt the tires slide on the compacted gravel. I brought the car to a stop. As soon as I stopped, around the corner came two dogs, running at full tilt. They stopped and began to bark at my side of the car. Leaping up as if to see who was in the car or to warn me that if I decided to get out, they'd tear my head off. Then I heard a voice.

"Come here. Now!"

Sitting in my car, I turned and there on the front porch was a heavyset lady with thick ankles that hung over the edges of her shoes. She had on a thigh length dress and a short coat that came down to her waist and the color clashed with her dress. It looked like the coat wasn't able to button up around her anymore.

"You two come," she said again more sternly.

It was then that I realized that her words weren't directed at me. They ran back up to her on the porch. I hesitated and then opened the car door slowly, making sure not to lock it so that I would have a quick escape if they decided to charge me as I walked towards the porch.

"Saw you pull up," she said. "Don't mind those two, all bark no bite; with the teeth they've got left they'd only be able to gum you to death."

I walked up slowly towards the porch, trying not to make any sudden movements. I kept thinking to myself; don't be afraid, they can always smell fear. Also, I nervously waited, thinking that at any moment she'd give the command "Sic 'em" and I'd be done for. I couldn't get it out of mind and it made me all the more nervous. I could feel the perspiration building up on my neck and under my arm pits I hoped the dogs couldn't smell my fear. Finally, I reached the porch.

"You're not what I expected, based on your voice on the phone. Thought you'd be bigger and a little younger. Come on in anyway," she said. With that she opened the door. I didn't know if she was beckoning me or the dogs. Then she turned to the dogs and said, "Stay." She opened the door just wide enough for me to enter with her. I almost felt like one of her dogs. She walked us through to the kitchen in back. There were three chairs with rounded backs braced by metal frames with worn and ripped vinyl seat covers. The oblong table was some sort of Formica with burn marks here and there. A dirty plastic ashtray sat on one side of the table. I could see the grey black floor, with a random pattern of odd shapes. I couldn't tell if some of the color patterns were dirt or dried food.

"I don't have much to offer you, in the line of drinks that is. Would you like tea, beer or I think I have a can of pop. Take your pick," she said looking at me with a thin smile that revealed a missing lower tooth.

"I'll take a can of pop," I said remembering my last adventure with tea.

"You betcha," she said opening the refrigerator. "Let me see where is that pop. I hope you don't mind if I have a beer. I don't get much company. This gives me an excuse to have a drink."

She came back with two cans and set them both down on the table. "Come now, don't just stand there. Sit down. I won't bite. I hope you didn't come all this way for nothing. After our discussion on the phone, I thought about it and I don't know that I can be of much help. As I said on the phone, I wasn't around when what's his name was alive. What was his name? Oh yea, Abaddon Magogson. Strange name to say the least."

"Well, maybe if I ask you a few questions that might refresh your memory. Is that OK if I start asking you a few questions?" I said popping open my can of pop while I finished my question.

"Sure. You betcha, no problem," she said, "Fire away."

"Do you recall anything at all about him? You seemed to suggest that you might know something more about him, when we talked on the phone." I was tense as I spoke. The chair I was sitting in creaked with my every movement. I was afraid it would break and so I kept my body stiff and in one place under my weight.

"Not really. To be honest I really just like having some company from time to time. I had a captive audience on the phone, you, so why wouldn't I work to get you here to visit me. Remember you called me."

"So you really don't have any information for me?" I asked a little annoyed, realizing that this whole trip might have been a waste of time

She took a sip out of her beer and shuffled over to the stove, pulled a cigarette out of a half opened pack, lit a burner and stuck the cigarette in the burner. It flared up. She quickly withdrew it shoved it in her mouth and drew a long puff.

"I don't care whether you like the smoke or not. It's my house and it's one of my few vices; and no, that's not what I said. I mean I do have some information. I just don't think you'll find it all that important for you to drive down for. That's just my opinion," she added as she shuffled back to the table. I could see the cloud of smoke and dust hanging in the kitchen air, thick in the ray of sunshine that entered the rear window and landed in the middle of the kitchen floor.

"Well, what do you recall? If you want I can keep this short," I asked, now realizing I may just need to be blunt to get to the point.

"You know, that is quite a long time ago, right before the turn of the century, if I recall. I wasn't even alive back then. I might look old, but I'm not that old. No, I was born right after the Great War, World War I that is. Evidently, it was as great as everyone thought so they had to have another one twenty years later," she said smiling at her own humor.

So she was born late teens, early 20's, I thought to myself. World War I didn't end until 1919. Wow, she was old. Pushing early 90's maybe. I moved into my questioning mode to keep things moving along.

"I'll cut to the chase. Your mother, Mary, was listed as the next of kin for Abaddon Magogson on his death certificate and on an autopsy report. I think the death was in 1899," I said leaning forward ever so slightly in my chair.

"Did your mother ever talk about him?" I asked.

"You betcha. I'm old but not too old to remember the stories my mother used to tell. Abaddon was her cousin. I guess we were related along his mother's side of the family. I don't know how far we're removed. I remember it because some attorney drove down one day, met with my mother at this exact table. Oh, I must of been nine or ten. He had some type of proposition. Evidently there was a question whether the Magogson farm was properly sold. Something about the deed maybe not being valid. But, he kept telling my mom that time was running out. Said they'd have to act fast if anything could be done. In the end my mom chose not to do anything. I think he was willing to waive his attorney fees until an award was made, but he still wanted money up front to file some legal papers to contest the deed. I think my mom just didn't trust him in the end. So she decided not to do anything about it. She always would mention that attorney, and say 'Don't think you'll ever go off to the city and find some rich lawyer you can live off. That just doesn't happen. It's more likely that they come to you looking to get something out of you and then leave you poorer than when they came.' Then she'd continue into the story I just told you."

"Do you know if your mom actually knew Abaddon?"

"You betcha, she mentioned him a few times. Nothing good to say about him and that whole family. Always said it was a blessing that that side of the family died out. Nothing but a sad lot them she'd always say. Never could put my finger on it. She did mention the death of his two younger brothers, the twins. But she actually only spoke about that when she was much older, near her death bed. And I was never sure if what she was talking about really made any sense."

"What do you mean?"

"By then, she was up in her years. She suffered from some dementia by then. You know they call it Alzheimer's now," she took a breath, took a sip of her beer and took a puff off her cigarette and then continued, "Where was I, oh yes, anyways, she always spoke as if Abaddon had something to do with their deaths. I think it was something he had told her maybe. Not really certain whether he did, but she said he was someone who she should have stayed away from at all costs. She regretted the day she ever met him. Said he was the devil she did, on more than one occasion."

"She called him the devil? When was it that she met him?" I asked getting ahead of myself question wise.

"She was invited up to the farm for the wedding, if you wanted to call it that. Some celebration. He married an Indian woman. The written invitation made it seem like it was going to be some big event. All it turned out to be was a small gathering with a justice of the peace, a few townsfolk and the bride and groom. You know, my mom went up there naive and all, wanting to meet her distant relatives. She said it was a mistake. Talked about it for weeks before, evidently wanting to go to a real wedding. That's what she said to me. Talked her dad into taking her up there. Well evidently, like I said, it was just a small gathering. Her dad and her stayed overnight on the farm. Well, she didn't tell me 'til years later, but evidently Abbadon cornered her in one of the rooms while the rest of the wedding group was outside preparing for the wedding. Basically he told her that he thought she was very pretty and would have made a better bride for him than the one he was marrying. But he was obliged to marry that woman because of his duty to her, seeing as he was the one that had a hand in the death of her family. He was responsible."

"Those were his exact words?" I asked.

"I don't know if those were his exact words. Like I said, she told me this many years later and I'm trying to recall it now," she said.

"How was he responsible?" I asked.

"You know, she never said. I don't know if he ever told her. But she did say if there was anyone that wasn't going to heaven, it was him. That he was bad and couldn't help it. She felt sorry for his bride to be. She never went back to that farm. Never really talked about him until she was near her death. She did say she should have done more. But that it was too late. It didn't matter anymore. Then she'd always close that story with a warning when she was older."

"What was the warning?" I asked.

"It wasn't so much a warning as a lesson about life I think. But it didn't make total sense. Let me see she'd say 'Spare the rod, but don't spoil the child. Use the rod and see the devil. I saw the devil one day and I never wanted to see it again.'"

"Is that what she actually said? What was she referring to, do you think?"

"I don't know, but she'd always used that phrase after talking about Abaddon."

"Was she serious?"

"I don't know. Like I said, she was pretty old at that point, but everything else she told me made sense. And I do know she never believed in physically punishing any of us kids. And, she always said that there are some families that are better gone and forgotten and that the Magogsons were a prime example. I don't know if those two facts tie together in any way."

"Anything else that you can think of?"

"No not really," she said puffing on her cigarette.

"Well, didn't she ever talk about Abaddon's death?"

"Yes. Yes she did. That was one story she told many times."

"Well what exactly happened?" I asked.

"Do you want a sandwich? I'm getting hungry. Let me make us both a sandwich before I continue. I've got some fresh egg salad. No one makes a better egg salad sandwich." she said taking another puff off her cigarette. "I don't just put eggs in there, no, lots of other special ingredients besides the mayo, celery, and pickles. I can't give away my recipe, but I know you'll like it. You betcha. Join me for a sandwich and I'll tell you all about the death of Abaddon."

I had fallen for the trap. I couldn't back out now. I was on her turf, in her kitchen. I really wasn't hungry; especially not for homemade egg salad with a touch of cigarette ash and who knows what else was in it. But I had no choice.

"Sure that sounds good. Egg salad sounds great. Is it your mother's recipe?"

"No, she wasn't that great of a cook. Thought she was, but in reality she could just get by. No I came across this recipe; oh I'm not really sure where, it is good though." She stood up and walked over to the counter. I was hoping I wouldn't regret this in a half hour or so.

Chapter 28
Abaddon Kills Rademacher

"What did you think of the sandwich," she asked looking at my plate as I finished off the last few chips.

"Not bad, huh," she said.

I thought the same thing to myself.

"Well, if I'm not mistaken, you promised me a story," I said.

"Let me grab another beer. I'd offer you another pop but you already drank my last one. Are you sure you don't want a beer?"

"No. I'm fine," I said.

She grabbed another beer from the refrigerator and then started in, "After my mother came back from the Magogson farm, she received a letter some time later from Abaddon. By then, his bride had already passed away. Basically, he lamented her passing and asked whether my mom would be interested in being his bride. He made it very clear that she would live with him on the farm and that now things could be as they were always destined to be. It was just too weird for my mother to comprehend that he actually wanted to marry her. Here, his wife had just died. Suicide from what I understand; and he sends her a letter wanting to marry her. Regardless of the fact that she was a second cousin, it was all pretty creepy."

"Did she respond to the letter?"

"You betcha, she tried to respond in a very matter of fact way. I asked her that too. She really tried to word it in a manner that it was way too early for him to think about marrying someone else given that his wife had just passed away. Then she added that she was already in a relationship with a local boy. She left it at that. I know at the time she wasn't dating anyone but for her it was a way to let him down easy, but also keep him from pressing on."

"And was that the end of it?"

"No, he contacted her by letter some time later," she said. "He asked if her situation had changed. He also said he just wanted to clarify that he was never in love with his first wife who had passed away. Instead, he had married her out of remorse, remorse that he was responsible for the deaths of her family. It was a rambling letter about how her family had been killed by local farmers who thought they were responsible for the deaths of his younger brothers. He then went on to say that he took full responsibility for the deaths of his brothers and that she or her family had no hand in it. He said he was responsible and didn't take that responsibility lightly. He wouldn't let it get in the way of their love, however and that true love could overcome any past obstacles, which he had created. He asked her not to think any less of him."

"What did he mean by that?"

"I don't know. He died shortly thereafter."

"Do you still have that letter?"

"No. The letter if it ever existed, remember this was what my mother told me when she was much older, was long gone. No, I never saw the letter," she said.

"How, did you hear about his death?"

"From my mother, of course. I'm not sure how she heard of his death. But the story she told me about his death was that it happened at the farm. The local sheriff evidently accompanied a developer who was finalizing some kind of foreclosure process to remove people from the farm, so he could go forward with a land development. There was some dispute about whether Abaddon had any legal right to remain on the farm. Evidently his parents had deeded away the farm before they died and they never told him. He must have been pretty worked up because he stabbed the developer and was then shot and killed by the sheriff," she said.

"Where were his parents when this happened?"

"All I can tell you is what my mother said about his death. It was always cloudy about why the sheriff was out there to begin with. I don't know if my mother actually knew all the details. Anyway, the developer was concerned about moving forward with the development of the land. He wanted to talk to old man Magogson.

"Was the developer a man by the name of Rademacher?" I asked breaking into her story.

"Yes, yes I believe so. The rest of the story was that he'd been unable to get a hold of Magogson. Abaddon had been threatening Rademacher, yes that was his name. Word had got out that Abaddon was now claiming he owned the farm because his parents had left it to him, that the land was his and his alone. You know, everyone in the area knew that Abaddon just wasn't right in the head. Now I remember, the county sheriff, even contacted my mom asking if she had been in contact with old man Magogson. Evidently, no one had seen the Magogsons in quite some time. Wasn't unusual, as it was my understanding that they kept to themselves pretty much. No sirree, my mom hadn't heard or seen them since the wedding. She told the sheriff as much.

It seems that Rademacher told the sheriff he had a deed to the Magogson farm but that there were certain rights that Marcellus and Eleanor Magogson still retained. He wanted to clear it up with them. So he told the sheriff that he was concerned about the way Abaddon was acting and wanted to have the sheriff accompany him out to the farm. To make sure there wouldn't be any problems. Evidently the sheriff was concerned enough about Marcellus and Eleanor that he agreed to accompany Rademacher out to the farm.

So those two head out to the farm together and who do they run into at the farm house but, Abaddon. He gets in a heated conversation with the sheriff and Rademacher about the farm. He says he doesn't know where his parents are, that he hasn't seen them in quite some time. He says they left and left the farm to him. Says that he is the owner of the farm and that any decisions about the farm need to be made by him. Then things evidently went from bad to worse. Abaddon pulls out a knife and kills Rademacher right there in the farmhouse kitchen. Then he tries to lunge at the sheriff. Yes sirree, it was lucky for the sheriff, he saw it coming. He pulled out his service revolver and shot Abaddon dead."

"That's the story? What about Marcellus and Eleanor?"

"I don't know. We assumed they died and were buried on the farm. We decided to stay out of it all together. Well, not me, it was really my mom. I was never involved in the whole mess to begin with."

"So you never did find out what happened to the husband and wife?"

"No, never did. My mom never wanted to get any more involved in that mess than she already was. My mom would just say from time to time when anyone in our family would bring it up 'You don't want to mess with the devil, Abaddon's the devil. It's best to leave well enough alone.' No, that's all I could ever get out of her.

And that was the last we heard of him until that attorney from the city came snooping around. I already told you about him."

"And that was it? There's nothing else?"

"Oh wait a minute, no, that's right. I knew that extra beer would help loosen up some of those cobwebs. Sometime after that, a person who claimed he was the owner of the house built on the Magogson farm wanted some information on the Magogsons. He called on the phone late one night. I remember the call because that was right after we first had a phone put in."

"What did you and he talk about?"

"Can't really remember. I really didn't have any additional info for him and I wasn't interested in going into all our family business."

"What was his name?"

"Let me see. That was quite some time ago I think it was Mic something, oh yes McMasters, same last name as the owner of the local grocery store here. Yes, McMasters. Couldn't tell you his first name though."

"What was he looking for?"

He asked some strange questions. Said he had built a new house on the old Magogson farm. He rambled on about using wood from the old oak tree that sat behind the Magogson farm house. He wondered if I had heard of any strange things happening on the Magogson farm from my mother. Like I said, I didn't want to air our family's dirty laundry so I just didn't really tell him anything. Mind if I have another beer and a smoke. My throat's parched from all this talking and a smoke will help me think better."

She walked over to the stove again and lit up a cigarette and then opened the fridge with cigarette in hand. An ash flicked and fell to the floor. She didn't seem to mind or notice. She came back with the beer and cigarette and sat down.

"Now where was I? You haven't even touched you pop."

"Oh," I said looking down and realizing it still sat full on the table in front of me. I quickly took a swig to make her feel better. It was still cold and felt good going down.

"You were talking about McMasters."

"Yea, yea, that's right. Yes sirree, of course I had to ask him why he would ask me something like that. You know what he said?"

"No, what?"

"He said, 'I'm not a real religious man and I don't believe in spirits but something is very odd about our house. I don't even want to say it, but I think it's haunted. I just wanted to understand a little background. I'd like to know more about the history of where our house was built.'"

"Did you give him any more information?"

"It would actually have been information that my mother had given to me. I didn't have any first hand information. But, maybe I should have told him what my mom had been telling me, looking back, but I didn't seem comfortable talking about it. Plus, the more you talk about those types of things the more they can come back to haunt you. Why, do you believe in evil spirits, things that go bump in the night? Not me I'm too old and ready to meet my maker to be scared by anything like that. But you, you're still young you've got your whole life ahead of you maybe you ought to be more careful.

Sometimes questions you ask shouldn't be asked and if you don't know what the answer is going to be well, that's an even better reason not to ask the question. No, with the stories my mother told, I got enough of a sense of the history of that place and I had no desire to go there or to ask any questions about it or for that matter answer questions about it. In fact, I think I've said way too much as it is. You can finish your pop and then you should go."

"Can I ask you one more question?"

"Depends, what is it?"

"Well, do you think there was something to McMasters question about the house being haunted?"

"I think I've already answered that question. I wouldn't even begin to know what to say more about that. All I know is that Abaddon Magogson had a strange hold on my mother even up until her death. A few weeks after she died, I was going through some of her things. In the back of her dresser drawer, long forgotten was a picture. Actually half of a picture. It was torn down the middle. It was of a man standing in what looked like his Sunday best. Poor haircut pasted back to one side; pants that didn't quite reach the top of his boots and a funny bow tie skewed to one side. He wasn't smiling; it was more of a frown on his face. You could tell that his hand was holding a lady's hand but the other half of the picture with the lady was nowhere to be found. That wasn't the odd thing about it though."

"What was the odd thing?"

"There were actually two odd things. One was on the back it read, handwritten, June 18, 18__, and forever yours, Abaddon. Yes sirree, June 18th was the wedding anniversary day when he married his Indian wife. My mother used to mention that date to me. Why would my mother have that picture? Secondly, when you looked at the picture of Abaddon you could see half of the large oak tree in the background. Funny thing was there were no leaves on the tree. What tree doesn't have leaves on it in the middle of June unless it's dead? Just odd.

"Do you still have that picture?"

"Can't say that I do, probably threw it out way back then," she said. And with that she took a final puff off her cigarette and put it out in her ashtray.

"Is there anything else you can add? Anyone who you might think of that would be worth talking to that might have some additional information?" I asked, not sure how to tie up my conversation with her.

"No, not really, just make sure to send me a copy of your article when you get it done; and make sure to spell my name correctly," she said smiling, revealing the missing tooth again.

"Oh, there is one suggestion, maybe the prior owner McMasters. But I don't know if he's even alive; that was many years ago that he called."

"Well, thank you for your time." I almost said I can show myself out, when I realized I didn't know where the dogs were lurking outside.

"Do you want to get me out to my car past your guard dogs?"

"Those puppies? Sure. And if you're ever back down this way, feel free to drop in."

Chapter 29
Discussion with Eloise Lafond Gives Me Some Ideas

I thought my drive back would be relaxing, but instead it had the opposite effect. Yes, I had a few more answers, but now additional questions kept churning in my head. Sure, Abaddon seemed fairly odd. Alright, he was downright creepy. But what would he have to do with a haunted house built after his death. And what about the odd picture sent to her mother? I wished I could have seen it. Without actually seeing it, I couldn't really be certain that what she was saying was true. Call me a doubting Thomas, but I wasn't sure how much of her entire story was true.

It was true; however that time really did have a way of eliminating mysteries. No, not really eliminating them. History had a way of changing the facts so it was more difficult to solve them. Yes, I was no longer dealing with facts that could be verified by first hand witnesses or tangible exhibits I could hold and examine in my hands. I was dealing with opinions, opinions and memories that may or may not bring me closer to the truth. It was my job to interpret, to sift through and find what was important and solve the mystery. But really what was the mystery I was really trying to solve? It started out with just getting background on an unusual house. Then that took on a life of its own. More of an entangled web of people, places and things all involved with one piece of land. It seemed like it was a black hole that sucked in all those that came in contact with it. So far everyone who had been involved with the land had met with a sad fate or was at least corrupted by the interaction with the land. But was it really the land? Maybe people just had a way of corrupting themselves, of seeking out evil if given the chance on their own. No, that couldn't be right.

People don't want to find evil, they want to live good lives, lives filled with hope and promise. It is the difficulties, the trials that one faces throughout life that make them take the paths they do, make the decisions, decisions made out of the necessity to survive. No, it is survival, I thought, that ultimately makes people who they are in the end.

Maybe, what I was seeing was nothing more than man's desire to survive at all costs, to thrive and rise above adversity. That couldn't explain all the hardship and death I had uncovered, no that was tied to something else, maybe greed maybe just inherent evil.

Maybe Eloise was right. I wondered where I could locate a McMasters' relative. I knew that name from my earlier searches at the land records office. At least I knew the name of the person on the deed to the house. I suppose that person was probably the owner of the house as well. But what was the tie between the ultimate owner of the house and the developer? Were they one in the same? That was my next step. I'd have to investigate the McMasters connection.

With my decision regarding my next step solved, my mind drifted off onto other thoughts.

All of a sudden, sadness overtook me. I realized I had lost my connection with my friend at the historical society. In the process of everything that had been going on, I don't think I had let it hit me earlier. I made a mental note I would have to show up at her funeral, it was the right thing to do. Maybe going to her funeral wouldn't be the wise thing to do. Let her family and friends grieve in peace. Yes, I decided I had worn out my welcome there. Plus, I had probably gathered up whatever information they had. There was nothing more to be gained by going back. For a moment, I was getting tired of the woven lies I put together and had to keep reweaving at any moment.

My made-up persona was getting stale, I thought, as I continued to drive. For each person I needed to talk to, I wove a different story of who I was and what I was all about. Sure small bits and pieces of what I said were true. But, for the most part it was all lies. I knew the replacement lady at the historical society would begin to wonder why my one simple article in the New Ulm paper was taking on a life of its own. Now Eloise would be waiting on an article as well. Was it all worth it? Was my ultimate goal all worth it?

I thought for a moment more. Sure I thought to myself, I was adding a little excitement to their dreary lives and to my life as well. It was definitely worth it.

My mind drifted off to other facets of my research. The autopsy report now made more sense. There really wasn't a trial then for Rademacher's murder. The only suspect for Rademacher's murder, Abaddon, was killed right there at the scene. That was why there was no trial. It was Abaddon who killed Rademacher at the farm after Rademacher came with the sheriff to evict him. In the end, Abaddon seemed pretty unbalanced. I wondered if there was any truth to what Abaddon was saying. I suppose those were times when unscrupulous people looked to take land. It seemed that Rademacher may not have been a real upstanding individual. Maybe he did do something underhanded to get a hold of the property. Anyway, I could picture the scene as it unfolded: Farmer's son stabs unscrupulous developer trespassing on his land. Son wounds sheriff and then is shot and killed by sheriff. It was probably the talk of the town. But, I needed to move forward. What would be my next step?

So I thought. Where else could I get more information? I needed another source. Maybe my recently deceased friend's acquaintance at the newspaper, Ms. Swenson could help me. But what additional information could I get from the newspaper that I hadn't already dug up? Plus, I wondered if Ms. Swenson didn't have a wealth of information on me by now. No, I'd have to think about that option for awhile.

I really needed to get additional information on the house. Darrah and Alona couldn't help. That's who I was checking up on. No, I needed to first find out about McMasters. I had to figure out if he built the house, if he was the one who called Eloise. That was the direction I now needed to go. I needed to figure out more about the house. But how? Maybe there would be city permits? If the house was constructed within the city limits then there would be a building permit on file. Maybe there would be additional information on the permit. I was back in business.

I was getting closer. Now I really just had a few loose ends to tie up, or so I thought.

Would there be a record of the building being constructed? That was my last thought as I hit the exit ramp back towards my house.

Chapter 30

My Discussion with the Son of Samuel Cartwright

I had searched high and low for a McMasters in the area. There was nothing to be found. No McMasters listed. I had hit a dead end. The only record I found on the internet under the search of the name McMasters was an old listing of the members of the Independent Order of the Odd Fellows, dated 1910, Lodge No. 2, St. Paul. But that was a listing from 1910. Somebody was doing research on the International Order of Odd Fellows and there it was, James McMasters. Other than that, nothing else showed up locally for a McMasters.

And so I decided to go at it from a different angle. It's amazing what records you can find, even after many years. It seems we as a society like to track and keep information on all types of things. Maybe it's so as a society we can somehow feel like we have accomplished something. It is under those piles of records that we stand on our accomplishments. But I can't help think that it's all just a waste the minute it is filed. In fact, whoever looks up those old records once they are filed? Well, I guess me for one.

Yes, I did check the city records, actually with a little help from the city clerk, and found a permit for the house. There it was: single family house, permit fee $1.20 according to the clerk. It cost me an extra $20, the cost of a copy, to see the rest of the information on the permit.

It looked like the permit was pulled in 1910. Interesting. Well after the death of Rademacher. I looked to see who signed for the permit. There was the name "Samuel Cartwright". There was really nothing else of value, information-wise on the permit. Samuel Cartwright, it certainly wasn't McMasters.

I thought for a minute, what if . . . it was a long shot. I looked back over my computer search for McMasters. Luckily, I had bookmarked the page on my computer. I pulled up the Odd Fellows page again. I scrolled through the list to check for another name on the list, and there it was "Samuel Cartwright". So that was how McMasters knew Cartwright. They were members in the same fraternal Odd Fellows Lodge.

That's when my curiosity got the best of me, I wondered what the Odd Fellows Lodge was all about, so I took a little research side track. I read on a little more. Evidently the Odd Fellows were a fraternal organization, based on belief in God as the father and men as fellow brothers. Members did charitable work on various projects in the community. Through the organization's teachings and ceremonies, they tried to improve upon the character of man, and make the world a better place in which to live. From what I could find it wasn't a religion, but Odd Fellowship required that no man could become an Odd Fellow unless he or she believed in a Supreme Being, the Creator and Preserver of the Universe, and was loyal to their country. The basic structure of the group was that they tried to teach friendship, love and truth. It was more of a philosophy of how to live your life. These lessons were designed to challenge the membership to elevate their own character and that of man as a whole. I wasn't too sure if the group was still in existence. Well, it seemed like a very noteworthy approach to living, but it was more than I needed to know presently; and so I moved on.

Now at least I knew McMasters and his friend Cartwright were of decent character, or at least they put on a good front. I wondered how they came to be involved with Rademacher. He really seemed to be a person of questionable character. Well, maybe they became involved with this property well after Rademacher had died. There was more than a ten year difference between Rademacher's death and the house permit. Maybe these two were involved in a totally different way. I had no way to weigh their character, other than by the fact that they were both members of the International Order of Odd Fellows. It probably really didn't mean much, other than it led me to think more highly of them both.

When I went to look, there was a whole half page of Cartwrights in the white pages. For certain types of name searches, I still used the hard copy of the white pages rather than going online. The problem with going online is that sometimes there is just too much clutter. You click on a link thinking you're going to the listing for Samuel Cartwright and you wind up at a listing for Cartwright Plumbing. There are so many sneaky people out there on the internet. I could only imagine what I would come up with if I Googled "newspaper reporter." Because I rarely used the white pages, I found myself wading through our front closet. Finally, under a pile of old bags I found a fairly current white pages for the city of St. Paul. That's the white pages where I found the half page listing of Cartwrights. Now, staring at the list I wondered who on the list would be the most likely candidates to be related to Samuel. I assumed most of these people listed were up in their years. My reasoning was that some old people now had cell phones purchased for them by their kids so their kids could stay in touch with them. But, unlike the younger generation, they still held on to their landlines as well. So, when I looked up names in the hard copy of the white pages I knew I was more likely than not calling on older people when I went down the list of names. As luck would have it, I again found the person I needed to speak with. I got a hold of Steve Cartwright. As luck wouldn't have it, it took me twenty calls to locate him. By the time I talked to Steve, I had my reporter story down to the point it was more believable than most. Too bad I wasn't making any money off it. In talking to him, I found out he was the son of Samuel Cartwright. As he stated on the phone, his dad was the lead worker for McMasters on many of the homes built in that subdivision. He said his dad had died back in '68. He didn't know what he could answer, but he was happy to sit down with me if I wanted to come over.

I expected a much older man. No, I don't mean older, I mean more worn out. Sure, he was a crusty old guy with graying hair on the top and wrinkles etched into his face, his skin was leathery from years in the sun, but he still looked to be in pretty decent shape, plus he had a full head of hair. From the looks of him, his build and the way he carried himself, I guessed he must have been in the trades. He shook my hand and all I felt was a massive scratchy pillow that swallowed up my long thin hand.

"I'm not going to mince words, never have, never will. So how can I help you? Hope I didn't get any grease on you," he said, as he all of a sudden pulled an old rag out of his back pocket and started wiping off his hands with it. "I was just out in the garage working on an old lawn mower engine. Heard the door bell ring and came right in. I'm always forgetting to clean up proper when I come in. I spend most of the day out in the garage, that's why I've rigged the door bell to ring out there. Well, like I said, what can I do you for? I'm not the real longwinded sort. Although, I do say what's on my mind. Now that you got me to come into the house, I'll take my afternoon break early. I'm going to grab a beer, need anything?"

"No. no thank you I'm fine." Feeling thirsty, but not wanting to impose more than I already had, I declined a beverage. Also, I made a mental note about my last run in with a beer. Instead, I started right into my purpose for coming.

"I'm the man that called you on the phone. I know I asked about your dad on the phone, but I really wanted to ask you about any information you might have on a particular house he may have constructed back around 1910," I said.

"So, coming into my house under false pretenses are you? he said.

I tensed up. I couldn't tell if he was serious or joking.

"Just kidding, ya know," he continued, "Here sit down. Are you sure I can't get you anything?"

"No. I'm fine," I said calming down again.

"So why do you want to know about the house?" he asked.

"Working on an article on turn of the century homes in St. Paul. I thought there might be some interesting background on this one," I stated.

"Oh. So then, to get back to your question about a house, my dad constructed a number of houses early on in his life. But he was really put out of commission much too early in life. In fact he had to drop out of the construction business altogether right around 1910."

"Why, what happened?"

"I'll just tell you what happened, he was working on a house right around that time, 1910 or so it had to be. He was constructing a house. He referred to it as "The Painted Lady". I haven't used that term in years. Not since my dad died. Referred to the house as The Painted Lady because of the multiple paint colors used on her. It was all wood and so back then people like to dress up the houses. They'd use three or four colors of paint, usually colors that would contrast nicely and sometimes not so nicely. They could actually be gaudy at times. They'd look like a woman all made up for a night on the town. Yes, sometimes those colors would be a little too much. That's why he called it The Painted Lady." He trailed off pausing to think.

I wondered, could The Painted Lady he was talking about be the same house.

"Now I'm not sayin, but she was an amazing house that one. They don't make them like that, no, don't construct homes like that anymore. That was a house. No it's all prefinished this, plastic that, cheap pressed wood byproducts. No, she was made of quality materials, mainly oak. I love those old oak floors and that hard wood trim, really adds class to a home. No, they just don't make 'em like that anymore. My dad really was proud of the work he did on that house. I'm not sayin, but my dad, he was a real craftsman. I went into the trades because of him. But, I didn't even come close. No, he was a real perfectionist. Really put his sweat and tears into what he did. Oh, sure people say they're craftsman now, but back then it was all hand tools, none of this power stuff. No, you really had to know what you were doing. Sad thing though."

"What do you mean?"

"I'm not sayin, but that was the last project he worked on due to the accident. For him I think he thought of it as his crowning achievement in life. After that he never was able to do the things he wanted to do."

"What accident?"

"Back then work sites were a lot more dangerous. Not that they aren't still dangerous today. But back then you didn't have any regulations, workers worked until they couldn't go anymore or until an accident occurred. Workers weren't limited in the number of hours they could work in a day, and overtime, there wasn't anything like that to speak of. So then, they were pushing to get that house completed. Near the end, he was working on the main chimney. It sat off to one side of the house. They had rigged up scaffolding around the chimney. Somehow a board that he was standing on broke loose. He started to slide down the roof. Almost caught himself on the ladder propped up against the gutter, but as he landed feet first on the ladder his weight shifted the ladder and it slid off. He tried to ride the falling ladder down to the ground but he jumped off at the last minute. Now I'm not sayin, but his back literally broke his fall. He landed on a small pile of bricks. He was never the same after that. Needed two canes to walk around. Even after the surgeries he wasn't the same. Surgery wasn't like it is today. Back then, they just did surgery to stabilize the injury, not fix it. Who knows, with today's modern medicine, maybe they could have done more. Strange thing though . . ."

"What?"

"Now I'm not sayin, but he always said there was someone up there with him, pulled his leg out from under him, that it wasn't his fault. Until his death, he would never talk to the guy working with him that day."

"Do you think his fellow worker had anything to do with it?"

"I can't believe he did. In fact, I talked to that worker once. I ran in to him. Actually he came up to me. I think he was trying to make things right about my dad. He said he was mixing mortar on the other side of the house and didn't even know my dad had fallen until he came around the corner with a fresh bucket of mortar mix. Maybe it was easier for my dad to just blame someone else. He didn't want to think that he could have caused his own injury.

But, interesting enough, that wasn't the only strange event with the house. No, my dad continually told stories about other things that happened during the construction of the house, in the days leading up to his injury. I always thought my dad told the truth about most things. But some of those stories he would tell about the house, I wrote them off to his imagination and having too much time on his hands or that he was trying to explain away his accident."

"Like what kinds of stories?"

"I'm not sayin, but actually, it went back, back before construction on the house even started. Back to when they started to clear out the old farmstead, back to when they started taking down the big oak that sat where The Painted Lady now sits. To my dad, it seemed like that's when all the strange things started. To him everything seemed to be interconnected. So then, let me start at the beginning when my dad first became involved with the land."

Chapter 31
McMasters Steps In

He took a sip from his beer, thought for a moment, and then he started into his story in earnest.

"My dad said the property on which The Painted Lady was eventually built, had sat dormant for many years. He never told me how many. It was originally supposed to be developed back in the late 1800's. But my dad said it probably just sat there for almost twenty years for a number of reasons. First there was the Panic of 1898. I wasn't around back then of course, but my dad used to talk about how tough it was. Heck, he was a kid at the time, how tough could it be. He used to say he'd go a day at a time without any food and how they'd have to scrounge for just enough food to get by. I'm not sayin, but he said it was pretty bad. As it turned out, it didn't compare to the Great Depression. Back then it was still fresh in everyone's mind and to them it seemed about as bad as it could get, I suppose.

Doesn't surprise me though, it seems that everything is cyclical. It seems like those depressions come and go every twenty or thirty years. Finally, the Panic subsided and new pressure arose to expand the city. More people were flowing into the city and St. Paul was looking for neighborhoods to expand into the outlying areas. It was right at that point that the original developer was killed. Murdered on the original farm that became the current subdivision. I think it happened in or right outside the farm house. I don't know about the details."

"Yes. You mean the Magogson farm. The son of the farm's owner killed the developer, Cornelius Rademacher out on the farm. I came across that information while I was doing some research. I think The Painted Lady you're talking about is the same house I've been looking for information on. Sorry, please continue with your story," I added.

"Could be, it could be that we're talking about the same house. Was that the name of the farm? I don't know. I don't know what their names were. My dad never told me. He only said that after that murder it took another twenty years before anything was done with the land. Maybe that land was a little too far out to be developed easily at the time. I don't know. Maybe the developer was just a little too far sighted and ambitious at the time. It does take time for a city to grow. Well, it was around then that my dad got involved. After that developer was murdered, one of his partner's sons came from out East to get the development back on track. I'll never forget his name, James McMasters, the second. Couldn't be a junior had to be the second. From the moment my dad talked about him, I didn't care for him. He was full of himself, my dad always said."

"How did your dad meet him?"

"If I recall correctly, my dad answered an ad in the paper looking for a construction foreman. At the time work was scarce. My dad needed the work and so he signed on with McMasters. As I've already said, my dad never liked the man. Always said he was one of those people who thought he was better than everyone else. Always interested in one upping you on any story; status meant everything to him. My dad grew to dislike him more and more the longer they worked together because he was the type of man that just took and took without giving back. My dad helped introduce him to different organizations and people in the community and he'd take advantage of the introductions, dump my dad to the side and take over those new acquaintances as if they were his own. No, he was a pretty self-centered, East coast snob. Those are my dad's original words."

"Well, how was your dad involved with the building of the house then after meeting McMasters?"

"Seems to me, he was involved from the beginning. McMasters used him to help tear down the farm house that sat there and get a hold of some locals to take down the large oak behind the farm house, and process the wood from the oak and reuse the lumber from the farmhouse for the building of The Painted Lady. He had this grand idea to use all of the wood from the oak to build his grand house, you know "The Painted Lady" and also reuse whatever wood he could scavenge from the farmhouse for The Painted Lady as well."

"I didn't think they recycled things back then, especially building materials?"

"Oh, of course they did. To save a buck, man has always tried to reuse construction materials. A lot of the wood on the farmhouse was in bad shape, but much could be reused. Some of it was used for framing The Painted Lady. If it was a little rough, it didn't matter, because it would be hidden under plaster or finished wood. No, it wasn't unusual to recycle materials, not at all."

"Had your dad done anything like that before? I mean had he worked on larger projects like that?"

"I'm not sayin, but he had worked construction his whole life. Started out at five or six collecting nails and scrap wood for a few pennies. Basically learned his skills on the job. He had a fair amount of experience but this was by far his most difficult project. I think McMasters hired him on thinking he could get top talent at a cheap price. My dad was no slouch in bullshitting at times. He was probably very capable of selling his skills to McMasters and knowing McMasters, well he probably was just looking at the savings he was getting. I'm sure my dad probably talked up his experience a little more than what was true. Anyway, he had connections to some pretty skilled workers back then and probably thought he could handle the project with their help if he needed it."

"Why, you don't think your dad should have been handling the project?"

"No. I think he was able enough. And I don't think his experience or lack of it had anything to do with the accident. If my dad set his mind to it, he could complete anything. It's just that I couldn't see him reading blueprints and constructing a house from start to finish. But who am I to say what he did and didn't know at the time. I was just interested over the years in all his construction stories."

"From the beginning you said that strange things happened at the work site. Things he couldn't explain. What did he say about those things?"

"Well, truthfully, I think that fall scrambled his brains. He always felt like the house was responsible for ruining his life."

"Well it did. That fall cost him his livelihood and left him a cripple for the rest of his life."

"No, it was more than that. He felt there was something there at the worksite, some sort of negative power contained within the house and the land that the house stood on that ruined him."

"Like an evil spirit?"

"No. Not as much of an evil spirit, as an evil power, evil itself."

"Isn't that going a little far?"

"That's what I always thought. Some of his stories were way out there."

"Like what?"

"So then, as I said before I should go back to the beginning. He and some of his buddies were hired by McMasters to demolish the old farm house. That was the first part of the construction my dad was involved with on the project.

Now I'm not sayin, but they get up there before dawn to start the work on the first day. As they approach the house, there's a light on in the kitchen. Almost looked like a candle was lit. Well, they get up to the door and go in thinking they'll have to get rid of some squatters. They go into the kitchen and its pitch black. Well, they light up an old lantern they brought along and low and behold the only footsteps in the coating of dust on the floor are their own and some bird tracks, probably those pesky crows. Except they could smell smoke as if from a fire and a strange herbal smell. He said the only other time in his life that he came across that same smell was when he went to a Native American powwow exhibit he attended through the Boy Scouts. He said the smell of their fire smelled the same."

"What did he mean by that?"

"As I recall what he said, they were doing a traditional Native American dance at the Boy Scout exhibit which included them throwing an herb mixture in the fire from time to time. He said it was that same smell that he smelled in the old farm house. Now you're talking many years in between both events, but he swore it was the same smell. He always thought that was just creepy. He swore that his two friends would back him up and tell the exact same story."

"Could it just have been the smell of the old farm house?"

"Yes, could have been. But he swore it wasn't. Probably were those crows," he said smiling at me.

"Was that it? Was that all that happened?"

"No. Not at all. Back then they didn't have heavy equipment to demo buildings. It was all about using your brawn to dismantle. And that's what those three did. They started by pulling off the wood molding and railings, anything they could salvage they did; and so they were careful not to damage the wood as they removed it so it could be reused. I'm not sayin, but it was a multi day project. Those three decided it was easier to stay out there at night rather than head back to town. The first night he said he had the strangest dream. After that he never slept inside that house nor would he step foot in it after the sun went down."

"What was the dream?"

"He told it again and again. I think he was always trying to figure it out in his mind. But he never could get a grasp on it. He said it was a group of Indians in a circle passing a peace pipe between them. Smoke was rising in a cloud that mingled between them and growing out of the cloud of smoke was a large creature. It was as if something was collectively created by all of them. What startled my father was that when he looked at the creature it grew wider as if branches of a large tree were expanding. Then two red dots grew larger focusing on him and where a mouth should be a black hole grew wider, slowly opening up as if to swallow him whole. And then all of a sudden he awoke with a start. He found himself lying in a cold sweat on the floor of the room off the kitchen. Next to him were a small pile of crow feathers."

"How many feathers were there? Were there seven?" I asked.

I don't think he ever told me that. He did always say they were crow feathers. He always swore that those feathers weren't there when he went to bed. He initially thought his two friends played a prank on him, but they always denied it."

"Well, so it was a bad dream. People have weird dreams when they're in strange places for the first time." I said thinking to myself as I spoke. I kept the image of the statue in the courthouse to myself for the moment. The images were very similar, I had to admit. I couldn't help but think that this whole story was just something he had concocted for my benefit. What if there was more to this whole story though? Parts could be true, but which parts.

"Have you ever been to the County Courthouse?" I asked.

"County courthouse? You mean Ramsey County? Why do you ask? That's an odd question to ask right now. But no, I can't say as I have. Almost got married there, though. That's a whole different story though; it'd take me a six pack to tell. Why, what does that have to do with anything I'm telling you?" he asked.

"Oh, nothing. Something just came to mind. It's nothing at all. Please continue," I finished.

"As I recall, that was just the beginning. Other strange things happened too. Remember I told you they had carefully removed as much wood as they could so that it could be reused."

"Yeah," I said, my interest continuing to grow.

"I'm not sayin, but the next day they go out to start adding wood to the pile they made the day before, except when they go out there all of the wood from the day before is splintered and broken.

Literally unusable. They didn't hear anything that night. Who or what would have done that?"

"Maybe a bear?"

"Maybe, but wouldn't they have heard the commotion?"

"You'd think so."

"As I recall, he said after that they tried to pick up the pace. None of them wanted to be out there longer than they had to. That next night they slept under their wagon. The horses seemed on edge the whole night. The next morning they go to start removing some of the exterior wood siding and trim and there in the soft ground around the house are numerous footprints, not shoe or boot footprints, but moccasin prints, and not just one set, but a number of different sets. Indians hadn't been or lived around there for years. What do you make of that? I just thought my dad was telling a tall tale. But he always said it was true, all true."

"Well, that is odd. All explainable though, I think."

"How so?"

"Maybe your dad was just telling you a tall tale. Maybe those footprints were there before he arrived and he just didn't notice them. Maybe it was kids playing a prank. Nothing strange about footprints.

"You didn't know my father. He was a straight shooter. As straight laced as they come. To the day he died I never knew him as one to exaggerate. No, I took everything he told me as the God's truth. And. well I've saved the strangest for last."

"What do you mean?"

"Now I'm not sayin, but finally they started to dismantle the walls of the old house. He said they were thick plaster and hard to break up. Back then they'd add horse hair to the plaster to stop it from cracking. He said it was slow going. They had to crack open the plaster and then pull back the lathe underneath to slowly strip back the walls from the studs. Just like peeling an orange. So then, they finally get working on the bedroom off the kitchen on the first floor. They're moving along the wall and all of a sudden they hit the edge of a sheet buried in the wall, actually plastered over. They slowly unearth the edges of the sheet which is tacked to the studs.

When they pull back the side of the sheet, the sheet and center part of the wall falls forward and there standing upright in the wall cavity were the dry mummified bodies of a man and a woman. It was hard to tell how long they had been in the wall. And that wasn't all. Written in blood on the sheet were the words "Spare the rod and spoil the child". Also, lying in there with the two bodies, wrapped in a cloth at their feet was an old hand axe."

I just about fell out of my chair. "He told you that story?" I said in disbelief.

"No, I'm not just sayin, it was no story, it was true, he said."

"So you're telling me after all that, he still continues working on the project, working out there?"

"He said, 'yes'. He did say he called out McMasters to the property right away, though. They all got the authorities involved. It was the authorities that determined that it was the owners of the farm who were buried in the wall. Evidently the axe had blood on it, but it couldn't be definitely tied to the two victims in the wall. After that investigation was all over, I think my dad figured the worst was behind him. He thought the strange occurrences were all tied to the death of the two old owners of the farm. With the recovery of the bodies, he figured everything would be fine going forward. Plus he really needed the money. So once the house was torn down he figured any evil spirits were eliminated. The husband and wife were then properly buried and everything was right with the world. My dad wasn't all that religious and for the most part wasn't superstitious. So in his mind it was just another thing that had been corrected.

I think as he got older though, all these pieces, these occurrences, slowly ate away at him and made him think he was done in by The Painted Lady, it was just that he didn't put all the pieces together until it was too late for him, at least that's what he thought. He probably thought he didn't heed the warnings, and because of that he was crippled for the rest of his life. I don't know. I wasn't there. I just got to hear his stories over and over. I think he believed them more and more the older he got and the more he told them."

"Did he always tell the same versions of the stories?"

"Now I'm not sayin, but from what I remember, yes. But I've heard them so many times I couldn't tell you whether there was an original version which changed over time."

"Well, did he tell you more about what happened with the construction of The Painted Lady?"

"So then, as I keep saying I need to start at the beginning, but you're right, there are other pieces to the story that I didn't tell yet. I need to tell you about some events before the construction of the house started. I need to tell you another one of his stories, the taking down of the big oak. That happened before the construction of The Painted Lady."

Chapter 32

Bringing Down the Big Oak

And so he continued on with his story describing how the big oak was finally brought down.

"Now I'm not sayin, but I'll tell you how my dad used to tell me what happened. I'm going to tell you in his own words.

My dad was actually the one who found the men to handle taking down the big oak tree. As I mentioned he had a lot of connections with people in the area. The men he found were retired loggers. Actually you never really become a retired logger. It's always in your blood, my dad used to say. They had worked in northern Minnesota when the big trees were still there for the taking. Back breaking work for months at a time, stuck with just your logging crew for company. They had given it up for city life, but they still looked forward to the challenge of taking down a big tree from time to time. And so it was that they took on the challenge of the big oak at the request of my dad that fall day.

They loaded the wagon for the ride down to their worksite for the day. The air was crisp and cold, like any other standard fall day in Minnesota. You know how the fog holds close to the ground in pockets that warn you of a snow fall coming soon. Each exhaled breath by the men and horses came with a visible cloud of vapor, body heat and energy was being expelled in one long slow process. The horses stood nervously, moving and shuffling in their harnesses knowing that they would be called to task shortly to carry the three men to the day's work site.

With each passing day, the days were growing shorter. It was only October, yet the chill in the air felt like winter. Motion, work, was the best way to keep the men warm. It seems that as you get older, every year as fall arrives it takes a little bit longer to adapt to the dropping temperatures. For the two older men especially, each passing year was indeed a little harder to adapt, as if they were counting down the measured breaths that they had yet to exhale.

The three, actually two men and a teenager moved about the wagon and went back and forth from a small shed carrying a wide variety of tools and equipment. It was all the tools of their trade; ropes, tackle, chains, short, one handled saws with long v shaped teeth, a long two handled saw, and a large and small can of oil with some blackened rags draped over. They moved almost in unison, quietly completing their tasks. These three were just getting warmed up. The heavy work would come soon enough. It was their job today to do the heavy work of bringing down the big tree. If that wasn't enough, they knew they'd have to get help from the day laborers to pull the cut logs out once they were cut into manageable pieces.

It was a complex process. The cutting of the tree into pieces had to be thought out in advance. Sections of the tree were going to be sawed up into useable timber, as much useable timber as possible. So the men would have to work around areas that were rotted out or large knots, to make sure they wound up with as much quality timber as they could.

Usually Clem, that was the name of the older man, he would bring along his youngest son who was wiry enough to move about the upper branches of a tree. He was the youngest of eight kids, but was now well into his teens. I think my dad knew their whole family.

Ya know he would lead the way up into the tree, climbing up to some of the taller branches in the tree with a rope tied around his waist. Once he reached a specific height up in the tree, while being directed by his dad, he would begin loosening the rope around his waist. Then he would move on to one of the closest main branches and he would toss the rope over it; tying it tightly to that large branch. Then the loose end of the rope would be lowered to the ground; and Clem would tie another rope to the end of that rope. The process would be completed three or four times until a number of ropes were tied off on branches high up in the tree. I don't know why, but my dad would always describe the process. I think he was fascinated by it.

Finally, each rope would be positioned over this branch or that, either tightened or loosened, so that they could be leveraged to direct how the branch would fall as it was cut. Next, once this was all planned out, Clem would pick out an appropriate saw, tie it onto a loose end of one of the ropes and his son would hoist it up into the tree. It was up to his son, high up in the tree to judge which branches to start trimming first. The key, my dad always said, was maintaining a balance on one of the larger branches while sawing off the uppermost branches. It was dangerous work. The person in the tree had to make sure that when the branch being sawed broke off it cleared both the person sawing and the other lower branches on the tree cleanly. It was a time-consuming process. The saws often needed to be sharpened or rubbed down with machine oil to make them saw more smoothly. Once some of the top canopy branches were removed it became more of a process of picking the next largest branches to fell the tree. At a specific point in the process, the cutting was switched to the ground where the main trunk would be sawed off and the tree would fall in one large chunk. Even then the job wasn't finished. The tree would need to be stripped of its bark and further divided into more usable sections, sections that could be placed on a heavy sled or wagon and pulled out of the field by a pair of heavy draft horses. Then they'd be taken off to a mill where the wood could be processed into usable timber. Each tree was different; there were knots, imperfections and cross running veins that might allow the wood to splinter and thus be unusable. It was up to the tree climber and the two experienced lumbermen to determine the best way to go about dismembering the large oak . . ."

My mind drifted off for a moment on what that day must have been like. I started to daydream about my own idea of what happened that day.

"Well, I guess we saved the best for last", McMasters said to Cartwright. "I hope your men know what they're doing."

"They're seasoned lumberman. You don't have anything to worry about," Cartwright added. McMasters stood next to Cartwright, with his two tree men, Clem and Michaelis and Clem's son Joshua looking up into the big oak.

"How much timber do you think we can get out of her do you think," McMasters said looking in the direction of the woodsmen.

"A big oak tree like that should yield three to four hundred board feet of wood. If everything goes well," one of them answered.

"That would be good for a number of new houses here in the new subdivision," the other lumberman added.

"No. No, I'd like to use the wood from this tree all for finishing one house, one grand house that could sit here overlooking the creek. It would be my memorial, no a monument, a way to maintain the glory and memory of me and this great oak. It would be a way to create a grand new house out of a grand old tree. The tree would finally serve a true purpose," McMasters stated in a rambling excited tone. The other four held their thoughts back. They knew from years of experience that it was best to let the boss ramble on, spew out his ideas and then at the end assess whether it was worth saying anything. "Well, what do you think, will this yield enough wood for a grand old lady?" McMasters added looking over at his workers.

"Before you say anything, just look at the size of her, what is she twenty or twenty-two feet around at the base at least. Yes sir, she's something alright. Almost sad to see her go. But that can't be helped," he continued. "Got to cut her down, gotta take down the tree. She's worth more down than alive in that location plus that canopy would take up too much area. I've decided to fit in another lot down in that area," he said pointing off further down the creek.

"With the tree down we can probably fit in another lot or two. Plus, if I divert that pesky creek, or fill it in all together, it opens up a whole lot of additional space. That's it. Maybe we just grade over the creek and then it would just go away." He finally stopped talking, not because he didn't still have things to say. He stopped because he knew he was running late for a meeting back in town with some of his investors on this project.

He turned to the workers. *"Well, what do you think how long will it take you to get this tree down and get the carcass to the wood mill?"* The taller one pulled back the hat on his head and pushed it in to his head at the same time. What was left of his hair pushed forward popping out and falling down on his forehead.

"I don't know. Probably take a couple of days, three tops. With Joshua here helping we'll get 'er done."

"Well, I'm counting on you. We need to keep this project moving forward. I don't need any more problems." He turned his back and walked over to a single horse buggy. The reins were tied loosely to a small sapling. He untied the reins pulled them back as he got in the small covered buggy. He yelled over to the men *"I'll be expecting the wood at the mill in two days."* If they heard him they didn't acknowledge it. They were already over at their wagon starting to organize the tools of their trade. They knew they had a deadline to meet.

Clem, the older of the two, was stocky with broad shoulders; Michaelis was taller and more lean and muscular. They worked well as a team, one filling in the gaps that the other missed. Michaelis was more talkative, usually rambling on about what happened over the weekend, the exciting poker game or a night out on the town. He was single and able to take in the finer things in life. At least in his mind. Clem was more reserved, sticking closer to home with his family comprised of his wife and two kids. He was especially more deliberate and watchful when his son was with them. His son was a thinner, somewhat shorter version of him with a brighter look in his eyes, not worn down by the years of labor and life's lessons Clem had experienced. At every chance, Clem would try to impart those

"Say, are you even listening to me?" The words abruptly broke my chain of thought. Startled, I realized I had wandered off in my mind, not really paying attention to what Cartwright was saying. I didn't know how much of his story I had missed, but I couldn't ask him to start over.

"Yes. Yes I'm listening," I lied, "You were telling me about them taking down the big oak."

"Yes, that's right. Well, my dad and the lumbermen were out there with one of the lumbermen's sons. That's when it happened," he said pausing.

"What happened?"

"The son was high up in the tree. He was working on loosening up one of the upper branches that had been cut, but it was tangled in some other branches. Now I'm not sayin, but the kid leans up and back to dislodge the branch, it comes loose, the rope catches him and before anyone can do anything it wraps around his neck; the branch falls with the rope attached and he's lifted up in the tree hanging by his neck. His neck snapped. He was dead instantly. Nothing anyone could do."

"That's awful," I said now fully focused back on his version of the story.

"Now, what I'm going to tell you next, I'm not sayin, but it's one of the few things my dad ever told me that I didn't believe."

"What did he tell you?" I asked.

"So then, I'll tell you just like my dad told me, but I still don't believe it. I'll tell you anyway. When the three of them were looking up in the tree for a split second they saw more than the one body hanging in the tree. He always said it looked like others up there and they were wearing Native American dress. Even my dad thought the image was caused by the shock of what had just occurred and that they were looking into the sun. He couldn't explain what he saw or if he even really saw it. To this day, I don't know why my dad would even tell me that."

"How many others did he see up in the tree?"

"I don't know if he ever gave me a number. He always said there were a few bodies, not just one. But he did say they looked old, like they had been up there for awhile. He said they all wore moccasins, tan leather leggings and then breach cloths and colored bead and feather necklaces adorning their chests. He said he could see the boniness of the legs underneath the leggings, as if they were just skeletons. And the most unbelievable part . . . ."

"What was that?" I asked.

"Now keep in mind, he really didn't tell me this part of the story until he was way on in his years; and keep in mind he said they only saw the images for a brief moment. But he said, their faces were gaunt and boney without expression, chins sitting on their chests each with two neatly braided lengths of hair hanging down on either side of their faces. Two black feathers protruded from the braids where they met the scalp. He said as they looked at the bodies from the ground, the eyes opened up revealing black sockets and then the mouths turned up into grins which opened to reveal blackness within. He knew the other two men saw it too, because they let out a scream as well. Then, he said that before they became calm enough to move, a huge flock of crows landed up in the tree above the hanging bodies and they began to caw in unison. This went on for quite some time. And then as quickly as they came the birds and the Indian bodies disappeared from the tree altogether. All that was left was the body of the boy hanging there in the tree. That's what he told me."

"That's terrible about the boy. Do you believe the rest of the story?" I asked.

"I'm not sure. I don't know why my dad would have told me it if it wasn't true. It may have been what he thought he saw. It may have been that he was just getting on in years."

Chapter 33

McMasters Meets His End

"I guess neither of us really knows what happened that day when the big oak came down," I said looking at Cartwright with an odd look on my face.

"You're right. However, what I'm telling you, that's what my father told me happened."

"I suppose that accident with the tree really held up things, then."

"Not really, sure it was tragic, but McMasters was all about moving things along as quickly as possible. My dad used to say he was a real ball buster, if you know what I mean. The next day he had my dad get another crew out there. Swore that if my dad couldn't get the job done, he'd find another foreman. So first thing in the morning my dad had another crew out there. There were always plenty of eager workers back then. It didn't matter what the risks were. No, they just wanted to get paid.

So then, the new crew brought the big oak down over the course of a few days. Then they set up a portable saw mill right at the site. It was a job back then, loading up pieces of the portable sawmill on horse drawn wagons and then taking it out to the work site and then assembling it. But it was easier than transporting all that wood into town to be cut. You just needed to make sure you had someone who knew what they were doing.

My dad used to talk about that sawmill separately. Whenever we were out in the shop in the garage, he would bring it up. My dad said it took awhile but they finally got the sawmill set up at the site, I think he called it a Frick sawmill. They had an experienced operator. Now I'm not sayin, but he said from day one it was difficult if not impossible to cut that wood. That sawmill is used to cutting pine and lighter woods. It took extra time and new saw blades to get that oak cut. In the process, they figured that the oak tree was nearly a thousand years old. They did that by counting the growth rings in the trunk of the tree. Can you imagine that?"

"Man, that is old. That's for sure," I said. I couldn't gauge whether he was intentionally laying it on a bit thick just to make the stories more interesting to me, his audience. I was having a hard time sizing up whether he was sticking purely to his father's words or ad-libbing here and there with his own version of things. I'd just have to listen to him a little more closely to see if I could tell what his version was and what his dad's story was. Everyone has a little tell, a twitch or a giveaway. Some people look down when they're making something up; some use catch phrases; others raise an eyebrow; and still others fidget with their hands. I would look to see if my friend here did any of those things as he continued to speak. "Go ahead, what else did he tell you about The Painted Lady?" I said trying to get him to continue.

"Now, according to my dad, McMasters had a lot on his mind financing this project. My dad could tell because McMasters was always on edge, pushing my dad and the other workers as hard as possible, everyday. There was a lot riding on his ability to complete this project successfully. That meant completing it all fairly quickly. My dad didn't care for McMasters, but he also said he tried to keep in mind that McMasters was really only an inexperienced kid, trying to do good by a dad who was back East.

At the time my dad was constructing The Painted Lady, St. Paul was expanding rapidly; new immigrants were continually arriving via train or steam boat, Europeans were moving from the slums of the big cities back East looking for a better life. Originally St. Paul was settled by French, German, Irish, and Swedish immigrants, but by the early 1900's there were more Czechs, Slovaks, Italians, and Poles, immigrating to the area. As with any migration of new people, the established groups were always leery of the new immigrant groups which took over the less desirable areas of the city like Swede Hollow and the Lower Levee area along the river. But at least the current city inhabitants knew why these groups came, for jobs and for a way to improve their lot in life. It was different with the elitists, the wealthy from back East, they usually came to take the wealth from the land or from the community, wring it out as best they could and then take it back with them to the more "civilized" areas of the country. They came in waves, timber barons, iron ore men, railroad tycoons and then land barons, all looking to get rich not necessarily off their own hard work but off the hard work of others because they had some seed money and what they thought was a smarter plan to succeed. Most didn't realize that it did indeed take hard work. No, the locals despised these get rich schemers. It was no different with McMasters. To my dad he was a necessary evil. He paid my dad's bills and provided him with steady work. Beyond that he could care less for the man; I can assure you of that. I hope that sets things straight."

"So McMasters never really fit in here then?" I added

"Oh, he tried, tried to get involved in local groups, meet the well known people in town. But he was one of those people who tried too hard. You could see right through his cheap suit, wasn't interested in getting to know you, just interested in getting to know enough about you to use it to his advantage, you know the type?"

I just nodded and allowed him to continue.

"Now then, by the time construction began on The Painted Lady, the investors had been waiting years in order to see any type of return on their investment. Some were in the process of writing off the whole project. A number of recessions had swept across the country. It seemed back then that people lost everything just as quickly as they made it. Maybe my dad was biased, but he always said you'll never go hungry putting in a solid day's work for a solid day's pay. I think my dad understood the landowners he worked for, the developers if you will, and the risks and rewards they faced.

Based on that, he chose to reduce his risk and take a steady reward that was a little less but a lot more consistent. In the end, was it the right choice? Probably not. I don't know. He wound up a cripple for most of his life. I don't know what he'd tell you today if he was still alive."

"Did McMasters finally finish the project?" I was hoping to get more facts or at least get information I could try to decipher as fact or fiction.

"Now I'm not sayin, but like I said, it wasn't easy. Things never moved smoothly on the building of The Painted Lady as my dad liked to call her. Back then construction was slow and tedious. No power tools, no big machines. It was all about these." He held up his two large hands in front of him and slowly rotated them back and forth. "These were what you used to get the job done. My dad always said there were too many layers of problems for the building of the house to turn out well. From the start things went wrong. I was never sure what was truth and what wasn't. I think it was a way for my dad to justify that what happened to him was just part of bigger problem with the whole project and that he just got caught up in the whole mess. To begin with, money shortages were a constant concern.

My dad used to always tell me how almost daily, they'd hear the far off clanking of a motor that would grow louder and louder. It gave them fair warning, to get back to work if they were on a break, or to tidy up the work site if it was especially messy. It was always the same car: a four door model T. It was red, stood out like a sore thumb. You could see it coming over the rise, slowly chugging along. Most of the time there were three people. A driver and McMasters who sat in the front seat and a man dressed in black with a long grey overcoat with fur wrapped around his neck where the collar should be. The fur collar looked like a sleeping raccoon." I gave him a funny look.

"That's what my dad said. To my dad it looked like a sleeping raccoon ready to awaken and pounce on anyone if the man didn't get the answers he wanted. That man would get out of the car as long as it wasn't muddy and walk around the work site here or there, use his cane to tap on any newly constructed wood window frames, brick chimney works or wood siding. Then he'd always ask my dad how things were coming and how much longer it would take to complete the next phase. McMasters would always be a step behind him trying to catch up and always trying to throw in his two cents about how things were progressing. The man in black never really wanted to listen to him though. He really wanted to get the details from his own inspection of the site and talking to my dad and the other workers. They usually didn't stay long.

My dad always made a point to tell me about the last time the man came out the work site. As usual, he heard the car in the distance, and then saw it was that red touring car that beckoned to be noticed."

"I thought model T's were black?" I interrupted, trying to catch him in a white lie and challenge his improvisation of the truth throughout his story. But, without hesitation he continued on talking.

"Now then that's a good point, it was true at one time. But back in 1908 you could get a model T in a few colors. Black wasn't one of them. Red was. It wasn't 'til Ford realized that it was cheaper, more cost effective beginning around 1914 when Ford set up his new policy 'Any color as long as it's black.' No, that 1908 Model T was red and back then in St Paul, very few people had cars. No, whoever that man was, he was important."

"Well what about that last visit?" I asked deciding not to interrupt again.

"Now I'm not sayin, but like I said the car drew nearer. This time though my dad noticed there were only two figures in the car, the driver and the well dressed man in the back seat. My dad stopped waiting for the car to arrive. It pulled up in front of him. This time the man just sat in the backseat leaning his gloved hands on his cane. 'Cartwright' he called. That's how he addressed my dad, not Mr. or anything like that. We've had to make a change. It just wasn't working out. We need to move along the completion of the house. I'll be the one paying you from now on. Same rate as before. If you can complete this project by the end of the month you'll get a ten percent bonus. Is that doable? My dad wasn't sure. But he figured he had no choice. What should I say to McMasters when he comes around? What should I say to him? My dad asked."

"Well, what did the man say?" I added not being able to keep my silence.

"He said, 'I don't think you'll be seeing much of McMasters anymore, but let me know if he does show up. So do we have a deal?'"

"That was it? Did your dad see McMasters again?"

"I asked my dad and he said he never did see him again. But he did say rumor had it that his body was found a few days later, floating in the river down by the lower levee hung up on tree branches and other debris."

"Was he murdered?" I asked.

"I don't know. I don't think my dad knew either. At the time my dad was more concerned about keeping some money coming into his pocket. Questions might have stopped that income stream all together, if you know what I mean."

"Well, who was the man in the suit?"

"I don't know. My dad never said. All he said was that some things are best not known. From what I could gather, McMasters was in with a rough set of investors. I don't know if the well dressed man was from back East or was a local character. Maybe McMasters just disappeared what with the stress of the project and all. My dad never told me the details, if in fact he knew the details."

"Was there anything else your dad told you about the house?"

"Now then, as I recall, through the years he talked about different bits and pieces of when he was working on The Painted Lady. As he got older, he seemed to have more and more time on his hands. As I've said before, he said, it seemed to have more than its fair share of worksite mishaps. But I don't know if he was just being a little paranoid in his thinking, especially after his mishap and all." He paused for a moment.

"There was one thing he always mentioned though."

"What was that?" I asked.

"Every morning when they arrived at the work site, from the time the frame of the house was up, there was always a flock of crows sitting on the framing before the roof was on and then perched on the roof after the roof was on. They'd try to shoo those birds away but they were always there the next morning. Treated it like their own roosting place, just like a giant tree."

"Well that is odd. You also mentioned there were other mishaps on the site as well."

"Yes. More like numerous little setbacks. Tools kept disappearing. Nails would appear pounded upwards in loose boards around the house, so that if you weren't paying attention you'd step on one and it'd go into your foot. My dad always wrote it off to someone on the site playing pranks. Or a disgruntled person who didn't get the opportunity to work at the site. It really added a whole layer of tension each day my dad said."

"Anything else, you can think of? Did your dad know who moved into the house once it was completed?"

"He spent a long time recuperating from his injury. And the last thing he wanted to do was think about that house. A number of years later though, McMasters' nephew swung by out of the blue. He was trying to get things squared away with the house he told my dad. It took a lot of balls to come by. Basically he just wanted to check up on my dad and thank him for his work in constructing the house. My dad was cordial to him, but that's as far as it went. It was probably a fifteen minute conversation at most and then he was gone. Never saw or heard from him again. That was pretty close to when my dad passed away."

"Did you meet McMasters' nephew then?"

"I don't know if meet him is the right word. I met him, but he wanted to talk to dad alone. I was in the other room, couldn't make out much of the conversation. It sounded like McMasters was doing most of the talking and my dad just listening. I came out when McMasters was getting ready to leave and walked him to the door. By that time my dad really couldn't move around well at all. Arthritis had set in and with his dementia he just wasn't too mobile. I was just glad we didn't have to put him in a home."

"Did he say what McMasters talked about?"

"Not really, all I could get was some babble from him, something to the effect 'I knew it, that house is alive, sure as I live and breathe.' But I didn't think much of that comment at the time. Plus, he wouldn't elaborate any more than that. Just didn't want to talk about it."

"Do you know if the younger McMasters actually lived in the house?"

"Couldn't tell you that for sure. That's all I know."

"Well, thank you for all your time, you've really been helpful," I said trying to wrap up the conversation. I sensed that everything he knew he had told me. I don't know why, it was just a feeling I had. I stood up. He walked me to the door.

"If you're going to quote me in your article, give me a call and let me know the exact phrase you want to use. I'd like a heads up so I don't sound like an ass. Is that a deal?" he said.

"You got it," I said, "Again, thanks for your time."

I headed out and down the street. I realized I needed to find McMasters if he was still alive. I had checked the internet and nothing. His name was still there in the tax records, though. Then it hit me: maybe the previous owners of our house might know. They were pretty nosey people. I was hoping that I wasn't opening another can of worms. But I'd rather ask them than someone who currently lived in the neighborhood. They were people I wouldn't run into on a daily basis if something went wrong. Plus, they had moved out of state so I didn't have to offer to get together with them.

Chapter 34

Phone Conversation with the Prior Owner

I started to lose my nerve. The more I thought about it, I had a problem coming up with a believable context to be calling the people we had bought the house from. If I used the old reporter angle, I knew they would want follow up. They'd pester me until I actually produced whatever it was I said I was writing. No, I'd have to go at it from another angle. It would have to be something related to our house. Something I would have a reason to call them for. Then it hit me. I could call with the pretext of whether they were still in contact with the prior owners of our house. Then I could transition the conversation into a quick question or two about the owners of The Painted Lady. I could use the premise that it was on the market. That might just work. I thought through my plan of attack. And when I thought I was ready, I picked up the phone in the early evening and called the last number I had for them. It rang a few times and I was beginning to think I'd have to leave an awkward message when all of a sudden a voice came on the other end.

"John, John Stogh is that actually you calling?" She asked.

"How did you know it was me?" I asked a little taken aback.

"You know this new technology they show you right on your cell phone who is calling. I'm surprised you called. Are you still enjoying the house? We hated to move. We just loved the house. Never would have moved if Phil hadn't been transferred. We just loved the area."

It was Jodie who had answered the phone. Lucky me. Now I knew why I had hesitated calling. The only thing worse than talking to Jodie on the phone was talking to her in person. She wouldn't stop talking unless she was hit by lightning and even then that might not slow her down.

"Well, we've tried to make the adjustment here and all. Oh, it's a nice community and all, I'm not complaining, but I do miss the old place."

"Yes, we do still enjoy the house and we are really settled in."

I started in, breaking off her dialogue. "That's why I'm calling. My wife wanted me to put together a little background on our house, for a little memento, and well, I'm wondering if you still have the contact info for the owners who lived in the house before you?"

"Can't really help you with that much, we actually bought it through an estate. Phil did most of the negotiating and discussions with the representative of the estate. I could talk to Phil about it. But I don't know how to put this delicately; we aren't on the best of speaking terms since the divorce."

What she just said didn't faze me at all. I knew it was just a matter of time when I met the two of them at the closing. I didn't know how he could put up with her. Well, evidently in the end, he couldn't. He just had to reach his limit.

"Oh, I'm so sorry to hear that. No, I don't want to put you in a difficult spot. You know I could call him if that would make it easier? I don't know his number. If you want to give it to me, I could give him a call."

"I don't know he's pretty touchy about me giving out his number. Tell you what I'll give you his work number. Don't tell him I gave it to you; just say you looked him up on line. Can you believe he really doesn't want to have anything to do with me? I can't believe that. You know we had been married for fifteen years. I've had to make a whole new set of friends here. I just can't believe it."

I had to cut her off again or I could be on the phone for half the day. I just needed one more piece of information, actually the piece I had called to get. So I just cut her off.

"Do you remember that old Victorian a few houses down the block on the other side of the street? Well, it looks like they're putting it on the market. Isn't that just a wonderful old house?"

"Oh, the wooden one with all the great colors? So the McMasters are finally selling. Or should I say Mrs. McMasters is selling. I was sorry to learn that her husband had passed away. You aren't thinking of moving across the street are you?"

"No, I don't know why I brought it up. Just some local news. That house probably was getting too big for her," I said.

"If I recall, I think she had moved to a nursing home at least for part of the year. I know in the winter she had been staying at Happy Day Retirement Home. Sounds like a lovely place doesn't it? If I have to go into a nursing home that's the type of place I'd like to stay. . . ."

I had to cut her off once more. I had just gotten the information I needed; and when would I ever talk to her again.

"Say somebody's pounding on the door I'll have to get it." I said.

"I understand. If you're ever out in Colorado, look me up. I'm listed in the phone book and well you've got my phone number. We could catch up on the happenings in the neighborhood. . . . "

"OK, sorry got to go." I hung up the phone and breathed a sigh of relief.

Chapter 35
Meeting with Maureen McMasters

Finally I had the opportunity to meet with a McMasters. I hoped that what I had already heard about her husband's uncle wouldn't taint my open mindedness. But after talking with Cartwright, I really found myself despising McMasters and what he stood for. I didn't know if his nephew was built out of the same mold, or a very different man altogether. I didn't even know if I'd get a sense of what he was like from his widow. Anyway, I was looking forward to meeting with the widow McMasters.

I strolled up the steps. Happy Day Retirement Home here I come. I thought about it: could I really live in a place like this? The building was clean and new on the outside. Nice grey siding with white trim. It looked like a giant oversized ranch home with a long wide porch with plenty of room to roll the wheelchairs around. On the far end, I could see a shuffleboard outline in the wooden planking. Yes, I guess I could see myself here in a few years, hopefully more than a few years. That's if I could play shuffleboard all day. I pulled open the front door. No alarm, no doorbell. Don't they really care about who comes and goes. Well, I almost forgot this isn't a prison or mental hospital, it's a retirement home.

I found myself in a wide hallway with a somewhat antiseptic smell. I paused for a moment not knowing which way to go. Then I heard it. It was like a slow rumble, a clanking, and a mixture of sounds; metal on glass, shuffling and what sounded like low conversation all mixed together. I headed in that direction. As I got closer I saw an open door ahead of me. I walked into the open doorway. As I stood in the open doorway, all of a sudden the noise stopped. It was like walking into an empty gym, except there were a thousand eyes all leveled at me. People had stopped in mid sentence with their conversation or in mid bite of their lunch. All eyes had turned on me. I wondered if I was the youngest visitor or the only visitor for that matter that any of them had seen in quite some time. A lady standing just inside the doorway asked me, "Can I help you?"

"Yes, I'm here to see Maureen McMasters. Is she here?"

"Certainly, she is as a matter of fact, she's always here," she said with a smile. "Let me go get her, stay right there." She walked over to a table a ways away and leaned over to talk to a frail lady in a wheel chair. Their conversation went back and forth for a few minutes. Finally, the lady who I had just talked to gestured me to come over. I walked over to the table and with each step I took I could feel the eyes on me, questioning my every move and silently asking me what my business was here. I walked over to the table. The frail lady, who I presumed to be Maureen McMasters, spoke first."

"Ladies, I have a visitor here as you can see. I may be late for the afternoon bridge game. As you can see there's nothing I can do if I need to miss it." She then turned to me and said, "Sir, I would like to introduce you to my lunch companions."

She extended her hand outward to the lady to her right. She was a plump lady with blonde hair that I immediately realized was a wig due to the fact that it was tilted to one side.

"This is, Agnes, Agnes Pearly she's our expert on dry cleaning. She ran a dry cleaning business until she moved here. Across from me is Jane, Jane Martens. Jane is our world traveler, she fills us in on the far flung locations we all may have missed when we were younger and don't have the will or determination to go to now that we're older."

Jane had a brightly colored scarf wrapped loosely around her neck and her bright red lipstick covered too much of her lips and face in some areas and not enough of her lips in other areas. She looked at me and seemed to nod her approval at me, for what, I hadn't a clue.

Next she turned to her left, "and last but not least this is Malinda Scott, she's our youngest member, an accountant by trade. She helps balance the books on our weekly bridge game, keeping us all honest. Isn't that so Maly?"

Malinda just returned a sweet smile and kept her hands folded in her lap under the table.

"Well I'd like you all to meet . . ." It was at this moment that she turned to me and said without hesitating, "my newest boyfriend who has taken the time out of his busy day to accompany me on a stroll around our plush estate. Sir, if you will?"

Then she put her hands up slightly and motioned for me to grab the handles of the chair. I stepped forward, but before I could, an attendant stepped forward, grabbed the handles and started to wheel her around towards me.

"It's our policy that staff moves the residents around," she said to me softly.

"You know I'm not deaf," Maureen said.

As she was being turned in her wheelchair, she loudly exclaimed for the benefit of many in the lunch room.

"Ladies I will see you later this afternoon, after my gentleman caller has gone. Good day until later."

I turned and smiled at the attendant, shrugging my shoulders. As the three of us moved towards the door, that seemed to be the cue for the rest of the lunchroom. The noise level began to rise as people started eating again and conversations were renewed. Still, different people would glance back at me from time to time. I tried not to look in any particular person's direction. I didn't want to get stuck in some uncomfortable eye contact. And so we made our way through the room towards the exit.

I followed a step behind the attendant as she wheeled Maureen down the corridor. It was then that I noticed that she was seated in the chair as if she was a little child, taking up just a small area of the chair. She was a shriveled up wisp of a lady, head tilted down and to the side as if she was nodding off to go to sleep. It seemed that the brief conversation at the table had taken much of her energy out of her.

The attendant spoke up. "Maureen, it's nice that you have a visitor. Do you want to say hi," she said leaning down trying to make eye contact with Maureen who looked as though she was struggling to stay awake and alert.

Turning up to me she asked in a now quiet voice, "I didn't catch your name?"

"Oh, I'm sorry, I'm Roger." I put out my hand to introduce myself but neither Maureen nor the attendant moved to shake it so I quickly dropped it down to my side.

"Who are you?" The attendant asked. "I mean are you related to Maureen?"

"Ah, no. I'm friends with the owner of the house she used to live in. I've never been here to visit before."

"I thought so. Maureen here doesn't really get many visitors. Do you Maureen?" She tried to get a little response from Maureen which didn't seem to work very well.

"Not except for my gentleman callers. They do come by from time to time," Maureen added.

"Now, if you show me your ID, a drivers license will do, I can wheel Maureen into a visiting room down the hall if you like, then you can have a nice chat with Maureen. Would you like that Maureen?"

Maureen raised her head ever so slightly and gave a very subtle nod.

"A driver's license? Just to visit?" I asked, realizing that I had just said my name was Roger.

"Yes, it's the rules," the attendant stated.

"Alright," I said as I pulled my wallet out and searched through it for my ID.

Then the attendant turned to me and whispered in a low voice, "She really comes and goes these days, some days are better than others. As to the bridge game, she hasn't played in eight months. The stories she can tell one day and then the next day she's just a loss for words altogether. You probably should have come on one of her more interactive days. I think she will still enjoy the company though, even if it's just sitting with her. She may not be all too talkative today."

I thought for a moment, I had come out here; I might as well sit with her for awhile. I handed the lady my ID.

She looked at the license and then looked up at me.

"Didn't you say your name was Roger? Your driver's license says John," the attendant said looking at me strangely.

"Oh, that. It throws everyone off. I go by Roger because my dad was also John Stogh, so to avoid confusion I go by my middle name, Roger. I always forget to tell people."

The attendant looked at the picture on the driver's license then up at me then back down at the license and then handed it back to me.

"So I see it does look like you. No funny business now, please, Roger. My shift ends in an hour."

I didn't know what she meant by funny business, but I decided not to ask. Now I was committed. She knew who I was. I had to be on my best behavior. The attendant wheeled Maureen into a small interrogation size room with me following close behind. There was a small table with a couple of chairs and a vase with plastic flowers in it. A box of Kleenex sat off to one side. Except for a cheap landscape painting on one wall, the room was just four white walls with a single window overlooking the front porch of the building.

"Just ring the buzzer over there on the wall when you're done and I'll come get Maureen," the attendant said. "Nice to meet you, Roger," she said a little sarcastically.

"Likewise," I said.

With that she was gone and I was left standing in front of Maureen McMasters.

For a moment or so she didn't move and I couldn't tell if she was still alive. Then she tilted her head opened one eye and spoke.

"This better be good, you're interrupting my dessert. It's Tuesday and it's apple pie. I'll be lucky if there's any left when I get back to my seat. They're all vultures. Minute you turn your back they take anything that isn't nailed down. Last week I left my room for a doctor's appointment came back and all my belongings were gone, replaced with someone else's'. How does that happen? What type of place are they running here? Hmm, you're not my husband, he's dead. You aren't a salesman, you look too normal. Out with it. What's your business? I haven't got all day."

She really caught me off guard. So I quickly started into my purpose for being here.

"I'm doing a little research on your neighborhood."

"Why would anyone want to do research on this place? Nothing but a warehouse for old people, run by a bunch of white ghosts waiting for us to turn into ghosts like them. No, who would want to delve into this place anymore than they have to?" She leaned forward. I hadn't noticed that she had slowly shuffled herself, wheelchair and all, forward with her feet. She put her boney hand on my arm and said, "it would be great if you could get my belongings back."

I just nodded, not sure how to respond. I began to wonder if I was going to get anywhere with her.

"No, I'm not trying to do research on this place, I'm doing research on your home where you lived before here, you know the house everyone called The Painted Lady."

"More like the Decayed Lady," she said all of a sudden coming to her senses. "Never liked that house. More dead than alive it was. We were supposed to live there just a couple of years. My husband promised we'd only live there for a few years. You know he won that house in a lottery."

Lottery, I thought to myself; she must be nuts.

"Yes, won it from his uncle when he died. Sorry excuse for a man, that uncle. My husband was his namesake, what a worthless proposition that was. His uncle thought he'd be the next James J. Hill. All he was, was a pompous ass with not enough character to fill a thimble. No, the best thing we ever got out of him was the house and that wasn't saying much. Trapped us, and let our dreams slowly escape like the air out of a balloon. No, I'm much happier here; if I could only get my belongings back and win a little more at Bridge everything would be great. Oh, and maybe a few more gentleman callers like you would help, too." With that she smiled ever so slightly. A smile I tried to ignore.

"Didn't your husband's uncle die before the house was completed, though?" I asked.

"Yes. How did you know? You're sneakier than you appear to be. I'll have to keep an eye on you. Are you a salesman of some sort?" She added.

"No, I 'm not here trying to sell you anything. I'm just here for some information."

"What kind of information," she asked.

"Like I said, just information about your home."

"Here?"

"No, your house."

"I don't live there anymore."

"I know, how did you get the house from your husband's uncle?" I asked figuring a direct question might get me the information faster.

"You ask a lot of questions," she said

"I'm just trying to help you. Trying to get to the truth about your house."

"I'll help you if you promise to get my belongings back. Will you do that?" she asked.

"Yes," I promised, hoping she would give me the information I wanted.

She looked at me for a moment and then started in.

"It was a drawn out process. Yes, my husband's uncle died before the house was completed. There were some legal matters that took forever to get resolved. It seems my husband's uncle died under suspicious circumstances."

She leaned a little bit closer in to me and whispered, "He may have been murdered."

Then she continued in a normal tone of voice, "anyway, the extended McMasters family from back East found a decent attorney to handle the whole mess. By the time the legal matters were completed and the house was finished, my husband was the lucky remaining heir. And I use the term lucky loosely."

By now I didn't know what I could expect to get out of her. I tried to change the angle of direction of my questions.

"Weren't there some things you liked about the house? You know, after staying there all those years."

"No. We were always the oddities in the neighborhood. It wasn't us, it was the house. People would want to get an invite over. At first we thought it was to meet us. Later on we slowly began to realize that people just wanted a chance to get inside and see the "Haunted Lady". That's what neighbors referred to it as. It was the oldest house in the neighborhood and stood out like a sore thumb from the rest. More of a curiosity than anything else. In my mind, it was just a big albatross around our necks. The longer we stayed, the more my husband got tied up in the house, repairing this, repairing that, painting this, painting that. It turned from a hobby to an obsession until it finally killed him."

"Killed him?"

"Yes. Killed him. Found him at the bottom of the basement stairs. He must have stumbled and fallen down. Broke his neck. That house threw him down the stairs like a pile of trash and then locked the basement door after him."

"You really think the house killed him?"

"I know he'd still be alive today if we didn't live there. It just sucked the life out of him and then locked him in the basement to die. That's all I know. Found him stone cold the next morning being watched over by a hideous creature."

"Hideous creature?"

"Yes, a black bird perched at the bottom of the stairs on the wooden railing. Just sat there silently, never made a sound.

"What type of bird was it, a crow?" I asked.

"Yes. Yes, Oh I don't know black bird, crow aren't they one in the same? It was probably what took my belongings here come to think of it. Now that makes sense," she added.

I decided I wasn't getting anywhere and thought it was time to leave. I started to stand up and then she switched gears.

"We really became the oddity in the neighborhood when they started digging."

"What, digging up the background on the house?" I asked

"No, digging, real digging with a shovel. Jim was breaking up a section of the back yard for a garden. He came across a section of stone wall buried under the ground. We thought it was an old lot line, but then that wall angled ninety degrees into another wall. It was about three or four feet off from that wall, that's where we found them."

"Found what?"

"Not what, who. The skeletons of two boys buried in a shallow grave they were," she said.

Something in the look I was giving her must have alarmed her a little.

"Well of course we didn't dig them up. My husband called the police. They came out and determined that the bodies had been there for years. Initially asked a whole bunch of questions. Thought we were killers, murderers. The neighbors were already spreading rumors about our house, but that just added a whole new layer of gossip.

Well, the police did some more investigating. They brought in some expert from the state historical society. He never really gave us the full details, but he thought the bodies were from a family plot by the farm that used to be located in the area. Imagine that, we were sitting on a cemetery, a cemetery in our own back yard."

"Did you find out who the boys were?"

"No, they never told us. They said the remains were in pretty bad shape. The skulls and skeletons were fragmented into pieces. The police said they looked for old records, but never came up with anything. They did say some objects were found with the bodies though. The boys' skeletons were intertwined facing each other. They appeared to be of similar build. The expert thought that the bodies had been moved after they had been initially buried. Looked too much like the bodies were posed. Plus, there weren't any remains of a coffin for either boy. Maybe that farm family was too poor to afford a coffin. You think they could have made one though."

"What other objects were found with the boys?" I asked.

"Well, placed on top of the skeletons was the remains of an old buggy whip and in two old tin cans were two dolls, one dressed as a man and one as a woman, each with a noose around their necks."

"Were they children's dolls?" I asked slowly being drawn into the story.

"No, from what I understood. They were pretty well decayed, but they were handmade. Both had human hair on their heads. From the analysis of the hair on the dolls, the hair wasn't from the two boys. Also, the clothes were more adult looking."

"Well, what did it mean?"

"I don't know. Maybe it was a warning, a ritual, a way to let the boys know their deaths had been avenged. How would I know? But that was really a story for the neighborhood gossip mill. We never got any peace and quiet after that. Everyone wanted to try to dig up our back yard or get invited over to see our house."

"Sounds like a difficult place to live after that." I added.

"It was, except one positive thing came out of the finding of those two skeletons," she added.

"What was that?" I asked.

"Those two never bothered us anymore."

"Who?"

"The boys, of course."

"What do you mean?"

"We used to hear them talking back and forth. Never saw them, but you could hear them moving about, playing, always downstairs in the kitchen when we were trying to sleep. Never heard them again after we found those bodies," she said.

"So, then I suppose you finally sold the house?"

"Oh, no we never sold the house Jim died and they put me in here. Haven't done anything with the house. Why? Is that why you're here, you want to buy the house? I must be slipping, didn't recognize you, you are a salesman. Sneaky lot you are. Can you at least help me get my belongings back?"

With that I stood up from my chair and stepped back towards the doorway, leaning up against the buzzer as I tried to exit the room.

Chapter 36

My Second Conversation with the Priest

My conversation with Mrs. McMasters raised more questions than answers and left me quite shaken. I did get one important answer about the house, though. In her mind it was currently vacant.

I knew I had to have another conversation with my friend the priest, just to tidy up some concerns I still had. Not really tidy up. I had another list of things I needed answers to. I hoped he could give me some of those much needed answers.

This time, he was willing to meet me at a neutral site. I felt like I owed him lunch for taking time out of his busy schedule to meet with me. Not just once, but twice. Plus, going to a religious location always had me feeling like I was at a disadvantage.

Meeting at a church, altered how I presented my questions. It tainted the conversation because there were certain things I didn't feel comfortable bringing up in the "House of God". It was enough that I had to stare at him while he was talking with that priest's collar on. but then I had to tone it down because of the location. It seemed like the church, the building, held onto my every sentence, the words echoing ever louder throughout the rooms and funneling up the spires like a broadcasting device to the general public, for all to hear. No, it was just an uncomfortable feeling.

Yes, I wanted his advice, but not as a priest, as a wise man, a scholar that knew much more than I did about these matters. Instead, this time I asked him if he would meet me at a local restaurant. I chose to meet him at a local restaurant where we could both take up half a booth opposite one another. Neither of us would have the advantage. We would be on equal footing. We'd meet at the Broiler. The food wasn't half bad: sandwiches, burgers, even cheese curds and the fries were pretty decent. It was one of those places you could smell driving by. If you didn't swing in that day, the smell was locked in your memory and you knew you'd be back in a couple of days if not for breakfast, then for lunch or dinner. I told him I'd pay and that sealed deal. When I walked in, I took a quick look around and then spied him in the backmost booth, eyes down writing something on a pad of paper. He didn't notice me until I was a couple of steps away from him.

"So, how's my regular Dick Tracy doing?" he said.

"I don't think Dick Tracy is the right term. I'm more like Sam Spade, a private eye," I said caught off guard about the comment and a little offended at the same time.

"No, I think you're more like Dick Tracy, someone out of the comics, more of a jovial guy, someone you shouldn't take too seriously."

I felt a little hurt actually, but tried not to show it. I was serious about this, this was a serious matter and I needed answers. I sat down without saying anything. I wasn't sure if he could see the scowl taking shape on my face that was my growing response to his last comment.

"So then, lay it on me Dick," he said with a little bit of a laugh.

That was too much to take. I responded with a bit of anger in my voice.

"Well, I'm glad you can laugh about it. Since the last time I met with you, I've found out that there's more to this whole story then originally appeared on the surface. This isn't just about an oak tree; it's about so much more. I'm beginning to wonder what this is all about; what I've gotten myself into." With that, I began my story about my encounters at the Historical Society and my meetings with the notary's granddaughter as well as the distant Magogson relative, the deaths, the murders, the intrigue. After I had filled him in on the details, I paused for a minute.

"This whole story plays out like a Shakespearean drama. Why can't you just finish reading it and come up with the ending," he said a smile widening on his face.

"Seriously, I don't have an ending. That's what I'm trying to explain. I need answers, answers to a number of questions that are helping keep this mystery or mysteries unsolved. The hardest part is that I'm talking to players, bit players in this drama who weren't there when the actual events occurred. The actual performers are long dead and buried and all I have to go on is bits and pieces that don't always make sense. I'm at a crossroads right now. I'm trying to solve this mystery and I need your help," and then without even waiting for a response, I started to lay the questions on him.

"My first question is more out of curiosity than anything else. I know there's an evil connotation for the numbers 666, but is there any religious significance for the numbers 777?"

"Slow down," he said. Are you ready to order something?" He added noticing that the waitress was standing in front of us. Based on the look on her face I could tell she had been taking in what I was saying for a few moments and was wondering what in the world I was talking about. I lost my train of thought, and said," Sure I'll take the Rueben with chips and a cup of your 'Soup of the Moment'. What would you like? Remember it's on me," I added.

"Just a bowl of chicken noodle soup," he said handing the menus back to the waitress, "I'm really not that hungry."

"Why do you ask?" he said turning his focus back to me and starting to get serious.

"No real reason. I just came across that number and it came to mind, that's why I'm curious," I said remaining a little agitated.

"Yes. Yes the number 777 is significant. Under Hebrew tradition both the numbers three and seven are considered sacred. It comes out of the Bible. The Book of Genesis talks about creating the universe in seven days."

"Yes. That's seven but what about 777?"

"Yes, 777 is considered the opposite of 666; it's like the opposite of evil. If one seven is positive then a trinity of sevens is extremely positive. That's where the three comes in. People outside religious circles also feel it is a sign that angels or the positive energy in the universe is trying to contact you or is with you. So the positive nature of three seven's goes beyond religion. It's a very positive sign throughout many diverse cultures. "

"How do you know that?"

"I don't just limit my readings to the pure religious context of things. Plus, I once had a long and interesting discussion with a spiritualist. Numbers have played an important part in man's history and certain numbers stand out like 7. In mathematics, seven is a prime number. In numerology seven is the thinker, the seeker, the searcher of knowledge. "

"Seven shows up as an important number in many areas then it seems," I added.

"As I recall, there's even a theory in psychology. They refer to it as the 'magical number 7'. The theory is that seven is the number of objects a person can hold in his or her working memory at any one time. It's a theory first put forth by a psychologist, George Miller, back in the 1950's. Some might say it goes as far as being a building block to understanding the relationship between stimuli, man's ability to think, and where man reaches the limits of making proper judgment decisions. It's like a building block that defines how man reaches the limits of deciding right and wrong, through analyzing how much memory input overloads the brain; and the theory says seven is the limit. That's my Psychology 101 lecture.

"Is there any other reference to seven in the Bible though?"

"Yes, there definitely are. There are numerous references to seven in the Book of Revelation, the last book in the Bible. But, there is serious debate about the Book of Revelation's meaning and the various references to the number seven."

Before he could continue, I cut in.

"Isn't the Book of Revelation about the end of days?"

"Not necessarily. There's debate about that as well, whether it's about the end of days, a prophecy of what might happen if certain things are set in motion, or words of encouragement to a growing, young Christian church. There's still much debate to this day about what it really says. The Book of Revelation is a dream or revelation that came to John. And so maybe it is meant as that: a dream of what might happen."

"Was it the Apostle John?"

"Well, that's even still up for debate. Anyway, if you look at The Book of Revelation, there are all types of references to the number seven. God's seven churches are referenced; John is visited by seven angels, there's a reference to seven stars in God's hand that represent the seven churches. There is even reference to the seven angels carrying forth the seven bowls with the seven last plagues. Each angel pours out a plague carried in that specific bowl, it's poured out over the entire land. Then there's the reference to the seven seals that the Lamb breaks open. The references go on."

"Well, is seven a good sign or a bad sign then." I interrupted

"Seven is a sign of power, from what I've read. It's God's power as seen in his churches at that time, symbolized by the seven angels. They mete out their justice through the final seven plagues. As I understand the Book of Revelation, it's meant to show what will happen to those who don't believe. It was a way to show the early Christians that God was on their side, he was coming soon, and he would punish those that were punishing the early Christians."

"So it's all about the ultimate battle of good vs. evil then."

"In a way yes and in a way no. We're still waiting for that final outcome. If indeed that is what is supposed to happen; and it may be simply a foretelling of a transition from one era to another. Maybe the Mayans weren't that far off with their calendar that was cycles within cycles that eventually came to an end. Remember people were all concerned that the world would end in 2012 because that's when the Mayan calendar ended? What if the Mayan calendar, like the Book of Revelation, isn't about an end but about a transition?"

"You don't believe then that the Book of Revelation is about the end of days?"

"I don't know that it is a question of believing or not believing as it is how you really interpret it. Is it really just a big parable? There are so many of them in the Bible. Maybe it shouldn't be taken literally, but more figuratively that a god is watching out for us.

"A god? Do I sense you're hedging your bets? Shouldn't it be just "God"?

"Now, I for one do believe that people perceive or interact with God in many different ways. There are so many ways to interpret or explain who or what god is. That's what makes the idea of a god interesting. Ancient Greeks and Romans split the idea of a god into many faces, each with a different defining characteristic. The Native Americans came up with a middle road: a mix of a Great Spirit found within the plants, animals, and the world around them, the world they interacted with on a daily basis. Each culture throughout history has tried to define God and has come up with varying interpretations. Who is to say who is really right or wrong about that? Does that help? What if each culture's god or gods throughout history are just a different way of looking at one great spirit?"

"So you think the Native Americans were right?"

"No I'm just saying, go into it with an open mind. There are many different ways to look at something. There are many interpretations. That's all I'm saying."

"Yes, well that's clear as mud. It does help clear up the meaning of the sevens though."

"You said you had other questions. I sense we haven't finished yet?"

"Right. Remember I had mentioned the prayer my neighbor said at dinner, that it was strange, that I hadn't heard it before."

"Ah, yes. Yes I do"

"I remember the words now, at least the start of the prayer. It actually went something like:

"Be watchful, and strengthen the things which remain, that are not yet ready to die: for I have not found thy works perfect before thy spirit."

"You're sure those were the words? The words are a little bit different, but that comes right out of the Bible out of The Book of Revelation that we were just talking about. Chapter three, I think."

He pulled up a Bible off the bench next to him. "Here let me see. Yes, I think its Chapter three. Ah, here it is. Are you sure you heard the second sentence right that he recited? In the Bible it reads that 'God' has not found thy works perfect and the word 'spirit' isn't there, it's 'God'. Are you sure you remembered the prayer correctly? I don't think that the word 'spirit' is in that phrase."

"Yes, I know he used the word 'Spirit' and not 'God'.

"Do you know what denomination your neighbors are? There are many interpretations, of the Bible. No, interpretation isn't the right word. There are many different versions of the Bible. Some people feel the King James Version is the true version others think the Good News translation is the right one. How do we really know? The original writing of the Bible may have been in Hebrew or Greek. The bottom line is the Bible has been translated many times before it was put into its current English, or French, or Spanish, or Asmaric versions. I think you get my drift. Who's to say which one is the correct translation? Maybe they all are at the same time because they speak to everyone at the same time. Anyway, for whatever reason your neighbor has changed the wording of the prayer. Who knows why?"

I looked up. I had been writing this last bit down so I wouldn't forget his words. Now I was more curious than ever about my neighbor's background.

"Well, to answer you, I don't know my neighbor's background. That's a good question you ask." I paused and thought for a minute.

"Now, is that it?" he asked looking at me.

"No." I said "My last question may sound strange, but I've been thinking. Can something, can something be made evil?"

"What do you mean?"

"I mean let's say you have something. Let's say some object."

"Does it have to be alive?" he asked.

"That's a good question. I'm not sure. And I'm not sure in what sense you'd call something alive," I added.

He thought about it for a moment and then he replied.

"It really isn't about something being made evil. Are you talking about nature vs. nurture, the debate about whether something is inherently one way or whether you can change it through its interaction with people, places and things over time? Me, I'm in the nurture camp. I believe people soak up what and who they come in contact with like a sponge. It doesn't matter if it's good or bad, it all gets taken in. However, no two people transform what they take in the same manner. No, that's where the nature comes in. We're all a little different, unless we're talking about twins and that's a whole other discussion all together. Now, getting back to your question, can something that is basically good become inherently evil? I'm not sure. But given my initial discussion, why can't things take in, soak up what around them; and if it just so happens those are mainly negative energy moments, then maybe, just maybe it can be made evil."

"Now, what if we're talking about an object, not a live person?"

"Then maybe, maybe it gets into the whole yin and yang thing: can something take on the positive or negative energy from things it comes in contact with, both living and inanimate objects? All I know is that the mysteries of the universe are much bigger than either you or me. We may never know. But why couldn't there be negative energy that can take hold of something and transform it?. There are many different types of energy. Why can't there be an energy, a negative force that ebbs and flows based on actions of people, places and things that it comes in contact with? We see it all the time: people are nurtured to act in a certain manner. They take on bad habits or good habits depending on what they see in others around them. Why couldn't it be the same with objects? I don't know. You've really got me out there on the 'what if' thought process. I think I'd just like to finish my soup and put my brain back in its charger," he finished.

I took a sip of my coffee and just sat for a moment, thinking to myself. Then I broke the silence.

"You know what; I'll fill you in with all of the rest of the details once I finish my investigation. Your information has been very helpful, as usual."

"It's an investigation now, is it? Well, I guess I'll have to wait for the complete write up," he said joking, "By the way, how's the job search going?" he added, changing the subject.

"Great. Just great," I said trying to convince myself, but not wanting to face the fact that I had totally put any job search on hold while I wrapped up this most important investigation.

Chapter 37

My Discussion with the Police Officer

I finally realized I had talked to all these different people over the course of a couple of weeks. The one person I hadn't talked to was someone from law enforcement. It wasn't like I needed to include them just for the sake of saying, "Yes, I've talked to law enforcement." And I wasn't doing it to give law enforcement a heads up, that if people started calling wondering why some newspaper reporter was pestering them, that it was me. And yes, reporters really do travel around the state, yes that was the case, they just needed to ask me.

No, I needed to know if what I thought were the facts surrounding the different deaths I had come across could indeed have happened how I thought they happened. Talking to an expert would help me understand how the deaths occurred and who might have committed the murders. It was all about tying up loose ends. Even though these events happened in the past, I assumed people didn't change all that much, motives for killing still remained pretty much the same. People still kill for the same reasons that they did a hundred years ago. What better way to get to the potential truth than to check in with someone who deals with murder cases on a regular basis. And so I decided to look up my friend at the police department. Well, he was less of a friend, more of an acquaintance. Actually, I hadn't seen him since high school. He was someone I went to high school with. I heard he was a now a detective, homicide detective. He would know.

It didn't go as smoothly as I had thought it would. I did get him on the phone. That's when the questions started.

"You want to come down here to the precinct to talk to me? I haven't seen you, what since high school. And even then I didn't know you very well. Why would you want to come to me and why after all these years?"

I had to salvage the conversation at all costs. So I started with my background, the reason for my call, realizing that he was probably an expert in seeing through bullshit.

"Well, it is your area of expertise. You know criminal matters and all. I just have some questions to ask. I'm putting together a book that I'm writing. I want it to be as authentic as possible. So I have a few scenarios that I need answers to. I'm just trying to see if from a police perspective they make sense and aren't too farfetched. There needs to be realism in my book. That's what I'm looking for. I don't want people to read it and say, no that's too unbelievable. It would never have happened that way. No, I want a factual thriller and so that's why I'm here on the phone with you. Are you up for it? Are you willing to answer some questions I might have on my plot scenario?"

There was a pause on the other end of the phone.

"Oh, alright," he said.

I could sense the interest and uncertainty in his voice at the same time

"But if this goes big time you will have to mention me somewhere that I was your police consultant, but only if it does go somewhere. If it turns out to be lousy then I don't want my name associated with it all. Is that clear?" he said in a joking, relaxed manner. I knew I had salvaged the conversation. Quality reporter skills again.

"When can we meet?" I asked

"Well, I'm rapping up some cases and then I have to be in court this afternoon. How about tomorrow morning some time? Would that work?" he asked.

"Yes. It will have to work. I'll bring by some donuts for your trouble." I almost began making a comment about police and donuts, but luckily I held my tongue long enough for the thought to pass.

"Yes. We've got a deal. Do you know where I'm located? It's the 5th precinct right off Lafayette, downtown. Do you know where it is?"

"Yes, I can find it. I'll see you tomorrow."

I expected the precinct building to be set up differently than it was. I was used to old movies where people would be ushered into an open floor area where desks lined the floor and I could pull up a seat next to my friend. Instead everything was behind glass. I entered the first floor and there behind a glass enclosed area sat a uniformed officer. I didn't know if he was trying to keep the public out or just making it look like they had everything under control. I walked up to the officer.

"Purpose of your visit?"

"I'm here to see detective Johnson."

"I'll need to see some kind of ID?"

I was relieved I had used my real name on the phone; it would have been difficult to pull out a fake ID on such short notice.

"Here you go," I said, sliding him my driver's license under an opening in the glass enclosure. It was at that moment that I worried about the unpaid parking ticket I had. I hoped they didn't check that out. I relaxed when he just did a quick look at my ID and then looked up at me.

"OK," he said passing the license back to me, "Detective Johnson is up on the fifth floor. Let me buzz you through the door to your right, go through the door and take the elevators there up to the fifth floor."

"Thank you," I said. I turned and could hear the door click open. I pushed it and felt an uncomfortable feeling like I would be trapped inside once I let that door close behind me. I reached the fifth floor and there was more glass. A woman came up to the glass.

"Can I help you?"

"I'm here to see detective Johnson."

"Is he expecting you?"

"Yes. Yes he is."

"Please wait right here, I'll get him." I didn't know where she thought I might go. There was nowhere to go except back down on the elevator. A couple minutes later she came back and pushed open the door.

"Detective Johnson will see you. What's in the bag?" I had almost forgotten it was the donuts. The officer downstairs hadn't even asked. I wasn't too sure what the security was all about anymore.

"Just donuts. I said I'd bring him some."

She gave me a smirk and then said, "Follow me. He's back in the corner."

We walked back past floor dividers to a desk in the corner. There he sat, I didn't even recognize him, not that I recognized him in high school either. But he was balding, a bit on the chubby side and wore a thin mustache that broke up the boredom of his face.

"Hey, John," he said standing up, "Thanks for coming by and bringing the donuts," he said loud enough for the woman and anyone else in the area to hear. "Here, sit down."

He grabbed a stack of papers on a chair next to his desk and plopped them down on the floor.

"It certainly has been a long time, hasn't it? You look a little older. I guess we both look a little older," he added trying to break the ice.

"Yes, it has been quite some time," I added.

"So you keep up with anyone from high school?" he asked.

"No. Not really. Didn't even go to the last reunion." I didn't even know when or whether it had occurred. No, staying in touch with high school acquaintances just wasn't my scene.

"Oh," he said.

I waited for more but there wasn't anything further out of his mouth.

"Well, as I said on the phone, I'm writing a book. I just have a few questions. I know you're probably busy so I'll keep it short."

"Ok, then fire away," he said becoming a bit more serious.

"Well, first I just have some basic background questions. If someone is murdered and the way they are murdered is by blows to the front of the face, what does that mean?"

"What's the murder weapon?"

"Let's say an axe or a hammer."

"Well that depends. There are different schools of thought here. First, it may have been just a murder of convenience, the hammer or axe may have been lying around and the suspect picked it up trying to protect himself or picked it up in the heat of the moment. That's if it wasn't planned out. The suspect could have killed for any number of reasons. You really need to look at the motive of the suspect."

"What if it was premeditated?"

"That's different. Then it's a murder of a very personal nature. To allow the victim to see your face when you're killing him or her and then striking the victim repeatedly, no, now that's very personal. The suspect wants the victim to know who's killing him or her. Usually there's rage, emotion, or a perceived wrong all wrapped up into this culminating event, this murder. Normally, with a murder of this type, the suspect would know his victim. Now the motive, that's different with each set of facts in the case."

"So you're saying that in that instance, the victim would know his or her attacker."

"That's not always the case, but more often than not."

"Now let me ask you another question. You know anything about river drowning?"

"What do you mean murder or just a drowning?"

"Well, let's say I'm writing in my book that a person was found drowned and it's the turn of the century 1900. And there's a drowning in the Mississippi River. Any thoughts?"

"I don't know. That's a little out of my league. I'm old but not that old. Back then drowning was more commonplace. There was a fair amount of flooding all along the river. Plus people, communities I should say, lived close up, right along the banks. It wasn't like it is today where the flooding is controlled for the most part and flood walls protect the inhabitants from the flooding river. Most of the lower levee communities were all cleared out. Back then though, it wasn't uncommon for people to wake with a foot or two of water in their houses due to a rapidly rising river. No, people back then wouldn't give a second thought to a body found in the river. Wouldn't suspect foul play either. Probably just write it off as an accidental drowning and leave it at that."

"Thank you. That helps. I have one more question," I said.

"Shoot," he said.

"Why do they have such tight security here?"

He smiled, "I don't know probably to make us feel safe," he said.

"Well, thanks for your time," I said.

"Now, you know as part of the deal, don't forget to mention me in your book. In fact send me an autographed copy. I'll be waiting for it."

"You got it," I said wondering if now I really had to write a book. I shook his hand and said, "Enjoy the donuts."

"I don't know why people get such a kick out of cops and donuts. We just don't see the humor," he said.

He led me out to the door and I rode the elevator down hoping that the door on the first floor wouldn't be locked.

Chapter 38
The Last Meeting

I came that night with my list of what I had found out about the grand old house, The Painted Lady. I had no intention of destroying the myth Darrah Braddock had created about the house in his mind. I just wanted to make it clear to him the exact nature of what he was living in, the complexities, the history, the sadness that all had gone into the creation of this house. I needed to disclose my finding to someone. Someone who would understand what I was saying. Someone who appreciated the information I had, information that had been hidden all these years, information that someone needed to care about and appreciate. I had unraveled a mystery, no, actually a chain of mysteries all linked to the house. It wasn't just about someone appreciating the information, but someone appreciating my efforts.

Whether we still remained friends after that didn't matter. I had to let him know that the delusion he lived under was one that had to be brought to an end. And most of all I wanted some answers from him. Why did he and his wife not show up anywhere in records of the history of the house? What was the true history he was trying to hide? I needed to know. This had gone on too long. I had spent too much time working through the clues and searching for answers. I had a right to know. I had worked too hard not to find out the answers now. I needed to get the rest of the answers directly from the source.

I was hoping it would go well, but I was really heading into uncharted territory. I wasn't good at confrontation, and I really wasn't good at direct confrontation. No, I was best at denial and fantasy. I worked best when I could conjure up my own world created just for me, compartmentalized so that only I could weave my way through my own private maze. But this time I had facts, plenty of facts to discuss. They couldn't be ignored. I needed to get those facts out. Hopefully, Darrah would have additional facts to supplement what I would present. I hoped he wouldn't dodge the issues that I wanted to discuss. I hoped we could discuss this on an equal footing.

It took me most of the day to work up my nerve. I reviewed and then went back over the facts as I had put them together. Then I looked over my list of questions that I was going to present to Darrah. I walked up to his front door. The sun had just set. Coming from within I could see a dancing glow. A fire was burning in the fireplace. I raised the knocker on the front door and let it drop. A slight echo of a sound could be heard throughout the house.

In a moment the door opened and there he stood, pale as ever, yet tall and upright, thin from toe to head.

"John, come in. To what do I owe this pleasure? And where is your lovely wife?"

"Thank you." I said. "She's not with me. This isn't pleasure though, it's strictly business."

"Business? Are you going to try to sell me something?"

"No. Nothing like that."

"Well, come in, can I offer you something, take a seat and tell me about what is on your mind. You want water, or juice, we have sparkling water or tea perhaps. It seemed you so much enjoyed the tea last time. I can't remember which type you chose. Also, I know you don't usually take anything stronger than that, but we do have some liquor."

"Do you have some brandy? Brandy would do just fine if you did. I think given the nature of my business brandy would be appropriate."

"Yes. I'll get you some. Here sit down. I'll be right back."

He came back in with a medium tumbler with a dark liquid in it.

"Thank you," I said, "Your wife isn't around?" I asked.

"No, no she stepped out for awhile. Don't worry she'll be back shortly. Why, do you want to discuss this 'business' matter with her as well? Now what do you have on your mind?"

"No, she doesn't need to be here. What I have to say can really stay between the two of us. Well, I don't know how to tell you this or where to start."

With that, I took a long sip out of the glass. I hadn't felt the taste of alcohol for a long time. It had a strong taste at first but then went down smoothly. I could feel the warmth invade my body. Yes, it had been quite some time. I had sworn off the alcohol. Actually, it was really my wife's idea. She had a notion, or a belief that it wasn't good for me. I had had just a few too many instances where one too many drinks got me in an argument or compromised my better thinking. At least that's what she said. This was different now. The sip gave me strength and clarity and I was prepared to move on with my disclosure. I had real issues I was dealing with here. One drink didn't matter, in the big scheme of things; in fact it would actually clear my head. No alcohol, and you'll have a job in weeks, maybe a month tops. Well, did that work? No, here I was eight months later and still no job. Well, I couldn't say that. I had found a job. I had searched down these clues, found information that hadn't been unearthed for a hundred years and now I was going to present my case to the person that needed to hear it. No, I was a damn good detective, I was better than most everyone else. I'd start into my presentation. He would have to listen and then he would take notice. Finally everyone would take notice. Everyone would have to take notice once they heard all the details that I had unearthed. I had solved the mystery. Through my hard work, determination, and thorough investigation, I had solved the mystery. And so I began to put my thoughts into more concrete words, when he interrupted me again.

"Based on the look on your face, it seems like you have a lot on your mind. Why don't you start at the beginning then, that's always a good place to start," he added.

"Yes, let me start at the beginning. I'd like to make it clear to you that I know exactly what the story and history of this house is all about and you my friend haven't been quite truthful in the whole process."

Before I could go on he added in.

"Really, how so? Can't you make yourself comfortable, you're getting a little worked up? Here just relax a little."

"Worked up, no I'm not worked up. I just don't like being lied to. When my wife and I were over the other night, some of the things you brought up got me to thinking. And, well, once I start thinking, I get to doing."

"Before you continue, do you want some more to top off your drink?" he cut in.

"Sure you can freshen up my drink, but please let me finish what I have to say, I think my words might go on for awhile. After I'm done you can speak your peace," I said leaning forward in my chair and setting my drink down in one motion.

He calmly reached to a glass carafe that he had brought in with my glass of brandy and gently tipped it forward filling my glass sitting on the table. I looked up at him and I made eye contact. It looked like he was debating whether or not he should say anything, but then he just leaned back in his chair without a word and settled back to listen to me speak. Then not being able to help himself he said, "There. You're free to continue."

I know I gave him a clenched mouth glare, but I couldn't help myself. He was trying to control the situation and I didn't like it. I was tired of people trying to control every little facet of my life. It was getting old fast. Pieces of my life were out of my control. And yet I had pulled them back within my grasp. The investigation had done that for me. I took control and searched out the facts. Waded through fact and fiction and boiled down everything into the truth. It wasn't anyone else that had taken the time, no it was me, me alone, and now it would all pay off. I took a quick sip and started flowing into my one way discussion.

"Well, you got me thinking about this house, about that oak tree over there," I said pointing to the picture over the mantel, "And I got to thinking about you and your wife in this big house. It all seemed odd and interesting at the same time. Well, I've done some checking and you are not who you seem to be. Yes, this house does sit where that oak tree once sat. That I was able to determine through my investigation. The tree sat here or very close to here, situated on what was originally part of the Magogson farm. But it would seem that there, the greatness, the charm, the benevolent nature of this grand "Painted Lady" ends. Yes, it is true that for the most part this big house is the oak tree that once sat here. All this wood, the floors, the trim, the guts of it came from that one big oak. But there it ends. This structure is just an empty cold shell built on the backs of dead souls who toiled and gave up their happiness so that this edifice could stand here as a constant reminder of what everyone thinks happiness and prosperity should be, but isn't. No, it is just one big fallacy that you continue to perpetuate. This house isn't about truth, greatness, and inner wealth. No, it is all about something that has been corrupted and altered; it's about decay and death and deceit. Not the true beauty, if it was ever there to begin with, and nature, if it had been left untouched was in the living oak and the landscape it looked over. It would have continued to grow unmolested, but is now long since gone. And do you know what? You aren't who you say you are. You and your wife don't appear anywhere in the history of this house, not now and not in the past. You don't exist, not in any records, not as owners of this house, maybe you're real for I'm looking at you, but you aren't being truthful about your name. Maybe no one else has decided to confront you, but I am. I am calling you out for what you are. You my friend, are at best a fraud and you, you and your wife are at worst just a couple of squatters. I've talked to the real owner and she owns this house. She doesn't know anything about you and your wife. Your story about the grand past of this house and you being the current caretakers in a long line of related family members is an utter fabrication. You are not a Magogson, nor are you a McMasters."

I stopped out of breath and could feel my face turning beet red. I took another quick sip of my drink and gathered myself for another ramble. First though I paused to see what type of reaction I would get from him. I had gotten so wrapped up in my speech that I didn't even notice how he was taking this all in.

Before I could go on, he calmly responded.

"You are quite right," he said, "I am not a Magogson, nor am I a McMasters. I have never professed to be a Magogson, nor have I ever wanted to be a McMasters. The former is but an evil lineage long since gone from the face of this earth and the later a contemptible lot of posers, yet destined to populate this earth for a brief time more. I never claimed any direct relation to those two families, yet in a way I am connected to them. But, I am something different altogether, something greater, something of many pieces. I am not defined by time, but to help you understand I will explain, I am many thousands of years in the making. No, you are right, maybe in your eyes, I am not who I seem to be. But trust me I am who I say I am."

I listened in disbelief. Part of me was taking all of what he was saying in and the other half was thinking this can't be. He continued on.

"In a way you can look upon me as a protector of what once was, is and will be. A spirit realm alive within the confines of that great tree and alive well beyond what you can imagine. I don't know if I can explain to you, you probably wouldn't understand. But nonetheless I will try. Come here," he said motioning me towards him as he stood up.

For a second I wasn't certain if I should move towards him. What he was saying was beginning to scare me, even in my agitated state. I had really laid it on him and I couldn't really judge how he was taking it all in or what he was even talking about.

"No. Please come here," he said calmly, "I have something to show you."

With that he turned and walked towards the corner of the room. There sitting in between two low burning candles was an old dusty book. Funny, I hadn't noticed it before. He stood over the book and waited for me to come up beside him.

"This may help explain what to you is a great mystery, but to me a simple story, one of many that intertwine. You believe you have solved the mystery, but truthfully you have only scratched the surface, and that is just me being polite. No, you have really missed the true mystery altogether. I laid out breadcrumbs for you and you did follow them quite nicely. You in fact are part of the solution to the mystery and that is why you are here now."

He grabbed hold of my arm. With that I stepped up next to him and looked down at the book which he had his right hand on. It was a leather bound book and the title in sweeping block letters curled outward in a ornamental gold leaf read "Home Sweet Home" I thought to myself, great, a family album how quaint, Does he really think he can change my mind by looking through this book? And then he continued.

"Time and again man corrupts the good of what the spirit of nature brings forth, thinking he is improving it."

With that he opened the book and there on the first page was a picture of a grand oak tree, maybe it was the great oak that once stood where I was standing. I wasn't sure. The colors in the picture were vivid. It was more than just a simple picture on a two dimensional piece of paper it was alive, three dimensional, in motion trying to leap off the page; it was as if I could've reached into the page and pulled out a real leaf off one of its branches. There were words below the picture and on the next page, but they were not in any language I was familiar with, English and Spanish being the only two I knew.

"Is this not the spirit of true beauty?" he asked. "Unspoiled nature at its purest?"

I had to agree.

"In the end though, man only corrupts nature to make it adapt to man," he said. And then he turned the page, There was the picture

I had last seen when I had first visited the house. It was the dull black and white photo of the farm with the oak tree in the background and the serene family of five standing on the porch. Each of their faces from the two small boys to the older teen boy to the two parents looked worn and sad as if their lives had been played out, but that they just didn't know it yet. I was actually happy that I knew they were long since dead.

"This is man in his true form: one dimensional in a multidimensional spirit world. Man changes nature to make himself comfortable. He reduces the vivid spirit of real life to the one dimensional limited view he chooses to reside within. Man is just fleeting, memories breathed to life momentarily; beings that have and will tread but a short time on earth. Yes, it is not nature that changes what is, but man that changes what is. If man is two dimensional like the images in this photograph, and then the Great Spirit is many dimensions."

He turned the page again.

"Do you understand? These pictures are but a brief history, a brief history set in motion by man."

He turned the page. Staring back at me was a Native American Indian, a woman dressed in turn of the century traditional Native American dress with a short coat and broad hat sitting high on top of her head. I recognized her as Abaddon's Indian bride. It was the same picture described by Eloise Lafond. Except this was the other half. She looked serious and I felt as if she was going to speak at any moment. Behind her stood half of the oak tree, leaves bright green. He continued to turn pages and with the turning of each page and the presentation of each new picture, a new memory was etched into my mind.

He turned the page again, and there was the picture from the historical society. Seven lifeless bodies hanging from the branches of the large oak. Then he turned the page again, and there was the oak and underneath its broad silhouette stood hunched over a ghastly spirit like silhouette of a figure contorted, with his face looking back at me with a wide smiling grimace. It was Abaddon Magogson and he was standing over the outlines of two small human forms lying in the grass underneath the tree. I don't know why, but I was transfixed. Finally, he turned the page and there staring back at me was a color picture of me. I looked into the picture and felt as though I could see my soul. It seemed as if the story had come full circle. I began to wonder where the whole story began and ended. I began to grow faint. My knees began to buckle. And he continued on.

"The expanse of man is finite, while the expanse of nature, within the Great Spirit, is infinite. In time, man will fall away, the Great Spirit will not. The days of man are numbered."

With that last statement, seriousness enveloped his entire face.

"You are but a mere man who will shortly disappear and your footprints will be covered over, leaving no one to weep over your passing. You are not like the thousand year oak. You are but a single feather in the wind."

At that moment, everything around me changed. I stepped away from him, in the process knocking over one of the candles.

One moment we were standing next to the table over the large book, conversing about the truths that lay in the big book, the information I had come to present to him just a thing of the past, when all of a sudden his demeanor changed. And out of his mouth poured the following words

"I have tried, tried to repair the rift by maintaining the legacy of this house. Darkness, if left unchecked has a way of unraveling things. That darkness, that corruption, the mystery you have finally unearthed, was necessary to make whole the Great Spirit that once grew and thrived here. Cleanse as I might, I couldn't fully restore the inner strength and tranquility of its past. That could not be done until the darker, uglier past could be unearthed. Only then would that allow it to transition; transition on. And so you have written a chapter, but not the final chapter. With its true dark story revealed, now it has come full circle, withered and become but a shell, an empty pile of wooden bones no longer alive and no longer dead, changed by those who over the years brought on this dark and twisted form. The tree of life may change and transform, but you cannot kill it. Over time different peoples speak. Even though they speak in different ways, they all speak of the same spirit."

He then pointed an angry finger directly in my direction and continued.

"And so in words you might understand, I say, and when the thousand years are expired, he shall be loosed out of his prison, and shall go out to deceive the nations which are in the four quarters of the earth, Gog and Magog, to gather them together to battle. The tree is the root and the offspring of the righteous. In the midst of the street of it, and on either side of the river, was there the tree of life and the leaves of the tree were for healing of the nations. It is not time for the seven plagues of the seven angels to be fulfilled. And so the legacy shall be renewed."

As the last words were uttered from its mouth, for it no longer appeared human in form, the orifice ceased to be what it had been. In its place was a blackening void of a hole and the top of his head fell away into a grey mist. His arms and legs grew thinner and longer merging into long tentacles, fibrous root like shapes that slowly began to slither along and burrow into the wood floor all at the same time. Hair and the outline of his body ceased to be and what used to be his hand lurched forward at the same time it turned to a creeping vine. The howl of the last word "legacy" resonated throughout the room and into the far reaching corners of the house. I lunged backward, tipping over the table with my drink and the glass encased candle. Both fell to the floor as the upended table landed on top of them. I stumbled and tripped backward as I tried to exit the room with the grey mist following. Flames began to rise off the floor up the curtain hanging along the wall. I ran past the fireplace mantel and above it the picture and the tree within it was engulfed in flame. I barely made it out of the room with the flames racing me for the front door. Outside at the curb I caught my breath, leaning over I still didn't understand what had just happened.

Chapter 39
The End

Flames grew from the wick and wax of the overturned candle when it hit the floor. Old layers of varnish on the floor boards provided ample fuel for the flames as they began to run in patterned extensions like roots outlined on top of the ground. The fire was quickly fed by the dry timbers that were the skeleton of the grand old lady. Soon flames rose and spread through the roof leaping and dancing in bright yellow and orange spikes of bright heat. From a distance it looked like a huge tree, an oak tree, with its brightly colored leaves set in a fall moonlit sky. The burst of energy, the peaks of flame rose and fell. It was alive and yet dying at the same time. Fire consuming, fire growing.

The fire engines with their wailing sound were heard far off and slowly grew louder as they moved closer. Even as they arrived, the glass in the windows began to pop, and in random sequence, windows here and there throughout the house broke and cracked inward allowing new flames to shoot outward. Heat and flame together tried to escape along with the black sooty smoke that curled up along the side of the building. It was as if the flames realized they were slowly running out of material to consume and that eventually they would die out all together. They were looking to escape to find another source to feed its energy. It was alive in the moment, dancing wildly here and there.

The first fire truck responded in minutes along with fire rescue units. Each truck or vehicle pulled up as close as they could. Trying to gain access to the building on fire, but wary of the power and danger that the fire produced. Firefighters began working in teams hooking up and running hoses from the hydrant on the corner. Another crew ran for the oxygen tanks and heavy gear in case they might have to go in to save anyone. The fire captain walked through the growing crowd of neighbors assessing the situation and talking on his two way radio from time to time.

He turned to the crowd and asked, "Does anyone know if there was anyone in the house when the fire started?"

"I don't think so, the house has been vacant for over a year," one of the neighbors down the street said, coming forward a few steps from the rest of the crowd that was watching the drama unfold.

"And who are you?" the fire captain asked.

"I'm Mary Hanson; I live in the white sided house two doors down from the house on fire."

"What happened to the owners of the house?" The fire captain asked.

"From what I know the husband Jim passed away almost a year ago; and his wife, I believe she is in a nursing home. I don't know who was handling her affairs. Someone was keeping up the yard. I just don't know who it was. I don't think there should have been anyone in the house," she added.

I rushed up as I heard the lady's statement to the fire captain tail off. No one in the house? Impossible. I rushed forward to address the fire captain.

"You've got to save them. The old couple who live there. I don't think they made it out of the house when the fire started. Please you've got to send someone in for them," I yelled.

"Ok, slow down a minute," the captain said, "How do you know they're in there?" he asked.

"They live there and they're always home. I didn't see them come out."

"Please step back sir," he added as a large boom was heard and we both saw flames now shooting out of the front round turret of the house.

Quickly the round spire fell down into the house. Any secrets that room held were lost forever. The captain grabbed me by the shoulder.

"It's not safe to send anyone in right now. Maybe they got out back," he added. "How do you know they were in there?"

I hesitated for a moment. I wasn't sure if I wanted to admit that maybe it was me who had started the fire, even if it was accidently.

"I just know, that's why. The couple, they're always home. I see them when I'm out for a walk. I've been over to their house for dinner. You've got to save them."

I stood there face to face with the captain. My gut told me they hadn't survived. "Nobody is going in that house right now Mr., I didn't catch your name."

"It's John, John Stogh," I answered.

"Well John, don't go anywhere. Are you from around here?" he added.

"Yes," I answered, "I live right there," as I pointed to my house down the block, "Right down the street."

"We're probably going to need to get some additional information from you before this is all over. Please let us do our job, but stay nearby," he said pushing me back with his arm.

"You don't understand. It's going to be too late. You're not going to be able to save them. I believe they're in there, in the house helpless. You've got to do something. It's your job, your duty," I said, my guilt beginning to boil up inside me as I began to realize I might be responsible for the death of two people.

Why couldn't I just leave well enough alone? Why did I have to get involved? What an idiot. Just to prove a point. Now look at what had happened. It was my fault. All my fault.

Before I could think anymore, I felt a strong arm take hold of my arm. It wasn't the captain, but another man in a blue uniform. Before I could respond, he said in a soothing voice, "Here let's step back over here and let the firefighters do their job. You've done all you can for now. Here why don't we step back across the street?"

I nodded and stepped off the curb backing up to my side of the street as an additional fire engine pulled up. He stayed with me, but gave me space as I began to pace back and forth, keeping my eyes on the burning house. In the end the firefighters could only stand back spraying their hoses on areas where the flame moved closer to adjacent buildings. I stood transfixed across the street watching the building engulf itself in flame. I blocked out most everything around me. It became just me and the house. Worry and guilt mixed together. It began to sink in that the house was a total loss and that two bodies were likely to be found in the burnt debris. Even from that distance the heat of the fire was almost unbearable. But it wasn't until much later when I would know how complete the destruction was. At times, when I focused intently enough on the house, it looked like a couple was framed in the second floor window staring at me with twisted smiles. But each time I would try to make out the figures, I realized it was only the flames playing tricks with the shadow and light. I had caused this whole chain of events. I was responsible.

I stayed there, sometimes sitting, sometimes pacing along the edge of my yard, well into the wee hours of the night. Other neighbors came and went asking questions, taking in the spectacle. I couldn't leave; I had to see this through. At times, I think I nodded off lying in the grass in my front yard, only to awaken with the fire trucks and firefighters still in full gear.

Finally, I don't know how long I had nodded off, I awoke. Light was slowly breaking, not light from the fire, but sunlight. I looked across the street. As dawn broke, the number of fire trucks had dropped to one, its hose at the ready to water down any remaining flare-ups. But there really wasn't anything left to fuel a fire. The house had been totally consumed. There were no timbers remaining, except for one charred beam which rose above the ground level. Grey ash blew up from time to time but even that was sporadic. A single police squad was joined by a red SUV with the words "Fire Marshall Arson Unit" written across the door. I looked around. The captain was nowhere to be seen. The man who had helped me across the street was nowhere to be seen either. Two men in jackets stepped out of the truck. Before I could walk up to them, they crossed the street along with the policeman. They were coming in my direction.

"John, John Stogh, one of the men with a blue blazer with the words 'Fire Marshall' written across asked me, "last night you thought someone was in the house. Why was that?"

It seemed like minutes as the three people stood glaring at me awaiting my answer. I had been up most of the night and the chain of events from the night before began to unravel in my mind. Did I really start the fire? Was it me? At worst it was just an accident. Was I really there? Did I do it? What had I done? I was just trying to get to the truth. I grew uneasy; I could feel sweat beginning to bead up on the back of my neck.

That's when I blurted it out, "I think they're still in there. I don't think they ever got out," I said.

"Who?" asked the shorter of the two fire marshals.

"The couple who owned the house and lived there," I answered.

"And what do you base this on?" The tall one asked.

"I live right over there," I said pointing towards my house, "I live right here in the neighborhood, that's how I know."

"Then you should know that according to the tax rolls that house has been vacant for over a year," he said questioning me about what I was saying, "Are you saying there were some squatters living there?"

My jaw dropped.

"I've met them. I don't know what you want to call them but they lived in the house. I had dinner with them in their house. They have lived there at least since we moved in," I answered now not so sure of what I was saying myself.

"I don't know. According to our records it has been vacant for some time. I can double check. But according to the records, a couple used to live there. Husband passed away maybe two years ago and the wife currently resides in a nursing home. We're trying to get a hold of her now. It's been pretty much vacant since then." The short man nodded in agreement.

"Were you in the house when the fire started?" the short one asked. It was the moment of truth. What should I say? I couldn't say. I didn't want to get involved. Why did I get involved.? I was only looking for answers.

"I really thought there was a couple that lived there. Maybe it was my mistake. I'm new to the neighborhood and maybe I mistook other neighbors as living there in that house. I'm sorry for the trouble." My words were really disconnecting from what I was I thinking. I didn't even believe what I was saying. But what else could I say? The house was no more. They were saying there was no one in the house.

"We'll check it out anyway," the short one said.

Then the taller man turned to his partner, and said "Is the dog unit on its way? You know standard procedure to make sure there are no bodies."

"Yeah they're on their way. Should be here in five or ten," the shorter man added. The dog unit pulled up shortly. I sadly resigned myself to the picture in my mind of them finding the remains of the couple in the house. The rear of the van opened up and the handler snapped a leash on each dog as they jumped down onto the street below. They were all business, ready to take off the minute they hit the ground. The handler held them back trying to assess whether there were still some hot spots that the dogs should avoid in the building. Actually, it was no longer a building it was simply a grey and black outline of the foundation on the ground. Here and there a charred finger of wood poked out from under ash. Finally, the handler, or should I say the dogs, went onward towards the burnt remains. The dogs sniffed through the remains of the house. Moving here and there, pausing at times, and then moving on to the next area. However, in the end, they didn't come across a single set of human remains. Only the blackened embers of what had once been a grand old house remained.

Epilogue

It had been a year since the fire. The neighborhood had recovered. Stories still circulated about the grand house that used to adorn the neighborhood and what a tragic loss it was to the charm of the neighborhood. Otherwise, the quietness and calm had come back. Where the house once stood was now a gently sloping curve of spring growth. Grass had been sown in the fall and it was popping up in clumps here and there.

The neighbors who lived in the lot next door to the now vacant lot had purchased it shortly after the fire. They had already placed a picnic table and a swing set on it. Rumor was that they were hoping to turn it into a little neighborhood park for kids and families to enjoy. In fact, they were pleasantly surprised to see the start of a small sapling already growing in the vacant lot. From the look of the few small leaves on the tree it appeared to be an oak tree. It was interesting how nature just takes its course and repairs itself. Thoughts of a large tree providing shade and a place to hang a swing for their grandkids crossed their minds. They would enjoy watching the tree grow tall and strong along the far corner of the lot.

And me, well I don't go out much anymore. I am still in the market for a job. And now, I'm also in the market for a new wife. But that's a discussion for another time. But really, I spend most of my time quietly looking out the window at the vacant lot down the street, wondering what really happened that night.

Other Publications by the Author

Memories from My Mind: A collection of 9 short stories

Mind of Darkness: 12 tales of dark mystery

The Words and Photos of Shortypman: A collection of poems and
photographs by John Ploetz

Be the New 2.0 You!: Improve yourself to live a fuller life

You can also check out his blogs on his website at
http://johnploetz.com

www.ingramcontent.com/pod-product-compliance
Lightning Source LLC
Chambersburg PA
CBHW072257130726
47910CB00012B/2061